WHERE
THE
MISSING
GO

WHERE THE MISSING GO

EMMA ROWLEY

KENSINGTON BOOKS
www.kensingtonbooks.com

KENSINGTON BOOKS are published by
Kensington Publishing Corp.
119 West 40th Street
New York, NY 10018

All Kensington titles, imprints, and distributed lines are available at special quantity discounts for bulk purchases for sales promotion, premiums, fund-raising, educational, or institutional use.

Special book excerpts or customized printings can also be created to fit specific needs. For details, write or phone the office of the Kensington Sales Manager: Kensington Publishing Corp., 119 West 40th Street, New York, NY 10018. Attn. Sales Department. Phone: 1-800-221-2647.

ISBN-13: 978-1-4967-2311-6 (ebook)
ISBN-10: 1-4967-2311-2 (ebook)
Kensington Electronic Edition: May 2019

ISBN-13: 978-1-4967-2310-9
ISBN-10: 1-4967-2310-4
First Kensington Trade Paperback Printing: May 2019

10 9 8 7 6 5 4 3 2 1

Printed in the United States of America

For Mum

PROLOGUE

The night is mild, but the girl shivers. The few cars passing by her look so cozy somehow, their drivers ensconced in their own little worlds, hurrying home to shut out everything.

If any one of them turned their head to look at the slight figure on the pavement, then maybe they would notice that the girl looks a little nervous. Apprehensive, even.

But none of them do notice her, walking just outside of the yellow cones of light from the streetlamps, her long hair hiding her face.

It seemed like such a good idea, at the time. The best idea, in fact.

Now? Now, she's not so sure.

The girl pushes down her unease. Oh well. Too late now to go back.

He'll be waiting.

Article in the *Manchester Evening News*, 17 February, 2017:

MISSING SCHOOLGIRL CASE GOES COLD
By Staff Reporter

Detectives investigating the disappearance of a Cheshire school-girl are scaling back their inquiries, it has been announced.

Sophie Harlow, 16, was reported missing from her home in leafy Vale Dean village before her GCSEs last year, sparking an intensive police hunt.

However, officers downgraded the search in the weeks following her departure on the night of Friday 13 May, after the former Amberton Grammar student made contact.

It is understood that although the case remains open, detectives will no longer be actively investigating her whereabouts.

A spokeswoman for Greater Manchester Police defended the "scale and commitment" of their efforts so far.

"It is our belief that there are no suspicious circumstances around Sophie's disappearance," she said. "We are now treating her as a voluntary runaway. As with any missing persons case, we will of course follow up any new lines of investigation and we urge Sophie to maintain contact with us or her family to confirm that she is safe and well."

Miss Harlow's parents were informed of the decision in a meeting with detectives earlier this month.

Mark and Kate Harlow, who are believed to have separated since their only daughter's disappearance, declined to comment yesterday.

PART 1

CHAPTER 1

Two Years Missing

I'm a bad mother. You're not supposed to say that. Everyone was very keen that I didn't blame myself. At first, anyway.

And they were right, there were plenty of things that we—that I—did get right. Bedtime stories, balanced meals, a lovely, elegant home. Holidays abroad, tennis camp and piano lessons, a maths tutor when Sophie was struggling a little at primary school. We even made a brave stab at the violin when Sophie was seven, although she was so extravagantly out of tune, the sounds so painful, that Mark and I once cracked up laughing when we met outside the living room door, not that we'd ever have let our little daughter know. But if Sophie didn't have much of an ear for music, she had everything else. We even had a dog—of course we did—a black Lab called King, as friendly as he was greedy. Mark chose the name. He'd grown up with dogs like that and he wanted Sophie to have one, too. I miss King.

And yet maybe I'm getting it all wrong, even now. Maybe it wasn't down to me or Mark that we seemed to find it so easy, that our little family bubble seemed to be floating through life—but down to our daughter, always laughing and sweet-natured, eager to please.

"Your little shadow," Mark used to call her. She was always there, trotting behind me, happily joining in with whatever I was doing. She had a talent for being happy. When she hit the teenage years, she had her moments of course, but I knew that was to be expected. It'd be all right in the end.

I was wrong.

But I'm making excuses. Because all the stuff I did, the car trips, the noses wiped, the kisses-to-make-it-better, the years of love and care, none of that counts now. In the end, there's only one conclusion, when you look at it. I've failed.

Mornings can be the hardest. Just getting started, deciding that there is a reason to get up after all. "I don't know how you carry on, Kate," people have said to me. I don't know how they decided that I was doing so. For a long time, it felt like I'd just ground to a halt.

I'm past that now. I don't work in an office, not anymore, but I do keep busy, in my own way. There's so much to do: phone calls, emails, letters. Articles to read, online forums to keep up with.

Sometimes it can feel quite overwhelming. People think I'm hiding away here doing nothing, but they don't understand how much work I still do. Although, if I am being honest, I don't always manage to get out of bed until the cat starts padding around crossly, hungry to be fed.

The trick, I find, is not to think too much about it. Today, I was helped by the sunshine making a hot streak across my pillow, too bright in my eyes. The sky was already a shocking blue slice between the curtains I hadn't quite pulled shut. So I made myself put both feet on the floor and then sat for a moment, still light-headed from sleep, thinking about the day ahead.

It's not exactly a full diary these days. Not like those weekends where we'd be out every Friday and Saturday, dinner parties and work dos and big birthdays—there was always something to celebrate. Mark was so social and I was happy to be pulled along in the slipstream.

But I do have plans tonight, so that's something. And now I've showered and made strong coffee, to clear my head, because I've set myself a task for today.

The first photo album has a layer of dust on it that makes me sneeze as I pull it down from its place on the living room shelves. I was always good about keeping these updated and making sure that we turned our digital snaps into glossy hard copies that I could paste into their pages. But I don't dwell in the past, contrary to what some people think. I rarely look at them.

Today I need to, because I've decided that the picture I have been sharing online and in the letters and emails I write—Sophie's last school photo—could be misleading. As of this summer, she wouldn't have been at school, she'd have just finished sixth form. So I worry that it could give the wrong impression—that it could even be a bit unhelpful, to use one that's clearly of a schoolgirl: Sophie's white shirt bright against her navy jumper, her shining blonde hair pulled back into a neater than usual ponytail. She got her hair from me, though mine has long needed some help from the hairdresser to maintain its fairness. The smile's all hers though—sunny, with a twist of mischief, lighting up that sweet round face.

Today I want to find a good, clear one of her out of uniform. I wipe my gray fingertips on my shorts and carry the album over to the coffee table, opening it carefully—and I feel my stomach sink. I thought I'd put the albums in order on the shelf ages ago, but this isn't the one I wanted to look at. This album is one of the very first ones, the photos already looking dated in that peculiar way. How does that happen? It can't just be our clothes—they're T-shirts and flip-flops, evergreen summer wear.

Yet this first shot belongs to a different age. It's Mark, Sophie and me, sitting on some anonymous park bench, each one of us with an ice-cream cone in our hand. Mark's thinner than he is now, and I look rounder, rosier, but that's not what makes our photographic selves seem like strangers to me. Maybe it's something in our expressions: we're both so carefree, ready for a future that would, surely, bring only more good things. And of course there's Sophie, a chunky two-year-old with a tuft of fair hair, her legs sticking straight out in her dungarees, too short to reach the edge of the seat.

I turn the page.

Oh, I remember this, too. I took this one. Sophie had fallen asleep on the sofa, one little fist still clutching Teddy, the far-too-expensive stuffed bear Mark had insisted on buying her one Christmas. They're collector's items, not for kids to actually play with, I'd laughed. But she'd loved her new toy, dragging him around the house by one leg and insisting on him sharing her pillow at night. I'd had to sneak him away once she fell asleep to wash him in unscented powder, so that he wouldn't smell different. Even when she was older, Teddy would somehow end up tucked under her pillow every night.

I don't know where Teddy ended up. It didn't matter so much, keeping tabs on that kind of thing, when we still had her . . .

The phone shrills from the kitchen and I start a little, the sound too loud in the quiet house. I pad in, wiping at my eyes with my sleeve—I've no hanky, as usual—"Hello?"

"Hello, love?" It's Dad, his voice scratchier than it used to be.

"Dad, how are you?" I'm pleased I sound so steady.

"I'm fine, I'm fine. Now, we were just wondering, your sister and I, if you'd like to drive over here this afternoon. We thought we could go for a meal at this new Italian that's opened. They've got"—he pauses thoughtfully—"sushi."

"Italian sushi? Are you sure?"

"Oh, something like that. Tapas maybe, I can't remember all these things. But it should be very nice. Would you like to come? Charlotte says you can stay over in her spare room."

"Oh. Thanks, but I can't."

"Or you could stay at mine, if you think it would be a bit noisy with her boys running around, I could make up the sofa." Dad's downsized to a little terrace, a cottage really, even nearer my younger sister Charlotte and her family. He's been hinting that I should do the same—he keeps telling me that it's "so easy to look after, a small place." I think they both want me closer to them, where I grew up.

"Thanks, Dad. But I really can't. I'm going out."

"Oh!" He sounds pleased. "And where are you off to on a Saturday night?" he asks jovially.

"The helpline," I say crisply. "You know it's my night."

"Yes. Yes, of course. I just thought by now you might . . . do you think they'd mind if you didn't go tonight?"

"I wish I could . . . but I can't let them down. It wouldn't be right." I bite my lip. Actually, I'm sure they'd be fine. I've done more than my share of shifts, and I'm always ready to pick up others when a message goes round asking to swap. I've got more than a few favors I could call in. "Next time maybe."

"Next time, yes."

Suddenly I can see him, neat in the checked shirt he always wears for gardening, alone in his tidy little kitchen, stooping slightly these days. It scares me to think about how much he's aged in these last few years. They're sweet to keep trying, I know that. "Actually, I've been meaning to come over some time," I say. "I had an idea, the other day. You know that night when you were outside the cottage?"

"Hm. Now what night would that be?"

"That night, Dad, when you thought you saw Sophie?" He doesn't like to talk about this anymore, but something in me wants to push. "I know you've always said you couldn't remember what sort of car she was in, that it was too dark, but I was thinking—I've got some printouts of some car models off the internet, and I could bring them over to see if any of the car shapes jog your memory. Because I don't think the police ever bothered to do that, did they?"

He's silent for a second.

"Katie . . . I'm sorry. You know, that wasn't very fair of me."

"What do you mean?"

"I should never have mentioned that, and got your hopes up. I didn't realize that was so much on your mind still."

"Well, of course. I'm always trying new leads."

"You know, Katie, it's very common, after someone goes missing, for friends and family to think they see them around."

"I know that but—"

For once, he cuts me off, his voice firmer. "Katie, please. We've been over this, a lot. I'd moved house by then. There's no reason Sophie'd know that, even if she were to come and find me. It was dark. I saw what I wanted to see. Actually, it's not so unusual—it's part of the process of grieving."

Therapy-speak. "You've been at that group again." I try to keep my voice neutral, but it is stony.

"We've found it very helpful, your sister and I. And I think you would too, if you would try again."

"Maybe. One of these days—oh, you know what, hang on a second. Sorry, that's the doorbell. I'll have to speak to you later, Dad. Have a good night, love to Charlotte and Phil and the boys."

"Bye, Katie." He sounds sad.

"Bye." I hang up.

I've never been a very good liar.

I did try the group thing, but I only went once in the end. I couldn't bear it. The only stories I wanted to hear were the ones with a happy ending.

I didn't want to be sitting in a chilly church hall with a load of strangers trying to come to terms with what had happened to them. Of course they couldn't. The whole thing was so stupid.

I do know how it works. I did read the literature they gave me. And some of it was kind of useful, in the end. "For a minority of families," one leaflet explained, "one way of managing the intensity and all-consuming nature of searching is not to do it at all, or to stop doing it after a period of time."

I didn't do that. I couldn't, even if I'd wanted to. But I suppose it did help me understand Mark, just a little bit, after Sophie left. Because that was the final thing that we couldn't agree on, in the end.

When to give up.

CHAPTER 2

The thing about the missing is that they don't always want to be found. That's what they tell new joiners here. It's what I tell myself when another Saturday evening passes by without even a prank caller to liven us up a bit.

In her corner, Alma is knitting another vast yellow rectangle, a jumper she tells me, those evil-looking needles flashing away. I hope she doesn't plan to give this one to me.

They don't need two of us on, by any means, but it's best practice, the charity says. Responsible. They're very big on all that, making sure we volunteers feel safe and supported and cared for.

Bit late for all that, I want to say, but I don't. They don't all know my situation here.

New joiners tend to be surprised by how quiet this place is. They think it will be all high drama, phones shrilling and people rushing about scribbling down urgent messages.

I didn't. I knew how rare it would be if people phoned in. It's not the Samaritans. That doesn't make the hours pass any faster though. Tonight, I'm getting a headache from staring at the computer screen; I've been flicking through my usual websites, leaving messages.

I rub around my eyes carefully, not wanting to smear my makeup, and roll my head from side to side. Through the sixth-floor window a spectacular sunset is flaring out over the Manchester cityscape.

With a sigh, Alma sets down her knitting and pushes herself away from her desk. "Time for my break, Kate dearie. You all right manning the fort? I won't be long, I'll just pop down to Marks and Sparks." Like clockwork—7 p.m. on the dot.

I'll just about cope, I think, but smile brightly. "I'll be fine. Take your time." I listen to her stately tread as she heads for the lifts of our less-than-glamorous office block. Regional charities don't have the funds for slick corporate headquarters. Still, you'd think they could buy us some biscuits.

My gaze falls on the noticeboard: there's that puff piece the paper ran last Christmas about our work. There we all are in the picture, one smiling team. I'm in the back row. They worry we feel forgotten about, up here. Head office is in London, a much bigger organization the helpline was folded into a few years ago. But I don't care about recognition, or team-building. I just couldn't think of an excuse quick enough to get out of the photo shoot.

I've helped out here for a while now, taking the weekend late shifts when other people are busy with friends and family. I've let them think it is because I'm busy with work the rest of the time. I don't want the looks.

My shift started at five, and now I am feeling hungry too. I'll make another cup of tea for me, and then take my break when Alma's back and head to Pret, I decide. Alma's strict. She won't even go for a loo break unless the junior volunteer's sitting ready in their chair, which I suppose is as it should be. I wonder if I should go and treat us to one of those mini bottles of wine, half a plastic glass each as we face the night shift ahead. But no, Alma and her rules, she—

When the phone rings I actually jump a little in my chair. First one of the night for me. I pick up within the promised three rings. We don't even get headsets.

"Hello," I say, making my voice sound warm and calm. "You've reached the Message in a Bottle helpline. I'm Kate."

A click. Sometimes that happens, they lose their nerve, we were told in the training. There was less said about the prank callers, bored teenagers and men who'd like to hear a stranger's voice.

It's been slow tonight. Alma had been right onto the last few, dispatching each caller with practiced ease. "Oh, I know love, it is hard, isn't it, but it's never too late to build bridges, you know. In the meantime, I know they'll be so glad to hear you're safe, now are you sure you don't want me to take a phone number for you too, schedule a little check-in call from us in a day or two . . ."

That's what we do here: people who have run away from home call us and we pass on messages to their loved ones.

RAN AWAY?
Send a message to let them know you're safe
NO QUESTIONS ASKED
Just phone and give your message
We will pass it on
Send a MESSAGE IN A BOTTLE

That's what the advert says. They're all over the place, if you know to look for them: in churches, community centers, sometimes a local paper, if they can find the budget.

Alma's brilliant at it actually, wheedling out parents' names, half-forgotten postcodes, "how are things with you now?," sketching over sad details of treatment centers and "no fixed abode," the detritus of broken lives, sounding for all the world like some cozy great-aunt at a family party. She may look like the president of her local WI—that's exactly what she is—but Alma knows what she's doing. Building bridges, keeping lines of communication open, delivering messages to family desperate to know something, anything, about their beloved husband, cousin, son . . . daughter.

As for me, I struggle to build rapport with callers, I'm told, can come across just a little chilly—I even, according to one feedback form (they're big on all that here, inevitably, there's endless briefing and debriefing) lack "empathy" with callers' situations. Which I find somewhat ironic, to say the least.

But if I can't be Miss Popularity, at least I'm reliable.

The phone goes again, startling me out of my thoughts, and I pick it up again. The static bursts into my ear, making me wince, then the line quiets to a low buzz.

"Hello," I say. "You've reached the Message in a Bottle helpline." I know: the name is unbearably cutesy. "I'm Kate."

No response. Then another round of pops on the line.

"Is someone there?" Perhaps this is a misdial, some automated call-center system gone wrong before a worker gets patched in from his desk in Glasgow or Mumbai to try to sell me something.

"Hello?" I say again. There's a burst of static, but beneath it I can hear muffled sounds now, like someone talking through water.

It'd better not be a crank. We have rules of course, can't be rude even if they are drunk kids dialing in—"You never know why someone might be calling in," Alma will tell newbies solemnly, "even a prank call could really be a cry for help." So when I do get the odd heavy breather whispering obscenities or teenagers giggling into the handset, I make absolutely sure she is out of earshot before I give them a few sharp words, inform them I can trace the call and hang up. They don't need to know that I can't.

The line goes quiet again, then someone is there, suddenly real and breathing quickly.

"Hello, Message in a Bottle," I say. "You're speaking to Kate." There's static again and I pull the handset an inch from my ear. "Do you need me to call anyone for you?"

More crackles.

"This line's terrible, I'm afraid. Is there anyone you'd like us to send a message to?"

It sounds like someone's talking very far away, but I can't make out the words. I can stay on the line as long as I feel the need to. I swivel in my chair and look out of the window. The last of the sun is slipping behind the jagged skyline, low rays of light striking the wall behind me as it flares out.

I try again, starting to work through our questions. "Are you in a safe place?"

A lull, then ". . . hear me?" It's a woman's voice, a tinny whisper against the buzzing.

"Yes, I can. Take all the time you need." I sip my cooling tea. I never want to scare them away.

"You're there!" The relief's palpable in her voice, low and hushed. She's young—they often are.

"Don't worry, I'm not going anywhere," I say. "Whenever you're ready to talk." The Post-it I've stuck to my handset reminds me of our latest prompt, by order of the helpline's harried volunteer manager, Chrissie. "If you prefer to text, we can, no problem. We now do—"

She interrupts me. "I've got to be quick. I need you to tell them not to worry anymore about their daughter. That she . . . that *I'm* fine—"

The words are drowned out by static again. "Who? Who do you want me to tell?" Suddenly my heart is racing.

Silence, then the voice, now tiny, like it's very far away, ". . . not to worry if they don't hear from me after this, it only hurts . . ." and it's gone again.

"I can't hear you, sweetie." I'm gripping my headset to my ears, pressing harder, harder, straining to hear. The line pops and sings.

Then the voice again, now clear, one that I know better than any other. ". . . are Kate and Mark Har—" My skin is cold, all over.

"Sophie," I say. Finally allowing myself to say it. "Sophie, is that you?"

But then there's another burst of static, I can't tell if she's still talking.

"Are you still there?" I wait, my heart pounding. "Are you still there?"

"Yes, yes, I'm here," she says. "I'm still here."

"Love you, So," I say.

It's all I want to tell her, in the end. I don't know what she's going to answer, and then—

The dial tone sounds, too loud as I strain to hear. I breathe out, setting the phone back, slowly.

Every part of me knows that voice. My daughter, Sophie.

By the time Alma's back, I'm calmer, at least on the surface. I'm good at that. You're so *calm*, people kept telling me. And later: I can't believe how *calm* you're being about it. I knew it wasn't a compliment.

But I find I can't quite sit still, my mind replaying those few syllables over and over: "Kate and Mark Har—" She was about to say Harlow, I know. "Kate and Mark Harlow."

I've told Alma what's happened, the call that's finally come for me, that I've always expected. The reason, she will know without me having to tell her, that I started to volunteer here.

"Well, I'm so glad, dear," she said, after a pause. "I know you've been waiting a very long time, haven't you." I returned her hug, so she couldn't see my eyes fill with tears. Her soft cardigan had her perfume—rose scent and custard creams.

She's letting me skip the rest of the shift: she thinks it's best if I go home. She can handle it tonight. For Alma, a veteran of the helpline, family break-ups and reunions are the bread and butter of her life, as much as trips to the supermarket and walking her dachshund.

I find I am trembling now, despite the two sugars in the milky tea Alma's made me sip ("For the shock, dear"). I want to get out of here, itching to act. And there's something on the edges of my mind, if I can only grasp it . . .

I shake my head. Be practical. I'll leave a message on the extension of the family liaison officer the police assigned to us. If it's not too late, maybe I'll drive to Dad's. I want to tell him in person. And I need to get a message to Mark, I suppose. It's the right thing to do. As Sophie's father, my ex needs to know.

As soon as she hung up, I'd tapped in the numbers for caller ID, even though I knew what the answer would be. That automated voice: "The service requested is not available." We can't identify our callers even if we want to—it's a fundamental policy, and the system's set up to ensure that.

But I'd know that voice anywhere. She was talking quietly perhaps, and the line was terrible, but it was her. She wants to get a message to Kate and Mark: me and her dad. Not to worry about her—and not to worry if we don't hear from her? What does that mean?

I feel a burst of longing, raw and hurtful. If only I could have spoken to her longer, I could have persuaded her to come back, I could have. *Come home, Sophie*, I will her, as if I can convince her to do so through the sheer force of my emotion. *Come home.*

I am halfway to my car, keys in hand, when I realize. I check myself, stopping dead in the car park, suddenly rigid. What it is that's bothering me.

I've thought about this call before. I've imagined it so many, many times: all the things she could be. Distant. Angry. Upset.

But I never imagined that she'd sound so . . . scared.

CHAPTER 3

My coffee from the vending machine, lukewarm to start with, is now cold. It's not making it taste any better. With my back to the room, I pull a face.

"Well, there must be something you can do to find her," I say steadily, turning round. "There must. Some sort of log kept by the phone company maybe—something." I sound more confident than I am, I used to be good at that. "I mean, the police must trace calls all the time."

"I do understand your frustration, Mrs. Harlow. I really do." The young officer taking down a report of the call has been polite, even solicitous, making me go over every detail. Getting him to do something about it, and now, is another matter. "But we can't do anything until we take a look into the original investigation, get up to date with that. Which will be this week, I can assure you."

"This *week*?" I catch the expression on his face. "Look," I say, "I know how it sounds. But it's not what she said. It's how she said it."

"Yes, you mentioned. You've a feeling," he says. I give him a sharp glance, but his face is blank. "But did she say she needed help? Police assistance? Has someone threatened her, attacked her?"

"No, I told you," I say, trying to suppress my frustration. He already knows she didn't. "She said to tell us not to worry anymore. But—but she didn't say she was safe."

"And no one else heard her, no one else heard you take the call, even?"

"No," I said, "it's a skeleton staff on Saturday nights. My colleague had just gone out for her break."

"And this caller—"

"Sophie," I interrupt.

"As you say, Sophie—she ended the call—"

"Yes, of course I didn't end it, I wouldn't hang up on her."

"As I said, she ended the call after she realized it was you at the end of the line?"

"I think so, yes, but it would have been a shock."

"Well, then. Maybe she'll ring again?"

I grit my teeth. I was always so grateful before, so *guilty*. I'm the mother whose daughter had run away. But now I'm not just upset, I'm angry.

I don't know what I expected, really, but something a bit more than this. Some sense of urgency, at least.

There'd been no reply when I'd left a message on the number I'd saved in my mobile phone for Kirstie, our old family liaison officer. So I'd simply driven straight round to the police station in Amberton, the market town next to Vale Dean, the village where I live. I got ushered into a room before an officer came in to take down my report. It was early enough that it was quiet, the Saturday night drunks not yet starting to fill the town center, still calm under the pink skies.

Not anymore, though. I've been here for what feels like hours, waiting for them to swing into action. It's become clear that I'll be waiting a while.

"Now, in the meantime, you said she told you not to worry," he says. He fiddles with a page of his notebook. "You know, at eighteen, if someone doesn't want to come home, well. The truth is, Mrs. Harlow, this may not actually be a police mat—"

"Not a police matter? My daughter, who's been missing for two years, calls me and what? It's not a police matter?" My voice cracks on the last few words and he casts his eyes down. He's embarrassed for me. He thinks I'm grasping at straws.

"You don't understand," I say bleakly. "I know my daughter. Or I did. Please, Officer"—I try to remember how he introduced himself—"Jesson. You know . . ." I say slowly, the thought unfurling as I talk, "do you have a sister called Jessica, did cross-country for the county?"

"Uh, no. Jessica's my cousin," he says, a little more warmly. "That name's a mouthful, but people don't forget it. She's at uni now, doing law." He pauses, as he realizes the most likely reason I'd know the name. "She must have been a couple of years older than your Sophie. Was she a runner too?"

"Is," I say, meaningfully. "Not was, is."

"Is," he corrects himself. "All right," he says, more quietly. "There's really nothing we can do tonight. This will have to go to our detective unit, you understand. It's not a simple thing, pulling phone records, even—" He stops. Even on priority cases, I fill in silently. "Even when it's not a Saturday night. But I've noted your concerns. We will be in touch."

This is as far as I'm going to get this evening. What else can I do?

"Thank you," I say, getting up to leave. There's no point antagonizing him.

It's dark when I leave the station. I have to navigate a group of drunk girls in heels, weaving their way through the back streets, before I get to my car. I am used to being out of sync with the rest of the world.

Driving home, I turn the radio on loud, flicking through the club music until I find some call-in show with mindless chatter to distract me.

". . . so *do* today's teenagers have it tougher than we used to? A new report says that mental health problems are on the rise among the young—but what do *you* think, give me a call. Now, Dave from Stockport has quite a controversial view about body image, don't you Dave, he's on the line now, he—" I flick it off. But as I leave the fringes of the town, the built-up estates giving way to fields, the memories keep coming.

I'd been away, on the tail end of an over-the-top bachelorette party that I'd wobbled about attending. "She's more Charlotte's friend than mine," I'd said, looking at the program: a race day, spa treatments.

Sophie had encouraged me to go for the whole thing. "You should. You might enjoy it."

Afterward, the police said she probably knew then that she was going to leave while I was away: that perhaps—they phrased this tactfully—a mother might be slightly more observant than a father.

It had been a source of contention between us: me, always trying to keep our daughter at home, safe, close, concerned about her schoolwork; Mark, more confident that things turned out for the best, arguing that a teenager needed her freedom, that I'd end up pushing her away.

Maybe it was her age. Maybe it was because, contrary to what I'd thought, teenagers could get into just as much trouble out of London as in it. And they seemed to have so much freedom here in Vale Dean, all driving as soon as they hit seventeen, racing round the country lanes. It filled me with horror.

There were endless rows: Sophie, tear-stained, upset that I'd stopped her from going to another party or gig. "But everyone's going, Holly's going. Danny will drive us, you don't even need to take us."

"Oh, that makes it better. A seventeen-year-old boy who's just got his license!"

"You wouldn't mind if it wasn't them, would you. Admit it, you just don't like my friends."

"It's just not safe, Sophie. I can't let you go."

And then that last one, the week she left, about nothing at all, really. I wanted her to eat dinner with us, but she wanted to eat it in her room. "To finish some coursework," she said.

I remember how it ended, as always: Sophie slamming her way out of the room.

"Just let me go. I can't stand it! Don't you get it? I just want some space!"

"Sophie . . ."

I thought it had blown over though, even if she was a bit quieter than usual, before I went. She gave me a proper hug goodbye on Thursday evening, when Charlotte had picked me up, her pale brown bob in a careful blow-dry for the occasion. She's always hated how her hair frizzes, saying she'd rather have straight flat lengths like me and Sophie.

"See you Sunday," I'd said. "Love you, So."

"See you Sunday," she'd said, over my shoulder. "Love you, Mo."

Our little routine, for so long, since she was a toddler, and I was putting her to bed. So, my little nickname for her; Mo, for Mum, she came up with, just because she thought it was so funny to rhyme.

It just stuck. I still miss that.

We were already on our way back home from the bachelorette, Charlotte driving us, when Mark rang, "just to check in," sounding far too casual. "So, er, Sophie was at Holly's last night, she said. Is there another Holly from school? Am I getting them mixed up?" He'd never been able to keep track of her friends.

Of course it all came out in the aftermath: the day before, Friday morning, Mark had taken her to school as usual—Amberton Grammar was on his way to work in the city center. She'd run back into the house as he'd waited with the engine running, he told us, saying she'd forgotten something. "Sophie!" he'd called, tooting the horn. "Will you get a move on."

He hadn't noticed anything different, he said later.

But as he'd dropped her off at the school gates, she'd struggled to swing her rucksack onto her shoulder, and the flap had fallen back, just a little.

"Is that bag big enough," he'd teased. "What you got in there, anyway?"

She always seemed to carry the world around with her, carting the entire contents of her locker at all times. "Oh, just some—some overnight stuff," she'd said. Then: "You remember I'm staying with Holly tonight?"

"No." He raised his eyebrows. "Sophie, does Mum know about this?"

"Yes, she said it's fine." She shifted her weight. "We're just going to do some revision, have pizza. That's OK, right?"

"I don't know, Sophie," he said, thinking.

She did look a bit guilty, he said later, but he'd chalked it up to the obvious: both of them knew that I wouldn't like it. But he was late, in a rush to get to work, and what was the harm? She'd been working hard. Of course, there was another reason he didn't mind her staying away that night.

The car behind tooted at him. "So can I?"

"All right, but don't be back too late tomorrow. Home by lunchtime," he called after her.

"'K, thanks, Dad. See you tomorrow." It was only when she failed to come home by late Saturday afternoon that Mark had called her phone and then, when it went to voicemail, Holly's house. I'd pinned the number to the noticeboard—she spent so much time there. Did Sophie want picking up?

No, Sophie wasn't there. Her mum had put Holly on the phone. No, she'd repeated, Sophie hadn't stayed at her house. In fact, she hadn't seen her since Friday morning.

"I'm sure it will be OK," Charlotte had kept telling me, after Mark rang off, as I grew increasingly angry—and, underneath that, worried. I couldn't believe he'd let her go, right before exams.

When he phoned again an hour or so later, I put my mobile on speakerphone. I could tell instantly that she hadn't turned up, looking sheepish.

"Katie . . ." he'd said, sounding almost bewildered. "It's Sophie.

She's left a note." He'd cleared his throat. For a strange moment I wondered if he was going to cry. "She's run away."

Two officers in uniform—professional, serious—arrived that same evening after I'd called 999. No, we didn't have to wait 48 hours, they'd reassured us. That was a myth. We'd done the right thing.

They peppered us with questions, as we nursed cups of tea on the living room sofa.

No, we've no idea where she might have gone. Yes, we've tried her friends, all the ones we can think of. No, she hasn't gone to my sister's, her grandpa said he hasn't heard from her, he's very worried. No, there are no other relatives she might go to. No, she's never run away before. Is she happy at home? Yes. At least, we think so. Have there been any arguments, recently? Well, yes, but she's a teenager. . . .

I couldn't get over the unreality of the situation, the sense that any moment I'd hear the key turn in the back door and her clatter into the kitchen.

She'd left her bank card and her phone—I'd found them in the drawer of her bedside table. That was a good sign, Charlotte had said. Sophie'd have to come back soon. But while Sophie hadn't taken much, what she had was important. Her passport was gone. That was one of the first things they asked me, where we kept it, and I'd showed them the drawer in the desk in the study.

How much money does Sophie have access to, they asked at some point.

"Not much, she only just turned sixteen last month, she's still at school." Mark had been flustered. He spoiled her, I'd always said that. Meanwhile I was doing the sums. There was her generous allowance, money she'd collected from her waitressing job the summer before, birthday gifts.

"We let her look after her own account," Mark had told the police, growing slightly pink under their steady gaze. "She wanted to save for a car." We sounded so naïve. Comfortable, trusting—and unforgivably naïve. She'd cleared out her account completely, we learned later. With everything added together, she had a considerable sum.

And of course, there was the note, her round bubble handwriting on a sheet torn out of one of her exercise books for school.

I'm sorry everyone. But I need to get away.
Please try not to worry about me, I'm going to be
fine. I love you all, Sophie xxx ✿

Three kisses, like we always left for each other in our family birthday cards and, once she was older, the notes I'd leave stuck to the fridge. One for Daddy, one for her, one for me. And a little flower doodle, like a daisy, in small strokes of ballpoint pen, next to her name. She always did that, since she was little. She'd started it for me: she knew flowers made me happy.

They wouldn't stop running over the details with Mark. "And when did you find this, Mr. Harlow?"

"This afternoon, after I'd phoned Holly's mum." He couldn't meet anyone's eyes. "It was on Kate's pillow, so I didn't see it."

I think Charlotte had snorted.

"It won't have made a big difference, will it?" he'd asked almost pleadingly.

They'd reassured him that they had every confidence, et cetera. But I knew, countless news stories and TV reconstructions flashing in my mind: the first few hours are crucial.

That was the beginning of the end for us. Of course he'd had to own up, and quickly, to what was already obvious to me. When Sophie ran in while he waited in the car, she must have placed the note on our bed, knowing he wouldn't see it until that night. But he'd had a sleepover of his own that night, elsewhere, so hadn't seen it until he came home the next day and, worried now, finally checked around.

"It might not have made any difference, Kate, if he'd found it sooner," Charlotte said to me, in the days after. And maybe she was right.

But I couldn't forgive him for that.

CHAPTER 4

It's too late to wake up Dad, I tell myself, as I pull up at the house after the police station. I catch myself sighing. Coming home to our pretty old redbrick no longer lifts my spirits as it used to. This place is too big for me now, but I can't leave. What if she came back and found us all gone?

In the drive, a small shape pads up and I bend down to stroke Tom—a ginger tom, unoriginally. Mark took the dog when we split. It was a surprise how much I missed him, I told my sister: King, not Mark. She didn't laugh.

At least it meant I could house Tom. Lily, my neighbor, had seen a sign in the supermarket advertising a "free kitten" and rung a number: a woman had rushed over with a cardboard box, the animal inside hissing furiously. He was already half-grown, I saw immediately, and—we soon found out—not yet house-trained. Lily had been so upset about it all.

Perhaps that episode was a sign: she was being too impulsive, not her usual sensible self. At least the cat doesn't require a lot from me. Suddenly I'm exhausted, the adrenaline that's borne me through this evening disappearing like bubbles from a fizzy drink.

I switch off the downstairs lights, listening to the noises of the house around me: soft creaks and hums as it settles, the warmth of the day evaporating. Climbing the stairs, I make a note to call the blinds company. In a rare burst of activity, I'd taken down the tired curtains at the landing window. I just haven't got around to doing anything more and I'm reminded of it every time I walk past the pane of glossy black.

In the darkness outside, I can see the bulk of the nearest neighbor, Parklands, its towers confused by scaffolding, alien shapes against the night sky. There are no lights on, of course. A bend in the road means we don't even have neighbors on the other side, not really.

I feel a sudden pang of longing for our smart London terrace—far too small for us, we thought, with a teenager and a dog.

For a long time, the idea of moving here had been just that—a "what if" to ponder after dinner with friends over dregs of wine, plotting our escapes from the smoke. Then Mark got offered the chance to expand the Manchester practice. An RAF brat, he was cheerfully unconcerned about starting over. "Everyone'll come and stay, it's just a jaunt up the M6. Have you seen the space we could get up there?" And we'd be closer to my family. Charlotte had stayed local to Macclesfield, near where we grew up. She, Phil and the boys were ten minutes from Dad, while Mark's parents spent half the year in France anyway.

There were things we didn't talk about: the distance between us.

I'd met him at a bar in the City, birthday drinks a friend had brought me along to—he was at the center of a big laughing crowd, as always. He was a golden retriever in human form, Charlotte had said to me, when I brought him home, rolling her eyes. She'd been with Phil, even more sensible than my sister, since sixth form and through her tough first years as a teacher. But in the end she was charmed too. When I'd got pregnant, early among our group of friends, there was no doubt about what to do. We'd married that summer, me fooling no one by slowly draining half a glass of champagne.

And if sometimes I wondered privately how much we really

had in common, if I was sometimes surprised to find myself with a husband, a house, a baby, even a dog, I can't really say it worried me much. Even when it became clear there wouldn't be any more to follow Sophie—after we both realized the other was ready to stop trying, too—we were OK, I think.

So we decided. We'd leave. There were tears from Sophie, an upsetting amount—she didn't want to leave her friends—but it would be good for her, surely. They grew up so fast in London.

And we'd been excited to find this place so quickly: leafy Cheshire, near enough to the city that Mark could drive in but still, to a couple of London transplants, all so shockingly green and quiet. Out here where the village turns to countryside, the houses sit far apart, most of them stately Victorian mansions built by the cotton merchants behind low stone walls. If you keep driving along Park Road, away from the village, you end up at the entrance to the deer park, once the grand estate that gave Vale Dean its name.

I took voluntary redundancy. I'd loved my job, fund-raising for an arts organization, but it didn't pay like Mark's, in the law, and I was sick of the endless cuts. I didn't need to worry about working for a while, Mark told me, I could focus on doing up the house. I squashed down the thought that he'd prefer me not to work.

Looking out at the shadow of Parklands now, I can almost hear his voice: "It's an eyesore, letting a good house get like that. Weren't you going to ring the council?"

I suppress a shiver. Enough of the past. I know where I have to go tonight.

On the threshold, I stop, and touch the pink wooden heart hanging from the doorknob. She'd got into decorating her room a bit, starting to take an interest in having a more grown-up space around her, and I'd let her. Privately I'd smiled to see her taste: flowered cushions in soft blues and violets, the walls "apple white." My sweet little girl was still there, I'd thought, even as she'd disappear to her room for hours, or rush out of the house—"out," the only answer flung at me as I watched her retreating back.

"She's a teenager, Kate," Mark would tell me, bored of the discussion. "That's what they're like."

I push the door open, slowly. I never keep it closed, just ajar. There's a tang of furniture polish in the air—Silvia, our cleaner, was good about that, she just carried on as if Sophie hadn't gone, until I said she could stop coming. There wasn't any need, anymore.

Walking over to the bed, I curl up against her wrought iron headboard—she'd paid half, promising she wouldn't complain it was uncomfortable—and let out a breath I didn't realize I was holding in.

My eyes wander around the room, over the school scarf flung carelessly over the cheval mirror; on the wall, the smiling faces of the boy band that's since split up; a dried rose, a gift from Danny; the stuffed animals sitting on her wardrobe, faded souvenirs of childhood. Everything's the same as it always is. I can't bear it— and at the same time I feel closer to her here. I can almost pretend that she's just stepped out, that she's taken the dog for a walk, maybe, and that at any moment might be back again.

But tonight I don't feel the usual sense of comfort. I'm antsy, even my skin itching, so I get up again. Maybe it's because I can't pretend now that she's just gone for a moment—I know she's out *there,* somewhere. I take one long look at the room, my hand on the door handle, and then go to bed.

I wake up suddenly, my heart thudding in my chest, my nightie sticking to my body with cold sweat. My mouth's dry.

I turn my head to the alarm clock: the green figures tell me it's still the early hours. Damn. I should have taken a pill. I've been trying to do without them, just as an experiment: to see if I could.

My dream . . . something niggles at my brain. Sophie . . . It comes to me in a sudden rush. I was walking around my house, looking for her. Another one of those. Nightmares sounds so childish. Night terrors, they used to call them.

I had so many in the months just after. They're always much the same. I come home and push open the door, unlocked. "Sophie,"

I call. "I'm home." Inside, it's like she has just passed through: a discarded school bag, books spilling out; her coat slung over the banister; hockey stick and tennis racket strewn on the floor, all the detritus of her school life. In the kitchen, I find a half-drunk cup of tea, the cupboard doors open, drawers pulled out haphazardly, like she'd been looking for something. I head upstairs, knowing, as you do in dreams, that I am only a step behind—that I'll find her if I'm quick enough.

And so it unfolds, like clockwork: I go into the blue bedroom, find the wardrobe doors open, our winter clothes pulled onto the bed and shoes scattered everywhere, like a whirlwind's passed through. It's the same in the next bedroom, the sheets and the pillows heaped on the floor. In the bathroom, the towels are hanging off the rails, all the taps running.

Still I know that if only I can catch up, it'll be OK. And so I keep going, passing through our bedroom now, where feathers are floating in the air; the mattress upturned, pillows ripped open, the long mirror smashed. I keep looking. And then, I climb the last flight of stairs, heading up to her bedroom, the door still ajar. I push it slowly, fear at last seizing me. . . .

And then I wake up, like I always do and remember: she's gone. Really gone, I didn't find her, I tell myself, as I pull open the bedside table drawer and rummage for the little packet that can soothe me. It used to drive me crazy, her mess. I'd follow her about, tidying and chatting. But now, I never catch up.

CHAPTER 5

Sunday's a waiting game. Despite the bad night, I'm full of nervous energy. I tidy the kitchen, half-heartedly, then check the fridge. It's embarrassingly empty. You get used to throwing family-sized packs of juice and pasta into the trolley, those big supermarket sweeps, but it's alarming how quickly you can end up living off scrambled eggs and wilting lettuce. Suddenly annoyed with myself—what if she did come back, what would she think of all this?—I pick up my car keys.

On my way into the village, I ring Dad on the hands-free. "I've some news, about Sophie—"

"They've found her?"

I wince to hear the lightness in his voice. "No, not that. But I picked up a call at the charity last night. It was her, I'm sure of it." I quickly fill him in on what's unfolded, giving him the facts.

He's typical, careful Dad, asking me questions about how long the call was, what time it came, what the police said. "And what about the connection—was there any delay on the line?"

"I'm not sure," I say. "It was a terrible line. Crackly."

He pauses. "But it's a good sign, isn't it? You said if people ring the helpline . . . that's what it's for. That they're trying to reach out. It's a step closer."

"Yes," I say. "I just—I do worry. She just sounded . . . not herself." I don't want to mention what I think she said about ending contact, how the call's raised my hopes and scared me at the same time. I forget how old he is. But I'm not prepared for what comes next.

"Katie, this call—I can see you're excited—"

"Excited's not the word I'd use, Dad."

He's not going to be put off course. "But what if—what if it's not what you think."

"You think I got it wrong? That I didn't really get a call?"

He stays calm. "No, no, I'd never think that. But what if—maybe you misheard her, you said it was a bad line. Can you really be sure, hand on heart, that it was Sophie? That it wasn't another young girl, ringing about her parents. And you so wanting to hear from her . . ."

I can't believe this. "I'm not imagining it. She said my name and Mark's down the phone. She did, she said my name." I can hear how I sound, my voice getting higher.

"OK." He sounds sad. "But even so. I just don't want you to . . . to get too carried away, even if it was her. It's been a long time, since Sophie left, and now Mark's gone too. You're all alone, in that house. I don't know whether you're looking after yourself."

I don't like it when he gets like this. It's better when he's telling me about what he's just picked up from B&Q or bits of gossip from the bridge club. Dad's done so well since Mum died, and he was left suddenly unmoored by the loss of his laughing, exuberant wife. I suspect, from careful references to his "new friend Trish" at the club, that he's recently taken another step forward, and I'm happy that he's building a new life. The only problem is, he wants me to do the same.

"So what's Clive been up to now, any news from the club?" I say, changing the subject.

"He's been busy showing off his new car. Walnut dash, very nice." Clive, kicking off with some rather orange hair dye, sounds to be well into the throes of a late-life crisis, and enjoying every moment.

But Dad won't be distracted. "Well, try not to worry, if you can. That's promising, it really is. Let me know as soon as you hear from the police." He pauses. "Have you spoken to your sister?"

I try to keep my voice light. "No, I haven't caught her yet."

"I'll be going round there today for Sunday lunch. You're welcome of course, you know. The boys would love to see you too, they're growing up so fast."

"Please don't guilt-trip me about my nephews, Dad, not just now."

"Just give her a ring, perhaps. When you can."

"I'll try. But you can tell her about Sophie's phone call, when you see her. I've got to go anyway, I'm just pulling in." Another lie. "See you soon."

"Bye, sweetie."

Don't get too carried away. My thoughts are whirling, as I walk through the car park, the hot tarmac filling the air with that pitchy smell—Sophie loved it. If only Dad knew where my mind could go. I know what happens to girls on the streets, I am all too aware of the stories. Drugs, men, bad decisions. And then the decisions get worse, to get money, to survive.

But not my Sophie. I won't think about that, I've trained myself not to spiral down that dark hole of possibilities. If she's talking, lucid, phoning home, it could be worse, I tell myself. Much worse. *She's alive. She called me. She's reaching out. That's all I need to think about, for now.*

I will buy a chicken and cook a proper roast for myself. I used to make lovely, careful meals all the time for the three of us, thumbing through my sticky-fingerprinted Jamies and Nigellas.

But I haven't made it halfway down the vegetable aisle when I spot the highlighted head. This is why I stopped coming here at weekends. I turn smartly on my heel to head toward the doors.

"Kate! Kate! Is that you?"

Too late. I lift my eyebrows, paste on a smile, and turn round to her. "Ellen, hi. How are you?" I hope my emphasis can pass as enthusiasm.

"Oh, you know, busy, busy, as always. I haven't seen you for *ages*. How are you?"

"Fine, thanks. How's the family, your . . ." I grasp fruitlessly for the names ". . . boys?"

"They're great, Neil's just had more exams, so we're holding our breath and hoping, he has worked very hard. But he's loved having his own patients." I nod, smiling. I cannot picture him at all. She tilts her head, her face more uncertain. "And you?"

"Everything's fine, thanks. I'm keeping busy." I wish I'd put on makeup today, that I hadn't just pulled my hair back in its usual ponytail.

"Oh really?"

"Mm, I'm still at the charity, I work on the helpline there, you know." It's not an outright lie. I didn't say I was full-time. Or paid.

"You know," she says carefully. "I'm doing a lot with the tennis club now, the social side and a bit of charity fund-raising. You should come along. Actually, what are you doing Thursday night?"

I know that crowd, and I had quite enough of them in the months afterward. "Thanks so much," I say brightly. "I'll have to have a look at my diary."

Not brightly enough. Ellen's mouth hardens into a little straight line. "Well, you do that." She gives her trolley a push, more for show than for the sign she's going anywhere. "I'm only trying to help. It's just . . . you out there in that big house. Lisa's very worried, you know," she adds, tucking in her chin and looking up at me meaningfully.

I can't help it, I laugh out loud. "Lisa? I'm sure she is." I'm remembering Lisa Brookland, all bleached teeth and tight bright sportswear, in the weeks when I was still trying to carry on as normal. She cornered me at the post office once.

"And you've really *no idea* where she could have gone? There was no sign she was so . . . *unhappy*?" The sharp interest in her face betrayed her thoughts: this doesn't happen to people like us. Not if you're doing it right. I never liked Lisa, even before.

And then one day I'd realized, when we'd gone to summer drinks at the tennis club, Mark saying it would be good for us. I'd stepped outside, just for a break from the questioning, the burden of other people's concern and curiosity. When I'd come back in I saw them in a corner of the hall. It was something about the way they stood, heads close together.

So now I knew: it was her.

I hadn't asked outright who he'd been with the night Sophie went missing. Because then I'd have to do something about it, and I didn't have the energy, yet. I suppose I assumed it was some impressed girl in his office. Wasn't that how it happened, when a husband worked such long hours? But no, he'd made time for the blonde divorcee from his tennis club. What a flipping cliché.

"Well, of course she worries," Ellen says now. "Wouldn't you expect her to?" Ellen, with her keen appreciation of social niceties, was always hovering around the local queen bee.

I'm lost. "Not really," I say.

Ellen opens her mouth, shuts it. "Well I must get on," she says, briskly. "I've people coming to dinner, and it's rammed in here, isn't it. Why I leave things to the last minute I don't know!" Her neck's going pink. "I'll let you go. But do think about Thursday—" She's flustered, trying to steer the wheels away.

"Ellen," I say. I put a hand on her trolley. "Why would I expect Lisa to worry about me?"

I think I know what she's going to say before she does. But I want to make her say it.

Her shoulders sag, her hand goes to her mouth. She always had a sense of the dramatic.

"Oh, Katie," she says. "I thought you knew, honestly. She and Mark—well, you're separated now, aren't you, have been for quite a while." She glances up at me through her lashes, slyly. "It's only natural that he . . . He's moved in with her."

CHAPTER 6

I keep it together long enough to get out of the supermarket. I can't remember exactly what I'd said to Ellen, enough to get her to stop talking—"Don't worry at all, it's fine, I'll see you"—then I'd dumped my basket, marched straight back through the entrance doors and into the car park.

I'd assumed their relationship would fade out in time, that he'd move on. But here he is, moving from his rented flat in town back into a family home. Lisa's got her kids most of the time, but then he's always liked family life. My face is wet, I realize.

This is what happens when you try to be normal again. The past lays traps.

Looking back, it's hard to remember those first days. I could answer questions and make tea for the police and Dad and Charlotte, who seemed to be here all the time, and do what was required. Then another great wave of terror would roll over me, flushing my body with panic: where was she?

The police talked to teachers and pupils at school. Sophie had signed in for registration on the Friday, that they could agree on.

But this close to exams, the timetable was pretty much abandoned, much of the students' time supposed to be spent in the library.

Then Jennifer Silver said she'd seen her heading to the changing rooms straight after registration, her big bag on her shoulder. Jennie Silver, I remembered Sophie telling me, laughing, was a total busybody. I held onto these nuggets of information. She'd got so protective of them.

They found Sophie's navy skirt and jumper in the changing room, hung neatly on a peg. She'd just walked straight out of the school's front door, as the older pupils were allowed to do, in her own clothes. In a letter to parents I heard the embarrassed head promised to review the sign-out procedure.

The upshot was the same: she'd been gone since Friday morning.

It didn't take the police long to get hold of the video footage. The bus station in Amberton had been full of people, but they'd freeze-framed a shot, where she'd swung round in the direction of the camera, and zoomed in on her, a grainy black-and-white figure on their computer.

"Mrs. Harlow . . . ?" the officer with me had prompted. "Is that your daughter?"

I'd had to clear my throat. "Yes, that's her."

I still couldn't believe it, that she'd actually done this. But there she was, in jeans and her winter jacket, too hot for the weather—at least she'll be warm, I'd thought—stepping onto a coach. I couldn't read her expression, as I tried to decipher the dots on the screen.

The coach was one of those on interminable routes that students love for their cheapness, winding south. They tracked down the driver; he thought he remembered her buying a ticket to London, but he couldn't be sure, and nor could the police. They weren't even sure where she'd got off.

"It's easier to disappear in a big city," said Kirstie, the officer assigned to us as "family liaison"—to hold our hand through the worst. She was Scottish, in her thirties, I guessed, and didn't shrink from telling me the truth, despite her warm manner. But there wasn't that much to report, in the end.

They went through her phone, email, her Facebook—nothing

out of the ordinary. Her internet searches though, on the laptop she used for homework and watching films, were another matter.

"Budget work"

"Casual work"

"Cash in hand"

"Travel work student"

Pages and pages, almost laying out her thought process for us.

"You'd know if she'd gone abroad, wouldn't you?" I said, my panic mounting. "She's taken her passport but it's all electronic now, isn't it, they must be able to track it. Right?"

"The records are thorough," said Kirstie, "especially flights."

"Of course, no border system's infallible," said the officer with her that day, a younger guy. "It's not impossible."

Sometimes my frustration spilled over: I wanted them to do even more.

"This is a—a child. She's still at school."

"She's sixteen," Kirstie said once. "And she's a clever girl, you say. Lots of teenagers leave home at sixteen." I think she was trying to reassure me.

"Not girls like Sophie," I'd replied.

I read her reaction in the swift glance around our spacious living room. She knew: bad things happen to people in nice houses, too. I knew what I meant though: I just couldn't see why Sophie'd gone.

Yes, we'd had rows; she wanted to go out more; she'd moaned about her revision workload. She loved art, and would happily spend hours hunched over her coursework, but she didn't understand why I cared so much about maths and science and the rest.

"Surely that's not enough for her to do—this?" I protested.

Kirstie didn't need to contradict me: Sophie's absence was its own rebuke.

At least there'd been no sign of . . . well, anything else. I could picture, all too easily, how it could have unfolded: long grass by a canal, a dog walker out early one morning, following their excited pet off the path: "Easy boy, hold on, what's that . . . Oh God."

I had to shut out the images that threatened to overwhelm me, that drove away sleep while Mark was snoring gently in the bed next to me. So I stayed busy. I started off local, driving around the streets at night, just to see. Then I went further, into the city, parking up behind derelict warehouses and near the railway arches, to show them my photos: Sophie, in her school uniform; Sophie, at the dinner to mark her sixteenth that April; Sophie, in a raincoat on a school trip to the Lakes.

Mark said it was dangerous. "We need to let the professionals do their jobs." But I knew they wouldn't hurt me, these tired people handling my photos so carefully under the streetlights. "I'll keep an eye out for you," they'd tell me. "I'll ask around." I said Mark should come with me, then, if he was so worried for me. He kept it up for a bit, and, later, at the weekends, after he went back to work.

The police had questions for us, too. Was there anywhere she could have gone? Anyone that she might have been in contact with? Anyone we could think of, at all?

Dad, Charlotte and Mark, we talked endlessly, racking our brains at the kitchen table, late into the night. Back to London? She hadn't lived there since she was, what, twelve—everyone she knew was up here. Some pretty seaside resort we'd once visited? We didn't think Sophie would even remember the time we used to holiday closer to home, before Mark started doing so well. Still, we dutifully wrote all our ideas down and passed them on to Kirstie.

And then there were the other types of questions, more personal. How was Sophie feeling about her GCSEs? How important is academic success in your family? Did Sophie go out with her friends? Was she allowed to? Could you run through again, just so we understand, what exactly you were rowing about, in that last argument you mentioned? And, once: you lost your mother in recent years, Mrs. Harlow, in distressing circumstances, we understand?

I'd drawn in my breath. I didn't know Mark would have told them about that. The driver had been heading home the morning after a wedding, after catching a few hours' sleep to sober up.

Except he hadn't sobered up, he was still well over the limit when he'd ploughed his four-wheeler into the car in front. Mum had been on her way to the garden center. It had been quick, at least.

"That—that was a shock, yes, but I don't think it changed the way I treated Sophie in any way. . . ." I trailed off. Maybe it had, just as she hit the age when she needed more freedom.

And, underneath it all, I heard the questions left unspoken but sounding just as loud: Is this your fault? Did you do this? Did you push your daughter away?

Sophie, I'm so sorry, I've failed you. I'm so sorry.

In the end it had been Charlotte, always such a mum, who told me I needed to go to my GP, that I should get some pills. And Dr. Heath was very understanding, writing a prescription that finally let me sleep; more for the daytime "if I needed them." I'd been grateful for that.

CHAPTER 7

Home safe from the supermarket, I pour a cup of water from the tap and drain it, twice. I'm hot and flustered—and I'm getting bogged down again. I need to stick to my routine, not get thrown off by changes. That's why Ellen bloody Fraser's slipped under my guard. I feel the old restlessness rise up in me, the electric buzz of anxiety. I want to soothe it. I know how I could. But I have to be careful, these days.

I just need to keep playing the game of distracting myself: I will go and see Lily.

Outside again, the afternoon sun is still strong enough to turn my pale skin pink. As I cut through the copse of overgrown bushes that separates our homes, heading up the slight incline, I tilt my head up to admire Parklands through the leaves overhead. Even for Park Road, it's a beauty under its torn plastic sheets and the plywood on the windows—it's all towering chimneys and carved stonework, that over-the-top detail the Victorians loved.

Lily's little redbrick cottage, once the mansion's carriage house, sits in its own small garden on the side of the drive that continues on to the big house, set far back from the road.

She was the house manager for Parklands, she explained once; it was rented out as rooms. I got the impression the residence had got increasingly shabby with the years. She'd stayed on with her late husband, after it was shuttered up for redevelopment: at least her rent can't be much.

I've got my own key, now, so she doesn't have to get up. That's what I said, anyway. I worry about her; I had visions of her falling and me assuming she wasn't answering because she was asleep or at a coffee afternoon.

As I let myself in, the smell of gingerbread slaps me. I sniff the air. There's a smoky edge to it. "Lily? It's me." I find her in her sunny sitting room, in her chair. Her eyes are closed. "Lily," I say loudly.

She raises her head and fumbles for her reading glasses. It takes her a moment to place me, then her face breaks into a smile. "Oh hello, darling, you look lovely."

I can't help but laugh—she always says I look lovely. "Lily, have you been baking again?"

"What? Goodness, you do mumble." I don't think she likes to admit her hearing's not as good as it was.

I repeat myself, and add: "I'm just going down to make us both a nice cup of tea."

"Oh yes, dear, and let's have something to nibble," she calls after me.

"Sounds lovely."

Down the steps, in her little kitchen built half underground, I crack open the small, high-up windows as far as they will go and open the oven, fanning the smoke away. The gingerbread men are black, welded to the tray. There's no saving them, or it. I'll chuck it later, when the thing's cooled.

I pull out the tin of biscuits I bought her and arrange a few on a plate. I know she'll only pick at one, still conscious of her "figure" even these days.

It's as neat as a pin in here, as ever, but under the sharp whiff of bleach—Lily's a huge believer in potent chemicals—there's a darker current. Damp. I make a mental note to have a think about what to do about that. Lily's vague about arrangements and utterly private about money, in that old-fashioned way.

We met my first winter here, when she drove her ancient Ford into the back of my car at the lights at this end of Park Road, as you head into the village. She blamed the ice on the roads.

"Oh dear," she'd said, as we stood by the phone box: her bumper was hooked over mine. "I am sorry. Shall we have a nice cup of tea in the warm, and sort this out?"

I'd walked her back down the road the little distance to the main drive to our houses and followed her into her hall. She walked stiffly: a hip injury, she told me later. "Just a little sore." She made us both Earl Grey. "I can't drink that supermarket tea, dear, who can? Or should we have a sherry instead?"

I'm not sure that was what Mark meant when he said I should make an effort to make friends locally, not spend all my time moping around the house when Sophie was at school. I'd found the not working harder than I'd thought—the days went so slowly.

"Why are you spending so much time with that old woman?" he had asked once, crossly. "Whenever I ring you seem to be at hers. Shouldn't social services be looking in on her?"

"I think she's got someone who goes round. I just like to check on her. She's fun."

She's nothing like my mum, really, who barely bothered to look in a mirror and would have laughed at the idea of spending time on a full face of makeup and polished pink nails, for another day of, well, a coffee afternoon at church, at most. But there's something in Lily's full-tilt approach to life, her heroic refusal not to have a nice time, that reminds me of Mum. Or used to, when we first met.

"Lily," I say, once I'm upstairs. "Did you forget about the gingerbread? It's all burnt." I put down her tea in front of her—in a proper cup and saucer, of course.

"Don't be silly." She frowns. "Of course I didn't forget. I just closed my eyes for a minute."

"Lily, you've got to be careful. The oven had started to smoke. Didn't your smoke alarm go off?" I'm sure I checked it just the other week.

"Oh, that thing," she says. "It would not stop that awful beeping. So I switched it off."

I get up to look in the hall. "Lily, there are wires hanging down. Did you take the batteries out?"

Her eyes look very blue, in the late sunlight. "No . . ." Almost childlike.

"OK." I can replace the batteries the next time I'm round, and tape the cover back in place. Despite this, I already feel soothed just being here, away from my life. This? This I can deal with.

I pull the worn pack of cards from the drawer. "Anyway, what are you going to beat me at today?"

CHAPTER 8

Finally, the call comes from the police, on Monday—a voicemail left on my mobile while I'm in the shower. Could I come into the station? It's a name I don't know. Detective Inspector Ben something. I play it again. Is it bad news, good news? I can't tell. Good, I decide, let it be good. It has to be.

I'm there within the hour, my hair still drying. And then I wait. Half an hour passes in the small windowless room they've put me in. Definitely more than that—but then I only started counting when the clock was at three. I make up my mind. I'm out of my plastic seat, hand on the door handle, when it pushes open and I'm forced to quickly step back.

"Somewhere to go, Mrs. Harlow? I'm so sorry to have kept you. Shall we sit down?" I haven't met this one before: dark hair, sleepy eyes, about my age, maybe. "DI Ben Nicholls," he says, pulling out the chair opposite mine. He doesn't hold out a hand to shake.

"I'm Kate," I say. "We used to deal with Kirstie," I carry on, suddenly nervous. There's not a flicker of recognition. "Kirstie Waller? Curly blonde hair? She'd told me a few months ago that she was going on mat leave, so she was passing on her responsibilities."

Neither of us had punctured the pretense that the investigation was going anywhere, even recently. I was grateful to her for that. "None of the officers I used to speak to are around," I say now. "Everyone seems to have retired, or be on leave."

He nods, unsmiling. "I'm up to speed on the case, I've read through the files."

"OK." So the small talk's clearly over.

"And I understand you're keen for us to get hold of some phone records from the charity where you work—"

"Yes, you've got to," I say, launching in. "My daughter phoned me, she's missing, she's been missing for years, she phoned me, and I need to know where she is, I need to talk to her—"

"Mrs. Harlow, can I interrupt?"

I lean back.

"I want to manage your expectations," he says. "A helpline has privacy procedures in place for a reason. And we can't necessarily overturn them to trace the call, even if you are concerned about your daughter."

"Well, why not?"

"Police officers have to follow rules, too. We'd have to have a very strong reason to break those protocols. The helpline's got a commitment to protect its clients' anonymity—"

"But I'm her mother!"

"And that's why she might not want you tracing her, isn't it? If it was her." I flinch. "She could have phoned home. But she called the helpline, you say, to let you know that you shouldn't expect contact anymore."

I'm not used to the police being this direct. So he's not so sleepy, after all.

"But I just know. Something's wrong." I've got to make them take this seriously. I catch myself: of course something was wrong if your daughter ran away. How can I make them understand?

"Mrs. Harlow, when someone goes missing—I know how very hard this is—"

"No, you don't know," I say simply.

"OK, maybe I don't. And the fact is that yes, in certain circumstances, different things are . . . possible. But, to be blunt, there's no immediate risk I can see here, or any other factors that would prompt us to get authorization to access the phone records, and try to trace the call in question. She's made it very clear, since she left, that it was what she wanted—"

"All right!" I say, too loud. "I remember." I don't want to think about all that, not yet.

He carries on. "So, frankly, we'd be acting with very little expectation that there'd be anything to show for it, or that there was any need. You may not like this, Mrs. Harlow, but everything about Sophie's actions so far have told one consistent story: she's a teenager—an adult now, at eighteen—who doesn't want to come home. But"—as I open my mouth to protest—"*but*, what I can say is that I'll make inquiries. See if there are any circumstances in which the charity might help, for a start."

"Well, OK," I say, uncertain of what he's promising me. "Should I ask them, too? Would that help? I work there, after all."

"Do *you* think that would help?"

"Well . . . no." I can feel my face flushing. I, more than anyone, know how much the charity prizes callers' confidentiality, how it would never pass on information to loved ones without their consent. It's the fundamental rule. "So, when do you think you might have something to tell me?" I can feel the situation slipping out of my control.

"I couldn't say. But here's my card"—he pushes it across the table to me—"there's my mobile number on it, too. Anything particularly pressing you've to tell us, you can let me know that way."

He stands up, ready to go, and for the first time there's a hint of something other than brisk professionalism. "Mrs. Harlow—can I suggest: try not to get your hopes up too much. When someone's been missing this long, well, the outcomes aren't always . . . what we'd like to see. People don't always want to come home. The longer they stay away . . ." He doesn't need to finish the sentence. "If your daughter called you, that might have to be enough for now. You might need to accept that she's not coming home."

* * *

"You might need to accept that she's not coming home." The words keep playing in my mind as I drive back, joining the beginnings of the rush-hour traffic out of town, the low sun flashing in my eyes.

So that's what the police say. That's what Mark said too, at the end, what my family now don't dare to say—but I could read it in their eyes, every time we talked.

Are they right? I make myself consider the question, seriously, just for a moment. Is it time finally to let her go—at least, as my stomach convulses at the thought, for now, until she's ready for more. I don't seem to have much choice in the matter, anyway. Perhaps it'd be best.

At the thought, I feel a strange sort of calm, lighter almost. Acceptance?

The feeling carries me home, as I let myself in, dump my keys on the hall table. What would it be like, if I could accept it . . . as I pad up the landing I realize where I'm already going, unthinkingly. I continue up the stairs to the top of the house, my steps slower now, and push open the door to Sophie's room. As I flick on the bright overhead light, the curtains pulled open as usual, the duvet forever untouched, the room looks oddly staged. This time I can't pretend Sophie's just stepped out.

Perhaps this is what Sophie was trying to give me, with that call, it occurs to me now. The chance to say goodbye, just for a while. To let her go.

Suddenly I'm overwhelmed with longing. I fight the urge to go into her wardrobe, try to catch the scent of her on her clothes. Instead I walk over to the dresser and rest my hands on the old pine. For a second I'm lost—what was I looking for? Of course, Panda. So beloved when she was little that his ears are long gone, the stuffing exposed at the seams. Only Teddy was more battered.

But Panda's on top of the wardrobe with the rest of Sophie's stuffed animals, tucked between the donkey and the tired-looking rabbit.

Silvia must have moved him, I think, when she was still coming here to clean, before it was just me. She must have knocked him and put him up there, forgetting where he lives. I need everything to stay the same, so I carefully pull the toy down and put him back on the dresser, as he always is.

He tips over. But I know what it is—Panda's always propped on his blanket, Sophie's old fuzzy pink blankie from when she was very little. It must have slipped off the dresser's glass surface.

I slide an arm in to pat blindly between its side and the wardrobe. It's not there. I put my hands around the top of the dresser and shuffle the heavy wood out a couple of inches, so I can look behind it.

Maybe Silvia put it in the wash, fabric can get so dusty. She was so careful about disturbing things, but she perhaps wasn't to know. . . . But I'm suddenly torn up inside, blinking away tears again.

Because I'm thinking of the start, when they kept asking me what she'd taken. Sophie would never have gone without her blankie, I knew that, even when she was sixteen years old and would blush to admit it. I knew that she couldn't sleep without it tucked under her pillow—a childhood habit that she'd yet to drop. But she had, of course, she had left it at home along with all the rest of the life she'd discarded so easily. I didn't know her that well, after all. And now, the one time I want it, I can't find it.

It's such a small stupid thing. I shouldn't even care. But the lightness has already dissipated, the familiar anxious buzz swelling up again.

No, I can't accept that she's gone. Nothing about this has ever felt right, has ever made sense, whatever they said to me. It still doesn't.

"Love you, So," I said on the phone. And then she hung up on me.

She'd never do that. It'd be "Love you, So," "Love you, Mo." Just one of those silly family jokes from childhood. She'd never forget that. But why would she punish me with that little snub, withhold that endearment from me? Is she that angry?

A chill goes down my spine. Have I got it wrong, so horribly wrong, that I don't realize I wasn't speaking to Sophie at all, just some confused, troubled caller, me hearing what I wanted to hear?

No. It can't be, it was her. I know my daughter, I do.

Something isn't right. Whatever they say. *Whatever she told me.*

And that's when I decide. That's when I know, with rare clarity.

I'm not going to rely on them to find her, not anymore. It didn't work the first time, after all.

This is my last chance. My last chance to find Sophie.

CHAPTER 9

My stomach flutters as I pull into the car park in the village. I'm nervous, I realize. I was surprised to find myself feeling buoyant this morning, the sense of optimism unfamiliar. I made the effort to scramble eggs and drink two cups of milky coffee, the cat prowling around my feet. Now it's all still churning unpleasantly inside me. But I'd decided. This time around, I'm not going to just sit tight and wait for the police to let me know what's happening.

I've got a plan.

First on my list is speaking to Holly Dixon—just to ask what she thinks, if there might be any possible factor I don't know about that's keeping Sophie away. And then maybe she'll have an idea, someone else I can talk to. Isn't that how it works? Anything to stave off that old trapped feeling. I'm determined to stay active, to hold on to this new stirring of purpose. My grief coach (Lara doesn't like the word "counselor," she says we are partners together in this) would be proud of me. If I still saw her.

Last night I left a message on Holly's mobile, hoping she hadn't changed the number. We haven't spoken in a long time. I left a long, rambling message about Sophie's call, that I could explain properly later, but did she think we could meet? Within about twenty minutes my phone beeped.

OK. Can do 11 tmrw, coffee?

We arranged to meet in the village, as she's still local. Not in the cutesy café, where you can buy the knickknacks that take your fancy. I know too many people in there. I've gone for the pizza chain one everyone disapproved of when it opened, staffed by breezily anonymous Australians. I like it.

I'm five minutes early but she's already sitting there at a table in the corner. "You've changed your hair," I say. "Blue!" Still so much makeup, I see.

"Oh, yeah," she says, touching a mermaid strand. "Well, I got bored of the lilac. Everyone was doing it, didn't you notice."

I smile, looking around. Today the place is fairly empty, but there's not a lot of purple hair around here, it's all tasteful honey highlights, from the girls in school to their mothers.

"It's pretty," I say.

She quickly covers the flicker of surprise. Too late, I remember.

Holly used to stay over all the time. She and Sophie would disappear upstairs and there'd be screams of laughter into the small hours, the two of them doing God knows what in Sophie's bathroom. One time, they'd emerged in the morning with pink hair— "It washes out, Mum, don't worry!" Sophie reassured me, Holly looking at me sidelong, amusement in her eyes as I tried to keep my temper.

Teenagers were always looking for a reaction, I knew. But it had been an expensive trip to the hairdresser to take Sophie's hair back to its baby blonde. She hadn't been grateful at all. "Well, I think it looks cool, Mum. *I* don't want to change it."

Holly and I order cappuccinos. Her mum's well, she says in answer to my questions.

I've seen her, since Sophie went, but after the first few encounters, we seemed to make a tacit agreement to smile and nod. I heard Holly didn't stick around in school after her GCSEs, but she seems to have done well since then. She has started at college and plans to be a nurse. Her tutor, she tells me, "is a total b—" she catches herself. ". . . a bit difficult," but she's enjoyed it.

What she doesn't need to spell out is the reason why I've avoided her until now. The wound Sophie left in her life is healing over. She's hitting milestones Sophie hasn't. I keep asking questions, suddenly wanting to hear the details, though it stings. But the lull's inevitable.

"So why did you want to meet?" she says.

I take a breath. "Obviously you and Sophie were really close." Quickly, I tell her about the call, the bare details of what I heard at the helpline. "I have a feeling . . . that she wants to come back home." It sounds weak even as I say it, but Holly's nodding, her face serious.

"I do too," she says. "I knew she'd come back, one day."

Another memory: Holly loved horoscopes, all that stuff— she even carried around a battered pack of Tarot cards that impressed Sophie deeply. I'd see them bent over the cards on the floor of Sophie's room, their heads—Sophie's pale blonde, Holly's a bleached mirror version—close together, both girls giggling.

"There's just a few things I wanted to get straight in my head," I say now. "About why she left. If she calls again I just—I just want to understand. If something might be stopping her, even now?"

"Well, it was all said at the time, wasn't it," says Holly flatly. "In the papers."

I flinch, remembering how exposed I'd felt. I'd gone along with it all—media appeals, articles in the evening newspaper, a video plea with Mark for Sophie to "Please come home. We're not angry, we just want to know you're OK" that they ran on the local six o'clock news.

Then we made the nationals. There were a few pieces, the longer ones mentioning Mark's job at the firm, and making much of the fact that Sophie's exams were approaching. Her school, the local grammar, was described as an "academic hot-house." There was a comment from a "neighbor" that we were new here from London, "only the one child, a lot of expectation." I'd read that article several times.

"They're saying she was under too much pressure," I'd said to Mark that morning. "That's what they're implying. From us."

"Well, no point worrying about what people write," said Mark shortly. He was starting not to like to talk about it so much.

"A lot of expectation"—I read the words again, in black and white.

"Well, that's wrong," Mark said aloud, reading over my shoulder. "That's only what we paid for this place when we bought it, it's worth a lot more now. See, they can't get anything right." I'd nearly hit him.

The coverage dried up soon enough, anyway. A pair of boarding-school sweethearts used their parents' credit cards to buy flights to Antigua and refused to come home, pushing Sophie's humdrum runaway story off the newspaper pages. Even before the investigation ground to a halt.

"Yes, they said what happened in the papers," I say now. "But what did you think?"

"Well," Holly says carefully. "I know it was hard for her, that she needed to get good grades. But I didn't always know exactly what was going on with her. She wasn't always that . . . easy to ask."

"But you were so sure of yourself."

"I was a teenager," she says, with emphasis. I hide a smile—she can't be more than eighteen, but I know what she means. "That's what I wanted everyone to think. Sophie liked me when I knew what I was doing, when we were having fun. She just didn't like it so much when I messed things up."

"Like when you had that pregnancy scare?" I blurt it out. Holly had been sitting at my kitchen table when I'd come home that night, her feet up on the chair next to her. "Hello, Kate. Isn't that a nice bag, been shopping again?" I'd said she could call me by my first name. I regretted it.

The girls had disappeared upstairs with pizza to get ready. They were going out that night, just round to Emily's from school, they said. They'd rushed out when someone's car beeped outside, and later I'd gone into Sophie's room to collect their plates. I had taken the wastepaper basket with me too, seeing the liner overflowing.

They'd buried it at the bottom, so it was bad luck really that when I'd tipped the contents into the outside bin that I'd recognized the packaging immediately: "99% accurate."

Mark was away with work, in a different time zone, so I poured myself a glass of cold white wine, and sat there at the kitchen table, thinking. Fifteen. Sophie still had a few months to go until her birthday. Under the age of consent, technically, but perhaps not all that surprising.

I'd still been there when the girls had clattered back in, their faces falling as they saw what I had on the table.

"It's mine," Holly said immediately, her usual swagger gone. "I'm sorry, but I couldn't do it at home. It's all fine, I promise. I just had to check. Please don't tell my mum."

Maybe I should have. But she looked so worried, I'd just nodded. "You need to be more careful, Holly." Sophie, bless her, had looked even more scared. At least she was taking it seriously.

They'd both sat there, subdued, while I'd booked Holly in online right there and then to an appointment at the family planning center in town. Afterward, I'd felt pleased with myself for dealing with an awkward situation so understandingly. I could do this, I could help Sophie navigate the teenage years.

"No, not the pregnancy scare," says Holly across the table from me, drawing me back to the present. "No. I mean when I would get upset. My mum and dad . . . I had a lot going on." She hunches her shoulders. "It was a good thing when they split up."

"Can I get you ladies anything else to drink?" The waiter's hovering over us, all smiles. "Tea, coffee?" He gives a happy little shrug. "Nice glass of fizz?"

"Fancy it? I will if you will," I say.

"I won't thanks. I've got to drive," she adds. "My parking will run out soon."

But now she's here in front of me, I suddenly want to keep her here, this link with Sophie.

"Do you still keep in contact with Danny, Holly? Sophie's old boyfriend?"

She pauses, fiddling with the pink pompom on her car keys. "I do, yes. Look—" she lifts up her head, looks me in the eye— "I talked about this with him. That's why I agreed to meet you. I don't want you stirring things up for us, it's not fair. It's been hard as it is."

I'm a step behind. "Stirring up—you're together?"

"Yes," she says, serious. "It's not a secret. We just haven't . . . been rubbing it in people's faces."

"Since when?" The words come out before I can stop them: "How do you think Sophie would feel about this?" I am suddenly angry: my daughter's best friend and her boyfriend. That old cliché.

"I don't know how she'd feel." Her chin's up now, patches of red creeping up her neck. "She's been gone a long time now. If she cared—"

"Sorry," I say, my flash of anger receding as quickly as it came. "It's not my place."

". . . if she cared about him or me," she's relentless, "if she cared about any of us, she'd have come back." She adds, softer now: "I missed her a lot. He did too. We started spending more time together. And, you know . . ."

"Fine, I get it. I'm sorry I asked." I want to go home and shut the door. Sophie's disappearing from their lives. Like a stone thrown into a pond, and even the ripples are now fading away. I motion for the bill, the waiter flapping a little—it's obvious the mood's changed—when it occurs to me.

"Sophie did care about you," I tell Holly. I really want her to understand this, for some reason. "When I found the package in the bin—your pregnancy test—I wasn't happy about it. At all. She stuck up for you."

Sophie had been so earnest in her defense of Holly: "You can't get her mum involved, you don't understand. She's a good girl." It's hard to remember a time when the specter of teenage pregnancy seemed like the worst thing that could happen to a family.

"She really stuck up for you," I repeat.

"Well, that was the least she could do," says Holly. She's looking around to catch the waiter's eye to hurry him, when she says it, casually: "After all, it was her test."

"It was her test? What—how?"

She shrugs, a touch impatient. "She was with Danny then. We were teenagers, it wasn't such a big deal."

It's now my turn to feel my face grow hot. I can almost hear Sophie: "God, Mum, you're so nosy. I need some space!" Her bedroom door slammed shut.

"I—I didn't realize they were that . . . serious."

Holly's mouth quirks. "Well. It's not something I talk about with him now. But, evidently."

"Why did you lie?"

"You'd have freaked out. That would've been the end of Sophie going out for a while, wouldn't it?"

I can't argue with that.

"Does it even matter now?" she says. "It's ancient history." She pushes her empty cup away. "You might not like it, but we don't talk about that time—about Sophie—now. We're thinking about the future." She picks up her bag, ready to go. "I know it must be hard. But I don't know why she never came back."

"OK," I say, with a slow nod. "I understand. Let me get this bill. Bye, Holly."

She's already out of her chair. "Bye, Kate."

It still doesn't sound right.

CHAPTER 10

I'm nearly home again, about to turn into my drive, when a flash of red ahead catches my eye: Lily's front door, swinging open. I feel a pulse of alarm and continue past the fork that leads to my house and up to hers, parking on the pebbled drive in front of her cottage.

"Lily?" I call, running in. "Lily, are you OK?"

I find her in the living room, standing in the corner. She's wringing her hands, her eyes unfocused. "Lily," I say softly, "what's wrong?"

"He's gone," she says. "The little boy. He's gone again. . . ." Uh oh. I settle her in a chair, head to the kitchen and make her a cup of tea. Normally she settles down after a minute or two when she's confused. When I come back she's still in her chair but staring out of the window, her blue eyes filled with tears.

"Oh, Lily, what's wrong?"

"My boy. I can't find him."

"Which little boy is this, Lily?"

"My little boy," she says impatiently. "I've been looking all over. I can't find him."

"Do you want me to help you look?" I say slowly. I seem to remember you're not supposed to contradict them when they're muddled.

"I've looked all over. I've been all round the house, I called in the garden. But I couldn't remember his name!" She's clasping and unclasping her hands in her lap. "He's gone, he's gone." She's so upset that I try to bring her back to the present. I kneel down by her side.

"I don't think there is a little boy. Do you remember, Lily? It's OK, no one's here now."

She seems to calm down, after that. But I make a mental note to find out what help there is for her. Because this is not working.

I don't bother making dinner myself. I assemble crackers on a plate, a smear of hummus, cut up an apple, and eat it standing up, trying to work out the source of my unease. Lily will be OK, surely. I can sort it. But my conversation with Holly has got under my skin. I feel fidgety, off-kilter.

Even I can see that Sophie's friends need to get on with their lives, that they can't stay stuck in the past, like me. But our conversation has shifted my view of their friendship, something that had seemed as clear to me as the sky was blue: Sophie was the quieter, responsible one, Holly the adventurer, pushing the boundaries. Was that not quite the case?

I wonder what else I might be wrong about.

I sit on the sofa and flick on the TV with the remote, scrolling through the channels, unseeing. I flick it off again, then pick up one of my old magazines from the coffee table. The silence I welcomed when I moved here presses down on me, a thick blanket I can almost feel. My beautiful, empty home. Suddenly I'm shockingly, furiously angry. How could she do this to us? To me?

I can feel the tears pressing in my throat, the grief about to come. I'd rather stay angry. I throw the magazine in my hand, the pages arcing through the air to the carpet. I don't feel better. So I go, quite deliberately, to the mantelpiece and knock the vase of flowers onto the floor, water and petals spilling everywhere.

It's satisfying. So I make a clean sweep of my tasteful ornaments. The heavy jade elephant, there it goes. And there goes the carriage clock, a present from Mark's parents. I never liked it much anyway! The cards behind it flutter to the floor in its wake.

I stop short, remembering that I keep them propped up there. I didn't know what else to do with them. I didn't want to hide them away: the reason we think she's OK.

I crouch, carefully plucking them out of the debris on the carpet. *I'm sorry, Sophie. I'm not angry.* Fat tears drop down. I make sure they don't mark the cards, as I lay them on my glass coffee table, pictures up, in a row. They're fine. Then I turn them over. No smudges. No bends. They're fine. The card on top is showing signs of age, the ballpoint pen ink darker. I'd recognize that handwriting anywhere, though.

The first one arrived a fortnight after she'd gone. I came downstairs that morning and saw it on the mat, under a gas bill and a circular for a new Chinese takeaway. The photo was of a beach, curving yellow sand under a bright blue sky, the red script in the top left-hand corner shouting: SPAIN! I turned it over. The address started "Kate and Mark Harlow." The message itself was brief.

> I know you'll be worrying. Please don't. I'm
> safe and I'm well. I love you.
> Sophie xxx ✿

The card trembled in my hand. Sophie had always written like she was in a tearing hurry, her words looping across the page. And there was her doodle in the corner next to her name, like she always did, a happy little flower.

Everyone had been positive. This was what we'd been waiting for: a solid development. Not only that, but Sophie had deliberately got in touch, reached out to us. We'd handed it in to the police. They'd been circumspect as ever, but I could see it in Kirstie's face: this was Good News.

What it meant was less clear. It was postmarked London. "Could she could have got someone to post it for her, maybe? A friend passing through?" Mark wondered aloud.

He took it upon himself to make the calls, spread the news through the web of friends and family, his parents, my dad, my sister, all the rest.

"Well yes. It's very encouraging really . . . we can all breathe a little easier." There'd even been some rueful laughter. I could imagine what they were saying at the other end of the line. That Sophie. Well, *really*. But we knew she'd come back home eventually, they always do.

Afterward, he'd opened a bottle of champagne, poured it out into our best flutes and handed me one. As I stayed silent, he'd gripped me by the arms. I'd been shocked. There were tears in his eyes, I registered, as he told me: "It's going to be OK, I promise. Maybe you can relax, just a little?"

I think I nodded. But I couldn't. It was like hoping that turning off a tap might halt a flood.

Soon, the police came back to us: the expert agreed that this was her handwriting. But as to how it got to us, they didn't know much more. My visions of them tracking the card back to the postbox where it was sent, pulling CCTV to show a small figure slipping it into the slot, soon faded. The postmark showed it was processed in north London, that was all.

We learned that what goes through the postal system gets covered in strange traces of all sorts, chemicals and blood and things you would rather not know about. Still, they managed to collect some prints off the card, ran them through the database just in case: nothing alarming came up, no matches with sinister prison escapees, anything like that.

And the news that she'd sent us a postcard sparked more media interest, the articles taking on a lighter tone that I didn't expect: Sophie appearing as a cheeky rebel on a jaunt, sending a postcard home to the parents. One columnist asked if she should be commended for her spirit of adventure, another if her departure would have drawn the same concern if she were a boy. There was a warning note, however, about the drain on police time, a reminder that serious cases needed attention.

And then . . . nothing happened. Not for a while.

Eventually I did stop going out searching, which made Mark calmer for a bit, reassured that I wasn't wandering through some abandoned warehouse in the city. Wherever she was, I'd realized, it wasn't within my reach—not physically.

Going out had got trickier, anyway, close to home.

"So. You only had the one child," the woman said to me, rearranging her handbag on her arm. "And then you went back to work?"

"Yes," I said, taken aback. I tried to place her name. A mother from the school? She'd come up to me outside the newsagent's, patting me on the arm: "How are things? Any news?"

"So why was that?" she said, then, not hiding her curiosity. No, I didn't know her at all.

"Why w—I'm sorry, my parking's about to run out. I'd better go."

So I went online, where I started trawling message boards, special ones for runaways, expat communities that a traveler might pass through, forums for postal workers who might keep an eye out on their rounds. I'd leave a photo with a note: "Have you seen Sophie Harlow?" Keeping my messages loving, worried, but encouraging. Never desperate, never angry. Keep it together.

There was no end to the task I'd set myself, really. There didn't seem to be so much reason to leave the house then, after that, or to step away from the laptop in our study. I drank, a little, to help me relax. And I had the pills, of course, to soften things round the edge, to help me sleep. I kept busy.

Mark tried to talk, a few times. He even suggested, sheepishly, that he "explain about that weekend." I knew he meant the night he missed Sophie's note. There hadn't been many slip-ups over the years. But now I didn't care. "I just don't want to talk about it,"

I told him. He looked relieved. He'd started going back into the office, just "keeping on top of things."

The journalists didn't bother to call me anymore. Though that was all the police seemed to be interested in, now: a phone call. Could Sophie please ring them so they could establish her safety? In my mind, I filled in what was unsaid: so we can close your case.

The second postcard came in December, dropping onto the mat like before.

> You'll want more than a postcard. But I'm fine, really, and I'm happy. I don't want you to worry.
> Sophie xxx ✹

With her usual flower signature. "France," read the script across the front, on top of a dated-looking photograph of the Eiffel Tower. Again, the postmark was London.

This time there was no champagne.

The next night, Mark'd come home punchy after his work Christmas drinks—I hadn't gone, of course. "Don't you think it's time to stop this? What's it all for, really?"

I turned to see him at the door of the study, where I was on the computer, as usual. There was a slurry edge to his voice. "You're drunk, Mark."

"Maybe," he said. "But you're one to talk. Holed up in here all the time."

I stayed quiet.

"With your pills," he continued, "hiding away."

In the argument that followed, I finally said it, what I'd held back from telling him for so long. "If you'd seen that note, if you hadn't been where you were, things might have been different."

He stiffened. But he didn't back down like I expected.

"And some people might say this all happened because of you. Overprotective, because of your mum. And now you're trying to make up for it."

"Oh, really," I said coolly, hearing the echo of someone else's judgement in his words. "And who exactly told you that bit of pop psychology?"

He colored at that. Bingo. So *she* was still around.

"The thing about you, Mark," I told him, "is that you are essentially . . . lightweight."

I turned my head away from his hurt expression. He'd never known how to fight dirty.

After that, I just—withdrew. We were polite enough after that, moving around each other in our big house with care. It was just a matter of time. He eventually left after that dreadful first Christmas, with both of us wedged round Charlotte's table trying to act normally for her boys. He told me we could sort out our stuff later, when things were more "settled."

The police investigation never ended, not officially. It's not currently active, is how they'd put it. I only realized what the last meeting meant, on that gray February day, when I read about it in the local paper. But I should have known: they said I could have the postcards back and her runaway note, they had all the information they needed from them.

When the third one arrived last summer—Austria this time, fresh mountains and gamboling lambs, the postmark London again—Kirstie took the details from me over the phone.

> I'm fine, I'm happy. I don't want to come home,
> not yet. I hope you understand.
> Sophie xxx 🏵

The same with the last one, roughly six months later, in January, this year.

> I'm OK, I'm looking after myself and I'm safe
> and well. Please give me space and time.
> Sophie xxx 🏵

That was Venice, beaming gondoliers, with another London postmark. I'd thought a lot about her request for space and time. Did that mean she knew of my attempts to contact *her*, somehow?

I imagined some quiet church somewhere, Sophie tanned—an inch taller, too, maybe—pausing, for a moment, and deciding to head in. Telling her companions—who? I pictured young men with scruffy beards, girls with long hair, in those global traveler clothes: baggy printed trousers, drooping cloth bags.

She'd go in to light a candle—she used to like doing that—her steps slowing as she sees the poster, with her last school photo, that I'd stuffed into envelopes and sent out with notes asking churches to mention her in their services and to pin her picture to their walls. "Sophie," it reads. "Come home."

Finally, my message has found its target. She walks closer, reaches out a hand to the paper. . . .

The cat mews, butting against my legs. He must be hungry again.

Now, I stare at the messages in front of me, as familiar to me as nursery rhymes. She was always so sparky, but these are dutiful missives home—not to connect with those she's left behind so much as to let us know that she's safe, no need for any more panicked efforts to find her. *Please leave me alone.*

I feel spacey, tired from the heat and what's happened. I just sit, with the postcards and the note scattered in front of me, but not really seeing them. I must remember to take the washing in, when I can be bothered. The letters go out of focus, so they jump and swim before my eyes. . . .

It's barely formed as a thought, but—I read downward, the first letter of each line, as they're arranged on the first postcard, trying to let a pattern appear.

I know you'll be worrying.
Please don't. I'm safe
and I'm well. I love you.
Sophie xxx ✿

I, P, A . . .

No. You'd have thought I would have learned by now. I've spent days in front of these cards, scrambling the letters, looking for anagrams and codes. There's no hidden message here. I lean down to rub the cat's ears. "Come on," I say, feeling his skull hard under the silkiness. "Let's get you fed."

CHAPTER 11

Nighttime and I'm dreaming, again. I'm following Sophie through my house, as I always do, always a room behind, a step too slow.

But this time it's different. I can't see her, I never do, but somehow I know, as you do in dreams, that it's not the teenage Sophie, the coltish girl I'm chasing after. It's toddler Sophie, all peachy chub, silken blonde curls, teetering into a run. And it's not the house I know now, soft carpets and tastefully chic. It's bare floorboards and half-painted rooms, like we've just moved in, or are about to leave.

We're playing a game. Shrieks of babyish laughter come from just outside the room, as joyful as sunshine. "One two three . . . ready or not, here I come!" And I rise from my hiding place behind the sofa and lumber toward her, my tread dramatically heavy on the bare floorboards. I still can't see her, she's still a step ahead, but I can hear her—the laughter comes again, high and uncontrolled.

Only it's too far away, I suddenly realize. She's wandered further than she should, in such a big house. "Ready or not, here I come!" I call again, louder. "Sophie? Sophie!" My voice bounces around the empty rooms. But already the laughter's silent, the house full of my echoes.

When I wake, struggling out of sleep, it takes me a moment to remember where I am. That was so real, I can almost still hear the laughter.

Another one, though—I thought these dreams had stopped, mostly. It must be the phone call, stirring things up again. I reach for the packet in my bedside drawer and swallow the pill down quickly, chased by a gulp of water from the glass by the bed. It will deliver me to the morning in one drugged whoosh. I can't cope if I can't sleep, and I can't afford to get off track.

I really will have to go tomorrow, after putting my appointment off again. I'm almost out of pills—I thought I could do without them. I turn over, and give my pillow a thump to plump it. Every time I go to the doctor half the waiting room seems to be checking me over, wondering if the strain's cracked me up yet.

Maybe it's the light in here. I don't keep my phone by my bed, I've read too many articles warning me about that wakeful electronic glare. But the moon is so bright tonight, you could almost read by it.

A thought passes through my mind, just as I'm starting to relax a little.

That there's one small comfort to my dreams, at least. When I wake up, when I'm coming back to consciousness, there's no moment of sinking horror as I remember my reality. I already know she's gone.

It's too early for someone to be ringing, I think, as I stumble downstairs in my dressing gown. Whoever it is won't just let it go to the house answerphone, keeps ringing off and trying again.

"Hello?" My voice is scratchy with sleep.

"Mrs. Harlow? Detective Inspector Nicholls. This call to the charity, from Sophie . . ."

"Morning. And how are you?"

"Fine. Now, did anyone hear you take the call?"

"I told you all this already." I prop myself up, glancing at the

clock: it's past nine. Not so early after all. That will be the pill.
"Well, Alma was on the shift with me that night. She'd gone
out. But I told her immediately after, when she got back into the
office."

"And how long would you say the call took?"

"I don't know. It felt like a long time but—" I know how time
can play tricks. "A minute, two?"

He pauses. "How many people work on this helpline, would
you say?"

"I don't know. Shouldn't you ask them?"

"Just a guess," he says. "An estimate."

I twist my mouth. "Fifty?" Maybe more. Not everyone can
hack it for long, they're always looking for new volunteers. And of
course we're not full-time.

"How many are normally on, would you say?"

"I don't know—three?" I like it on a Saturday night, when it's
just me and Alma: that's quite enough sociability for me.

"And how often do you shift there?"

Now I see where he's going. "I know, I've thought about this
myself. It was so fortunate I picked up. Just think . . . If I'd missed
that call. But—I guess it could have been anyone," I finish.

"Yes. Quite the coincidence, really," he says. "And is it always
that quiet—just you on your own?"

"No," I say, "not at all, but Saturday nights, that's when they
can get away with just the two of us. It's not a very big set-up, the
helpline. There's a call-waiting system." We don't normally need
to use it.

He nods. "That's what the charity told me." So he *has* been
checking up. On me?

"So have you found the call?" I say.

"We're still looking into it."

"Because I had a thought. . . ." I tell him about the pregnancy
test that might have been Sophie's; that her friend Holly's mentioned it to me.

"And you think a pregnancy scare would . . . what? Have made
her run away?"

"It sounds stupid, put like that," I say. I can feel my face heating up. "No, I don't. I just thought I should—let you know. In case it had been a factor."

"Ah, well, of course. It's good to know," he says, his voice neutral. "But I would suggest that you don't try to take investigations into your own hands. That's rarely . . . helpful."

"OK, well. It was just a chat, really, I—"

"Thanks, Mrs. Harlow." And he hangs up.

I'm still annoyed when I head out—the phone call distracted me, and then I realized I had to rush. But the GP surgery's not far, just the other side of Vale Dean, in Amberton. I'm not supposed to go too long without a check-up recently.

Maybe that was the biggest shock of all: realizing that life doesn't stop. That you have to keep on keeping on, and not just in that stiff-upper-lip way I'd vaguely imagined: managing a smile while people offer you sympathy. I mean in the way of just keeping up with all the tasks and chores that life offers: bills, insurance claims, keeping food in the cupboards, doctors and dentists and the rest of it.

"Kate," says Dr. Heath, as I sit down in the chair by his desk, "you look so tired."

"Oh thanks," I say. "Never tell a woman she looks tired!" I sound like some coy auntie at a Christmas party. "It always means you look terrible."

"No," he says. His pleasant face is serious. "I don't mean that."

"No, of course not, I was just joking."

He's nothing special, Dr. Heath—tall, glasses, that no-color hair that's not fair or dark—it's not that. I just don't like having a male doctor. Not for the first time, I think I should ask to switch to a GP who's not my age. Someone nearing retirement, or straight out of medical school. Preferably female.

Or maybe it's not that. Maybe he just knows too much about me.

"So how are things?" he says, interrupting my thoughts.

"All right," I say slowly, avoiding his gaze, looking at the photo he has framed over his desk: a glittering nighttime cityscape. He lived in Sydney for a while, he told me once: I think he understands why I can find village life difficult. "I'm still using the pills."

"And how's that working?"

"They help, definitely. I had a couple of bad nights, recently."

"Bad nights?"

I take a deep breath. "There's been a lot going on. I've told you that I work at this helpline, sometimes?" He nods. And then I explain, quickly, about Sophie's call to the helpline. I try not to sound too emotional about it. I've got to seem reasonable, in front of him.

He listens, frowning in concentration. "Of course, well, I can see why you might be struggling. That's understandable." He looks at his computer screen. "And you're not mixing the medication with alcohol in any way? You're absolutely sure about that?"

"Nope. All fine." I shake my head for emphasis. There is nothing like denying you have a problem to make it sound like you have a problem.

"OK. Well, for now, if you still think you need them, I'm happy to renew your prescription." It's anxiety and insomnia, officially. A fun combination. "But you shouldn't really be waking up on your dosage."

"You see, I *was* trying to cut back."

"Perhaps for now, while you're feeling under pressure, you need that crutch. Why don't you stick to the prescription, and then we can see about tapering off, sensibly, in due course."

I can feel myself sag with relief. He's always been supportive, even after—everything.

"But the side effects?" I ask. "I read that you shouldn't be on them for more than a few months and"—I can feel myself growing pink—"it's been a bit longer than that."

He shakes his head. "Nothing that you need to worry about." He glances at the screen. "But it says here in your notes that I referred you to a grief counselor. Remind me, are you still seeing her?"

He knows I'm not, but is too polite to call me out. "We're taking a bit of a break at the moment."

"Kate . . ." He looks at me over his glasses. "Medication is one thing, but it's important to tackle the root of the problem. If that counselor didn't work, there are others, you know, you might just not have had the right chemistry. There's a waiting list, but it's certainly worth referring you. Shall I?"

"Well, why not," I add, slightly sourly: "But the root of the problem is hard to get to, isn't it? She's not come back."

"I can't imagine . . . but I'm always here to help."

Maybe it's because he's not someone I'm close to, something in me can unlock. "I just feel like I've failed, in every way. I failed her, as a mother. And I'm still failing her, even now. Because I haven't found her." I can feel the tears welling up, never that far from the surface.

He leans forward, his blue eyes concerned behind the glass. "I know." I've told him before. And nothing ever changes. "I just think if we can get you to some . . . acceptance of the situation— your new reality—you might feel a little better. I know it won't make it right. But you might feel more at peace with what's happened, if that's the way to put it. That's why I really feel returning to counseling might help."

I don't want to accept it, I want to scream. I will never accept my daughter going away; you shouldn't ask me to. I told you: she just phoned me.

"OK," I say. I'm already regretting my outburst. So I shift in my seat and do the British thing. I change the subject. "OK. Also, I wanted to ask . . ." I take a deep breath. "If Sophie had had a pregnancy scare before she ran away, would you have a record of that?"

He sits up straighter. "And what makes you think she was pregnant?"

"Oh, I don't. Not really. Just something her friend said."

But it's been preying on my mind all morning. What if, what if. What if it was more than a pregnancy test, if that result wasn't what she told Holly. The trauma of going through that alone. A procedure. That could explain a lot, perhaps. . . .

"Well," he says. "That's not necessarily something her doctor would know about." He pauses. "Patient confidentiality is important, of course. But I think you can understand that perhaps she'd be unlikely to raise it with me, as her family's doctor."

He raises his eyebrows at me. I get what he's saying: she didn't tell him anything. "And there are a lot of other options. Young people's services. Clinics."

"Of course." I knew it was a long shot. I start getting my stuff together, aware that my ten minutes must be up.

"But you've mentioned this to the police?"

"Yes, I mentioned it, to this detective. He didn't seem to think it was important."

He frowns. "I would have thought all the details were important, even now."

"You think?" I feel vindicated—and a little worried. "Thanks. And I won't leave it so long next time."

"Any time."

CHAPTER 12

There's no wind, only a few puffs of cloud hanging high and still in the sky, as I drive through Amberton. Surely there will be a storm soon, this weather's got to break. It's not far at all to where I'm going, but I notice the change, the houses getting smaller, less cared for, as the town merges into the outskirts of the city.

I was already nearly home, when I decided, and turned back in the direction I'd come.

I'm going to try to see Danny, Sophie's old boyfriend, and ask him about what Holly said. I've been wondering if I am just being ridiculous, after what DI Nicholls said on the phone. Then I realized I was wasting time, and got angry with myself. Just do it.

There's a body in the garage, half under a car on a rig, as I drive in. That'll be Danny's grandad, Len. I came here a couple of times before it all happened, I was always pranging my big car before I got used to it, and keeping it quiet from Mark. So I knew him to speak to, I would nod if I saw him around.

Afterward I stopped coming. But that could mean anything, I might not have needed my car seeing to. I've a vague idea that

I'll book the car in for an MOT, its annual safety test, then see if Danny's about. Something tells me he won't be as amenable as Holly, so I decided, well, not to ask him if he'd meet me. I've got my running kit on, so I can run home after leaving my car.

I park in the small paved forecourt. An old collie uncurls itself from beside the garage doors and barks twice, more out of habit than warning.

As I step toward the open garage doors, Len's already emerging from under the car, wiping his hands on his overalls. He can't be much older than me, really, but he looks it. His hair's gone gray since I saw him last.

"Morning. What can I do for you today?" There's not a flicker of recognition.

"Hi, um, I don't know if you remember me but I'm Kate Harlow, my—"

"I know who you are." His expression remains blank.

"Oh right." The collie runs up and starts nosing my crotch. I push it away gently. "Well, my car needs an MOT."

He nods toward the office. "Step in and we'll fill out the paperwork. It shouldn't take more than a few days."

"The paperwork or the MOT?" He doesn't laugh as I follow him in. "So is Danny around?"

He turns round. "And why do you want to know?"

I stop too, the collie now sniffing around my feet. "I'd like to talk to him, if that's OK." Polite—but it's not a question. The dog's coat is dusty, but I pat his wiry back, avoiding Len's eyes.

"What about? Haven't you people done enough?"

I straighten up. "*My* people? Done what?"

"You nearly ruined my boy's life, got him locked up." His voice is stony, his arms folded.

"Are you kidding me? It was a police *investigation.* . . ."

"And who pointed them straight to Danny, made them think he had something to do with it?" His voice is getting louder. "I know what you're like, the lot of you, think you and your daughter are too good for him—"

"Hang on, hang on." I put my palms up. "I never said that. I never said she was too good; they asked us who she was hanging around with, that's all and—"

He takes a step toward me, the dog suddenly jumping around us, giving anxious little barks. "Do you know that people still talk? I told him not to get mixed up with that silly, spoiled . . ." I can see him grasping for it, what to hurl at me next—"*bitch*—" He spits the word.

My hands are still up, as if I'm warding him off.

"Grandad!" A tall figure lopes round the corner as the collie, seriously worried, butts up against me, whining. "What's going on?" He slows, clocking me. "Mrs. Harlow."

"Hello, Danny," I say, pushing the fretting dog off me. "Can I have a quick word?"

"You're not welcome here." Len's no longer shouting, but his face is red.

"I don't care," I say, any veneer of civility gone. "I need to speak to him, it's important."

"Grandad, it's OK," says Danny. "I'll deal with this." Len's undecided, his mouth half open. "Take Billie off, will you, he's going nuts."

Len takes the dog by its collar, patting it absently. The touch seems to calm him. "All right. I'll be here." He looks smaller now, the anger shifting into upset.

I'm shaky as I follow Danny into the small office, him pulling out a chair for me. Now emotion's ripped through me I'm quiet, shocked at myself for raising my voice. And at him.

"I thought we were fine," I say, finding myself suddenly on the verge of tears.

"I'm sorry about Len," says Danny in that soft voice. "He's just protective. He found it very hard. He's getting older now. The police—anyway." He sits down, waits for me to do the same.

"How've you been?" I say, then kick myself inwardly. We're not here to make conversation.

"I'm doing well," he says, a touch of defiance in his tone. "I'm basically running the garage, Grandad's handed a lot of responsibilities over to me these days, he prefers working on cars to doing the books, anyway. We've taken on an apprentice."

"Congratulations!" I'm slipping into my mum-at-the-school-gates mode. "Sounds like you're doing really well for yourself."

"Yes," he says pointedly. "I am. Better than everyone ex-pected."

There's a lull. I could swear he's got even taller. He's filled out, lost that puppy-dog lankiness.

"And you're with Holly now."

"And?" he says, hostile.

"I didn't mean . . ." I give up on the pleasantries. "I know we haven't spoken since Sophie's gone. But I"—I find myself veering away from the details—"I'm trying to understand a bit better why she ran away. To help me understand when she might come back. What do *you* think happened, Danny?"

"She'd had enough," he says. "Sometimes people just need to get away." *But you didn't.* The thought crosses my mind, unex-pected. *You stayed to help your grandfather.* "Why d'you care what I think anyway? You didn't seem to back then."

"But I did speak to you, so did the police," I say falteringly, "to see what you knew. . . ."

"What I *knew*," he echoes, opening the binder in front of him. "You know they thought I had something to do with it?"

"I had an inkling." Following up all leads, was how they'd put it, before her first postcard removed some of the urgency. Of course they'd look at her boyfriend, especially one like him. But I don't want to say that with him looking so, well, grown-up in front of me.

"They kept me there for hours," he says. "Asked loads of ques-tions about me, Sophie, what we used to do. And they went round the neighbors. Whether I was the type to—to do something. Hurt her. It made things difficult. For Grandad . . . kids threw stuff at our house."

"I didn't realize." I didn't know it had been quite that bad. "But of course they've got to follow all avenues," I add. "You were a, well, an unexpected couple. . . ."

Danny was a year ahead of her at school—until he'd left. And no, I wasn't keen when Sophie told me, casually, that she was seeing him. Running wild at his grandad's, his parents who knows where. It was just minor stuff, really: scuffles outside the pub; that time a teacher left his keys in his car outside school and it was taken for a spin. It turned up the next morning in his drive, with dried mud sprayed up the side. But somehow Danny Mason's name always got mentioned. Even I'd heard of him.

Now he bends his head over the paperwork in front of him. His eyelashes, I remember Sophie telling me, in an unexpectedly confiding mood, are ridiculously long—softening that face, all hard angles. She was right, I see now.

"It wasn't really like that," he says finally. "It was kind of . . . innocent."

"Oh? I thought maybe Sophie had a . . . that you . . ." I take a deep breath. "She did a pregnancy test, before she went. I wondered if you might have had a scare."

"That would have been a miracle."

"Oh, really." I don't mean to sound as sarcastic as I do.

"Yes, really." The tips of his ears are going pink. "We weren't much more than friends."

"Friends."

"Friends. We had nowhere to go, anyway."

I flash back, suddenly, to when I'd come home and found them all in my kitchen once, Sophie, him and Holly, the laughter drying up as I walked in. She didn't bring him round much once they were together, but teenagers find a way, don't they? Sophie was always off with him, at the cinema, she said, or someone's house.

"If you want to know, I think she liked the fact that it wound you up," he says now. "But she intimidated me, a bit."

I raise my eyebrows.

"It's true. It was the whole thing. Her life, her home." He looks away. "Her family. I mean, her dad was going to buy her a car! And he's picking her up from school and all that, it's not exactly easy to . . ." He trails off. "Do you have your car key? We've still got your details. You can pick it up tomorrow."

"Oh. Of course, yes." I'm being dismissed. "Here you go."

"I've got stuff to do," he says mildly. He stands. "I'm sorry you had all this upset."

He's polite, but I know our conversation's over. I stand too, automatically brush the seat of my leggings down from the tatty office armchair. I notice him watching me doing it and I stop, abashed.

"All right. Thanks."

Len's gone off somewhere with the dog, so my path to the road is clear. But some impulse makes me turn in the doorway, as I set off for home. "Sophie was a daddy's girl. But he didn't pick her up," I add. Petty, but I can't resist scoring the point. "I did, if she was late finishing. Mark was always at work."

He shrugs.

"Bye, Danny."

I should have got a taxi. I'm regretting running, at first, the pavements throwing up the heat of the day at me. My muscles feel stiff. Too much sitting in front of my computer. But soon, as ever, I feel calmer once I'm really moving, heading down the roads that will take me from these brick terraces to the fringes of the countryside. Why did I ever stop? I suppose I just got used to being indoors, these last few months. Or year. And once Mark took the dog, there seemed less reason to run.

I'm going to make my way home round the outskirts of the village. It's nicer this way, anyway, along the edges of fields and under the trees. I veer off the tarmac onto the track I'm looking for. It's instantly cooler, the leaves cutting out the sunshine.

My mind starts to wander as I pad along, my thoughts unspooling.

Holly says that pregnancy test was Sophie's. Danny says he and Sophie didn't sleep together. Someone's wrong. Or lying. And if so, who?

Maybe even today Danny just didn't want to admit to me, Sophie's disapproving mum, that she wasn't still my little girl in the way I thought. I suppose it's respectful, in a way.

Still. I could have sworn he was telling the truth to me.

Does it even matter?

I almost trip, and right myself. My lace is loose. I stop, bend down to retie it.

The thought occurs to me: what if it wasn't negative? Would that have been enough to prompt my sensible, good girl to run away?

I actually shake my head, almost stumbling as I start off again. I can't really believe that. I would have helped Sophie, wouldn't I? Mark and I, of course we wouldn't have been pleased, but it wouldn't have been the end of the world. We just wanted what was best for her. Surely that couldn't have been enough to prompt her running away?

But then I know that's what so many families say. I've read the research, the plaintive comments from case studies. "We couldn't think of a reason as to why he'd disappear." "She didn't give us any sign; it came as a total surprise."

Suddenly I picture Len again, red-faced with anger. It shocked me. Danny's always seemed so quiet, so still. But what if he's got his grandfather's temper too? The track's opened up into fields now, great torn-up stretches of dark soil under the huge sky.

A black shape bursts out of the hedge in front of me, leaving the branches moving. I pull up, my heart pounding, even as I register that it's just a bird—a big one, a crow or maybe a raven. I must have startled it. As I watch it wing its way across the field, low and fast, I'm reminded once again how quiet it is here. There's not a soul around.

I set off again, picking up my pace.

CHAPTER 13

I feel like I spend the next few days on the phone. I've left several messages at the charity, and emailed; not Alma, but the higher-ups. I dug out my induction leaflets, looking for contacts in head office. It's more corporate than I expected: it's been hard to get through to anyone via the switchboard.

What I want is a long shot: for them to give me all the details of the call I took—and the number that rang it. I don't know if they do keep a record, or how it works. And it goes against all the rules, but I've got to ask. What else can I do?

I've tried everyone I can think of, even the CEO. Eventually her assistant, a young man called Jason, told me, in the politest of ways, to stop calling.

"Someone will be in touch with you, Mrs. Harlow, to respond to your inquiry. When they're in a position to do so." From that I judged they're working out what to do.

And I told Mark about the call. Well, not directly. I didn't want to speak to him, so I sent an email to his work address, setting it out in the briefest of details: that when I was working at the helpline on Saturday night, I heard from Sophie, who was trying to get in touch with us. But that when she realized who she was speaking to, the call ended.

Put like that, it's not the most encouraging development, I know. He hasn't replied yet, but I know he'll have read it. He's always on top of his work email.

I haven't heard anything else from the police yet.

Every time I check my answering machine, it's my family: Dad was once the only person I knew who still left messages on a landline, rather than just hanging up and trying my mobile. But Charlotte's started now too. Probably because she knows I won't pick up.

There was another one this morning.

"Kate, I really need to speak to you. Is your mobile switched off again? I want to know numbers for Alfie's birthday party next month. He'll want you there." He's turning two, I think, he really won't notice as long as he's got his favorite wooden spoon to bang on the floor. "And I'd like you there, a lot." I sigh. "Can you get back to me, please? Also, I've been speaking to Dad. We should chat. About this call—what it means . . ." Her tone changes. "Kate, are you there? Are you listening? Pick up, Kate—" How does she do that? I shut the kitchen door behind me, muffling her voice.

I went out for another run, to the garage, to pick up my car. Danny wasn't there. I spotted Len in the garage itself, but he didn't make eye contact. It was a younger boy, the fluff on his cheeks not making him look any older, who returned my car to me.

But the run seems to have unlocked something in me. I feel more full of energy than I have for ages, despite my phone calls getting nowhere and my worry about Sophie. Despite all that, there's something driving me forward. For the first time in ages, I've got a reason to hope.

And I haven't forgotten about Lily. I finally got put through to an "away on annual leave" voicemail at the council and left a message. Well, it is August. I want to find out what's happening: I've yet to see any sign of anyone else checking on her.

In the meantime, I'm taking a new tack, starting when I visit her this afternoon: I'm going to stop contradicting her, however politely, when she gets mixed up, and try to draw her out a bit more. I've been reading about it: the idea is that it's less confusing. We can all do with a bit of time indulging in our dreams.

I'm not quite sure how to get onto the subject, as she chats about her programs—*Coronation Street*'s her favorite. Mark never liked me watching it, and the moaning got so annoying I'd switch over. Since he's gone I've made a point of getting back into it. And I chat to her about the charity, about Alma and her dog, the other volunteers who sometimes work alongside us. I've not much else to tell her, otherwise.

In the end she brings him up, as we sit on her flowered sofa with cups of tea. It's so soft you sink right in, knees almost higher than your head. "The little boy," she asks. "Where's he gone?"

"I don't know, Lily. When did you last see him?"

"A while ago," she says. She looks sad, unusual for her. "Why won't he come back?"

I don't know how to answer. "Tell me about him, Lily. What's he like?"

Her eyes brighten. "Oh, he's such a lovely little boy. Such a tinker. And those blond curls!"

"Blond curls?"

"Oh yes," she says confidently, "just like me, when I was a girl."

"Lily," I say carefully, "I didn't know you and Bob had any children."

I know they didn't. Bob, Lily's husband, is long departed but honored with a photo in pride of place on the hall table, in a fancy gilded frame. When I first met her, she made discreet references to their "disappointment in the family way." She'd run a shoe shop in Leeds before she met Bob, and they'd made a good life for themselves, she told me.

She doesn't reply. "So what's his name, Lily?"

"I don't know. . . . I've forgotten, haven't I. Do you know?"

"I don't. But I'd love to meet him," I add.

"Well . . ." Lily glances sideways at me. "I don't know when he'll next be here," she settles on.

I'm reassured by that. If Lily is imagining a little boy to keep her company—the child she never had?—then her reluctance shows that, deep down, she still knows I couldn't meet him.

"What about you, dear?" she says now. "Have you heard from your Nancy?"

I didn't know she remembered. It had upset her, when I'd explained that my daughter had gone away, and I didn't know where she was. I'd ended up telling her she was traveling.

I clear my throat. "I had a phone call, yes. Recently. But it's Sophie, not Nancy."

She nods. "Nancy was the other one, then. Oh, she was trouble." She looks downcast. "I get a bit confused these days, don't I?"

It's hard when she realizes what's happening to her. "Just a bit, Lily, but that's OK. Now. I think *Corrie*'s about to start."

I'm suddenly awake. I lie there, the bedclothes clammy around me, the dark room hot.

The run worked just as I hoped. I fell asleep quickly, no thoughts crowding in. Don't think, don't think, don't think. My mantra, until sleep descends.

But now I'm awake, in the dead hours. Yet again.

And then I feel it. It's not so much a prickling of the skin as something else, some older sense, the quiet, electric awareness. The presence in the room. Slowly, inevitably, I turn my head.

The figure in the doorway is quite motionless.

I close my eyes, reopen them. And still he's there.

He slowly takes a step toward me. . . .

And then I wake up again, for real this time, and grasp for the light.

Of course, there's no one there. But my heart is still thundering, my whole body flushed with adrenaline. Another dream I've had before. Quite common after trauma, my counselor Lara once told me. A physical manifestation of the perceived threat to my world—my brain making sense of things.

It still scares me though.

I reach for the pills in my drawer. This time, I take two. Just to be safe. They'll work, as always, and I settle down with a book, keeping my thoughts occupied, till I start to feel drowsy.

As I fall asleep, fragments of my day appear before me. Len's face, red and angry. That collie dog, whining and afraid. The black shape bursting from the bush. And Lily: "Nancy was the other one."

Just as I slip under, a question bubbles to the surface and stays, for a second. Who's Nancy?

CHAPTER 14

I'm so sick of staring at my computer screen. I've spent the morning falling deep into an internet hole, bogged down in the rules around teenagers and privacy. Dr. Heath's right, of course. If a teenager gets pregnant, medical workers don't have to keep her parents informed if . . . I don't want to think about it. But Sophie could have done anything, and I wouldn't know. They respect her privacy. And she can just go into any of the centers in town for help, there's no need for her to involve the family doctor at all.

Or maybe I've got this all wrong, am jumping to conclusions. This feels so pointless and familiar, immersed in web pages, digging and digging, getting nowhere.

I stare out of the study window. It's been so hot the trees are already yellowing. Or could it be autumn starting early? It's so hard to keep track. I feel stupid and drowsy. I could take a nap. . . .

And isn't there something else I'm supposed to do, something I should check? It's dancing on the edge of my consciousness, like when you can't remember something just as you fall asleep. . . . I fell asleep quickly last night, tired out after my run. But I'm sure I still woke up again, took a pill or two. . . .

And then I catch my thought again: who's Nancy? That Lily mentioned. I'm always intrigued by Lily's life; she can be really quite guarded.

I don't really expect to find anything, but I type it in anyway. Just to check.

Nancy—I pause, type more—Vale Dean. That's all I know. Oh. I see. I lean forward.

New appeal over missing Vale Dean girl

Sister of schoolgirl missing for 20 years
says she's never given up hope.
Twenty years after she vanished,
Nancy Corrigan is still missing
Missing
Missing
Missing

So there was another girl, who went missing too. Nancy.

It doesn't take me long to read what's online. The articles are sparse, archive stuff that local papers have put on their websites. The twentieth anniversary they're marking was back in 2012, before we moved here. But I quickly glean the basics.

Nancy Corrigan was a local girl, who went missing in April 1992. Sixteen years old.

She's not one of those that I've heard of, that I try not to think about anymore.

The housewife who stepped out and left a note "back in two minutes." The baby left in the rear seat of a car, just for a moment, and never found. The children known by their first names only—or over-familiar nicknames that their families never used. And all the pages devoted to them online, articles and discussion forums. What happened? Where did they go? Without a trace.

My family told me to stop torturing myself. Eventually, I listened.

And it's so very different to our situation, I tell myself. Thank God we heard from Sophie, that she didn't just disappear. But they fill me with cold horror, all the same.

I make myself continue, but I can't find much from the time it happened, just the few pieces marking the twentieth anniversary and repeating the appeal for information. There's a sister who's quoted.

"This is a difficult time of year," said Olivia Corrigan, 29. "I have never lost hope that we will hear from her again. I think about my big sister a lot."

There's not much else, but I keep scrolling.

Oh, I see. That's why I haven't heard of her. Not such a mystery, after all. She ran away. So that's why Lily got mixed up.

Nancy left a note, too.

I wonder, vaguely, if I'm going to be sick. Suddenly I've got to know. What happened next? So she never came back? Did they ever hear from her again? I feel caught out, like I should have known about this. But why would I? It's so long ago.

Think. It's a Saturday, so Lily will be out—she gets picked up by people from the church for a coffee afternoon, I know that. It's fine, I can just ask her later. If she remembers any details. My heart sinks a little. It's hard to get information out of her at the best of times. She hates to admit she's forgotten anything. Sometimes she pretends not to hear me. "You what, dear?"

Olivia Corrigan, 29. So she'd be 35 now. Younger than me. It brings Nancy's story closer, out of the past.

But it doesn't mean anything for *you*, I tell myself, it's not a sign. It's not. Don't think like this. There are so many families like mine, after all. That's what working on the helpline's taught me. So many parents whose children don't—*won't*—come home, I tell myself, even as I go into the hall and rummage for my car key in the drawer. The library's not far, it's just off the high street in the village. And then I can just settle my mind.

The phone rings as I'm going through the front door and I wait until it clicks to the answering machine, the voice carrying loud from the kitchen. It's Charlotte again.

"Kate," she sounds harassed, noise in the background: the boys. "Kate, are you ignoring my calls now? It's really not on." No, she sounds upset. Nothing drives Charlotte crazier than someone ignoring her. I should know; it was my last resort to wind her up when we were little. I'd compose my face, and block her out.

It's harder now. "I really need to talk to you, I mean it, Katherine." Like Mum used to call me. She's definitely mad. "You are not doing to me what you've done to everyone else. I'm not letting you. Call me back, or I'm coming round. Soon." Shit. I almost stop, pick up the phone to call her back, then tell myself I'll wait— I'll go now, before the library closes, then I'll call her. Maybe.

I have to speak to the librarian to get access to the archives and sign something promising I won't make off with any of their microfilm, but after explaining the machine to me, a sort of light-up magnifying box with a screen, he leaves me alone in a small dark cubby off the main room.

It's story time this afternoon; snatches of the book being read to the half a dozen or so children drift through the door left ajar. "Once upon a time, there was a princess, who lived in a castle. . . ."

They've only kept records of the very local papers here, the weeklies, they don't even have copies of the daily evening paper. But as I'm here, I might as well look. I've a pile of little paper boxes to go through, each containing weeks, months, of *Amberton Telegraphs* copied in miniature onto small rolls of film. The librarian's showed me how to do it; loading the right one into the machine for me to start me off.

I start scrolling, turning the knob on the machine, and watch the pages of old newsprint blurring on the screen in front of me till I near the date Nancy went missing, Friday 10 April, 1992.

I start to track forward more slowly. It's easy to find once I've got the hang of it: an appeal for a runaway Vale Dean schoolgirl. It's dated 15 April, the Wednesday after she went, so the first mention in the local paper. She's made the front page, alongside suspected arson at Amberton football ground.

The piece about her is surprisingly short, just a headline and a couple of hundred words, relating that police are appealing for information after Nancy Corrigan, 16, from Vale Dean, went missing. She left a note signaling her intention to run away, it says.

There are a few more details, but not much. I suppose it would all have been covered in the bigger papers already. She went to Amberton Grammar, like all the kids round here still do, if they can get in. It's still a good school. *Her family are concerned for her welfare.*

The next week's edition's missing—the film just reels right on to the following paper without a gap. But this time the article has a bit more detail: a sixteen-year-old boy questioned by police has been released without charge. The rest of it just repeats what I know already. It doesn't seem like anyone was panicking.

So what happened to the boy?

But I can't find another mention of him and I get sidetracked as I scroll through the pages on the reader, my attention wandering into details of decades-old mayoral visits and planning disputes. A Cabinet member visited Amberton and was egged outside the town hall, the photographer catching him furious in his gray pinstripe. The church is appealing for a new roof. It still is today, I think. The more things change . . .

I'm getting stiff, my lower back seizing up. Wanting to move, I wander out of the side room and over to the water fountain by the main desk. I feel grumpy and tired. I should be worrying about Sophie, I think now, not this. But what exactly can I do? I should be honest with myself: I'm just looking for distractions.

"How are you getting on?" says the librarian. He's tall, thin, with a friendly air. I've told him I'm researching local history.

"Not that well. It's missing some of the dates I'm looking for, the film I'm looking at. There's no paper for 22 April that year?"

"Ah, well," he says, frowning slightly. "It's all going digital so we're not exactly on top of it all, I must admit. What are you looking for, anyway?"

"I'm looking into a local girl, who went missing. Nancy Corrigan."

"They'll have more papers at the Central Library, in the city center. I think you'll have to make an appointment. You might need to be a student. Are you a student?"

"No." I can see he's waiting for an explanation. "I mean, it's a personal project. I'm looking into the social impact of—of missing persons on small communities."

"Ah well, it should be fine then," he says. "Fascinating story, too."

This gets my attention. "Nancy? The missing girl? You know about her?"

"Oh, it was all very sad," he says cheerily. "And of course, it was what, twenty years ago?"

"Nearer thirty. So did you know her? Are you local?"

"I am yes, grew up round here. But she was a bit older than me." He must be younger than he looks. "But we used to go and look at the house after the family left, dare ourselves to get into the grounds. You know how kids are."

"What house?"

"I forget the name. You know the big gray one. Park Road, the one on its own at the end."

"She lived at Parklands?"

"That's it. Parklands." He misreads my look of surprise. "It would have been different in those days, a lovely house. Grand, even. They had big parties on the lawns. . . ."

So Nancy lived at Parklands. No wonder Lily got mixed up. Another runaway girl. And then they all left. How could they? What if she came home one day and they'd gone? The door closed, a new family in the house, like Peter Pan. I push down the rush of concern. It's not my story. But now I'm curious.

"It said in the papers that a boy was questioned?" I ask.

"Oh, I don't know about that." He starts to tidy, moving books about, then he stops. "But my cousin went to school with her. Nancy. She might remember things. I could ask her if she'd speak to you, for your project."

"Uh, OK. Would you?" I'm always surprised at the friendliness here. I was in London too long. I pull out a piece of paper from my bag and grab the pen in front of me, before he changes his mind.

"I'm Kate," I say. I don't write down my surname, just in case. I've had enough of the questions.

"David." He gives me a little awkward wave from behind the counter.

"So here's my number, if she—" as my phone starts ringing in my bag. "I'm so sorry." I fumble for it as he gives me a look and tilts his head meaningfully at story time. "I'd better take it outside," I whisper. On the other side of the sliding doors I wrestle it out.

It's a withheld number. "Hello?"

"Hello, Mrs. Harlow? DI Nicholls here."

"Yes, it's me. Hello?"

"Can you come into the station today? Something's come up."

"Uh, OK. Now?" I glance at my watch. It's just after four.

"Yes please, if you could."

"What's this about?"

"Something's come up," he repeats.

Fear clutches at me. "Is it bad news? Have you—"

His voice is firm. "It really would be best if you came in to discuss it."

"Yes, of course. I can be there in ten."

I lick my dry lips as I end the call. Something digs into my palm. I look down, realize I'm still holding the librarian's pen, my knuckles white around it, and head back in.

"Oh, I thought you'd gone." The librarian, David, sticks his head out of the cubby. "Have a look at this."

I follow him in. "Sorry, I've left all my stuff everywhere, haven't I, I'll just get my jacket"—I want to get out now, my mind on what's ahead—"and here's your pen back." I start to shuffle my jacket off the back of the chair he's commandeered.

"I really should sort these archives out," he's saying, "but you know, with the amount they expect us to do now, we've two of us doing the work of three, and they're already muttering about a mobile library, which poor Lynn finds very alarming, she can't even drive. . . ."

The photo on the screen is in black and white, a poor reproduction.

"You're right, the film jumps right past that edition," he says. "I found it on a separate roll of film, a few of the issues that were missing. They were so thorough then, they must have added them later." He gives a rueful laugh. "If only we had the resources, these days. Um, are you all right?"

I can't reply. I'm fixed where I stand.

So they'd put her on the front page again, that second week— but with a photo, this time. Nancy's school photo, a headshot against that mottled gray background school photographers always seem to use. Nancy Corrigan. Blonde hair, round face, that sweet smile. Laughing eyes.

Nancy, not Sophie. Just breathe. It's OK.

"Thanks," I hear myself say. "That's really helpful, really it is. And you've got my details."

It shocked me, catching me off guard for a second, that's all.

She's the spitting image of my daughter.

CHAPTER 15

I wish for a breeze as I drive, opening all my car windows to cool the sweat prickling under my arms. It'll be fine, I tell myself. Don't think what it could be, don't think what they could have found. But I know what that means, that polished professionalism, before they break some new horror to you. "Mrs. Harlow, we have video footage of Sophie at a bus station." What could they need to tell me now—what have they found. . . .

Stop it.

I switch on the radio and turn it up loudly. It's the news. A shadow minister caught on a walkabout being rude about the voters, not realizing the cameras were still rolling, will probably have to resign. A big-name footballer's been caught up in a tax row. And now the weather: the hot spell is going to stick around. There's a drought warning in five counties, please don't use your hosepipes. . . .

It's soothing, to me. By the time I'm at the police station, waiting in another of their small rooms, I'm almost calm. The building's all carpeted corridors, muffling its sounds. I start as the door opens and DI Nicholls walks in. He nods at me and drops something bulky on the table, in a clear plastic bag.

The pages have warped at the edges. Brown spots fleck the cover—damp? The diary still has the sticker on, a large white rectangle—a car bumper sticker from our last holiday to Florida: "Mickey ❤ me." I didn't know you still liked Mickey, I'd teased Sophie in the gift-shop queue.

No, Mum, it's cool, she'd explained patiently. It's *ironic*.

I reach toward it, automatically, and he touches my arm, just gently. Hold on.

I sit back, startled by the contact.

"Do you know what this is, Mrs. Harlow?"

"It's Sophie's." I sound angry. Another shock. "Where did you get this?"

"Why do you think it's Sophie's?"

"I bought it for her. Back to school."

"Do you remember when you last saw it?"

"No. Yes. I mean—not recently. Years ago. When . . ." When Sophie was still around.

It must have been a few months before she went, just before Christmas. I'd been in her room while she was at school. They were finishing late that year, it was how the dates fell. I'd been putting away her washing, when I'd found it at the back of a drawer. I recognized the chunky little notebook, a week across two pages of thin paper, and I reached for it before I let myself think it through.

The first few pages were full of details of her homework, reminders of what she had to do for school, but after a few weeks she'd abandoned those good intentions. She'd started to use it like a normal diary: recording details of what had happened in class, funny comments that her friends had made. And all her little doodles and sketches, cartoon animals peeking out from the page at me, hiding behind flowers. I'd smiled to see them, as I flicked through. Danny got the odd mention; they'd got together earlier that year, not that she really told me. But it was obvious, when he and Sophie started doing more things together just the two of them, without Holly and that crowd.

> 6 December, 2015
> Cinema with Danny. Holly wanted to come too, so I said she could. He was a bit annoyed. I don't want to hurt his feelings, but why shouldn't she come? I don't care. The film was great, so interesting to look at, the colors they'd used . . .

She spent more time writing about what the film looked like than what happened.

I leafed through the rest quickly. There was nothing particularly personal, really. Still, I must have spent twenty minutes sitting there, glorying in getting to know my teenage daughter, always so closed now, and all the things she'd stopped telling me.

Then I caught myself. What on earth was I doing? I'd have been furious if my own mother read my diary, however innocuous. Embarrassed, I put it back.

She noticed, of course—I should have known. I replaced it in not quite the right way, displaced something balanced in the drawer. Or perhaps she'd just guessed: she'd always found it easy to read me. She'd stood at the door of the kitchen that evening, her face serious.

"Mum. Did you read my diary?"

I'd actually blushed.

She'd moved it after that. I hadn't checked where—I'd felt so guilty—but I'd never seen it again. After she left, we looked, of course we did—the police too, after we mentioned it—but there was so much that was missing. She could be ruthless in throwing things away.

"I haven't seen it for a long time," I say now. "Where on earth did you find this?"

"Amberton Grammar called in. There's a common behind the school, behind its own grounds?"

"Yes, I know it. The kids play sport on it sometimes, and there's cross-country." I'd gone to watch Sophie run a couple of times. It's a huge grassy field, far too uneven to mark a pitch, fringed by scrubby trees.

He nods. "The school secretary rang us. Apparently a dog walker saw it and handed it in—he thought it must belong to one of their pupils. Of course the woman in the office knew who Sophie was, and so it came to our attention."

"Can I have a look at it?"

"Let me." I notice now that he's wearing those plastic gloves. He opens it at the front page. "Do you recognize this as Sophie's handwriting?"

"Oh," I say. "She's filled in all her details."

It's one of those old-fashioned diaries asking you for your name, address and the rest. I don't remember her having filled it in when I'd seen it before. I follow the script with my eyes, relishing the familiarity of those shapes, her letters all fat round bubbles and short spiky stems.

Name: Sophie Harlow
Age: 15
Address: Oakhurst, Park Road, Vale Dean, Cheshire.
Contact details: Sharlow90@yaymail.com

He holds the paper down. She's used blue ballpoint pen, pressing down hard. She always wrote like she'd punch through the paper, her teachers gave up trying to get her to use a fountain pen—too many bent nibs.

"Yes," I say. "That's definitely her writing." I frown: there's something about it . . . but he's already turning the pages, then he stops.

12 November, 2015
Hockey today. Freezing cold rain. Mrs. Wilson—that was her PE teacher—was on at me again. Can you try harder, what's wrong with your attitude. I wasn't in the mood. It was too cold. Holly had skipped it. She said I should too. Took the dog for a walk. So much homework.

I nod. You'd never guess it from reading these entries what was to come.

He keeps flicking through the pages, slowly. But the words stop meaning anything. How can this have happened to us, I think, yet again. How can this be my life? Disassociation, my counselor called it—I've refused to accept my reality. She told me so, in the months straight after.

"Mrs. Harlow?" I've almost forgotten he's here.

He raises his eyebrows, letting the pages flutter back round.

"It's hers. Can I look myself, now?" I reach out again, wanting just to touch something of Sophie's.

"Just a moment, please." His gloved hand hovers over the diary. "You see, there's some detail in it that surprised us." He pauses. "Did Sophie tell you she was pregnant?"

"No, she didn't," I reply automatically. "I mean—No, she wasn't pregnant."

"She thought she was, according to this," he says. "So you didn't know then?"

"That—that's never been a line of inquiry." The phrase, out of officialdom, sounds somehow false in my mouth. "I mean, her friend—Holly Dixon from school—I told you I spoke to her the other day. She said that Sophie took a pregnancy test, yes. But that it was negative."

"I see." Carefully, he starts to leaf through the pages again and I crane to see Sophie's handwriting. But soon they go blank—charting the months after she caught me, I realize. The new year's empty.

But only for a while, I realize. Nicholls stops, then turns the diary around so it's facing me, and pushes it closer. In thick blue ballpoint pen, the words are almost etched into the pages.

10 April, 2016
I haven't written in this for a bit. She found it. I didn't
feel the same afterward. But now I just need to tell
someone, even if it's just this stupid diary.
Mum found the test, too. She's such a nosy bitch.
Holly took the blame. But I don't know what I'm going

to do now. I don't really want to tell Danny. He won't
react well, but he's got a right to know, I suppose. I
wish I could just get away—I just need to have some
time to think. I've had enough of all this.

He turns the page. She's left a few days blank, then just one
line:

I was right. I saw another side to him this time. He
scared me, a bit, that's all. It's silly, really.

"Is this Sophie's handwriting, Mrs. Harlow?" His tone is neutral.
My thoughts are a tangle. "Yes. Yes it is."
"There's not many references to it. Just a few entries after she
found out. You said her friend said it was her test?"
"That evening. Yes." I feel hot and cold, my head buzzing. He
won't stop talking: "There's something else." Does he look uncomfortable, just for a second? "This pregnancy test she did, she
writes about having to 'fix it.' This is the bit." He finds the section
and holds the pages open for me. The first couple of lines come
into focus.

22 April
So now it's all sorted. It was horrible. But I do feel
relieved. I went to school after, it was like it had never
happened really. I said I'd not felt well, I'd had to go to
the doctor, which was kind of true. No one checked.
No one knows anything.
I know though. I just wish I could get away. Start
afresh.

And on the following page, another entry:

Danny's being difficult again. I thought if I did what he
wanted, fixed things, he'd back off, but I don't know.
So I've decided, I'm going to go. I want to live a

different life. I've got a plan. I can work, cash in hand
somewhere. Then later, maybe I can go abroad. I
don't know how, not yet. But there will be a way. A
new start, just until I'm feeling better about everything.
I just can't keep on like nothing's happened.
I'm not sure what I'll tell him. If I should tell him.
P.S. I'm going to stop writing in this, too risky. I need
to hide it. Somewhere she won't find it.

"There's nothing after that," he says.

"Can I take it home?" Tears are thickening my voice. It's a
piece of Sophie, my daughter.

"We've got to keep hold of this, for now."

"So you'll be investigating again?"

"The case was never closed, of course." I give him a look—he
must know that nothing was happening anymore. "But we'll be
making a few inquiries."

"In what way? Danny said they didn't sleep together. He told
me to my face. Do you think—Do you think he did something
bad?" My breath quickens, but he's shaking his head.

"We've no reason to think that. But it might be a little clearer
now why Sophie's gone, and why she's stayed away so along."

Danny, I think. Or us? How we'd react?

"She sounds so angry," I say.

"I know this must have been hard to read. But you've done
the right thing: letting us know about the call, and about your
concerns. Because it meant that Sophie was on our radar again,
when the diary got handed in. These things shouldn't get missed,
of course, but sometimes the significance isn't always quite obvious. . . ."

I can picture it. The diary handed in, dutifully put in a file, left
somewhere safe with a note for Kirstie to look at it, maybe return
it to the family, once she was back from maternity leave. If she
ever did come back. The thought chills me; how lucky they realized what it meant.

"So you think that's why she ran away? Because she was scared?

Or that *he* scared her off?" I can't square it with Danny, that quiet figure. But, unbidden, I see his grandfather Len's red, spitting face.

"I'll let you know when I've information I can share," says Nicholls, standing up.

I do the same. There's so much to take in. "So what happens now?"

"We'd better take down a statement, confirming what you've told me about the diary, and the pregnancy test and the rest of it. My colleague will do that now, if you can just wait in here."

"OK." Outside there're voices, one getting louder. "But I mean, longer term, what happens?"

"I'll keep you informed," he says.

The words outside are suddenly clear: ". . . Well, *why*? Why can't you tell me—"

Mark. "Sophie's dad—he's here too?"

"I didn't think, necessarily, that you'd want to speak to me together," he says, his tone dry. "If you'd prefer not to see him now—"

I hear a woman's voice now, quieter, then his rises over it: "Well, I'm a busy man, you know. If you ask me to come in . . ."

"It's fine," I tell Nicholls. I pull open the door and Mark's right there in the corridor, an officer behind him, only her sharply arched eyebrow betraying her annoyance.

"Kate," he says, startled. "And *you*"—rudely, as Nicholls steps past me—"I believe I need a word with you. Well? What's happening?"

"Mrs. Harlow?" The officer is holding the door open for me. "I'm Detective Sergeant Hopper. Shall we go in?"

I follow her back into the room. I forgot how Mark gets when he's flustered, reverting to his most pompous. At least it saves me having to talk to him myself.

Afterward I stand outside the station, leaning on the wall, and breathe in big gulps of the evening air, cool in my lungs. The statement didn't take that long really. I've done it before.

She was good, the officer who took it, very thorough. She got everything down that I remembered about the night I found the test, what Holly said the other day, then Danny, and ran through again why I know it's Sophie's diary, how certain I am it's my daughter's. But I feel like I've run a 10k, my legs shaky.

Now I've time to think, my body's reacting to what I've heard. Sophie. My little girl, scared. Alone. I can't bear it. And Danny— what did he do? Threaten her, scare her—what?

But at least now we know. We are getting closer to what happened, what drove her away. This is it, this is what I wanted. Things are moving again. It was never going to be easy.

I breathe in, out again, then I straighten up. So maybe this is what it feels like. Progress.

CHAPTER 16

Over the weekend, it gets hotter still. The sky's a glorious, cloud-less blue by the time Monday lunchtime arrives, the weather hit-ting a new high for the month: 30°C. The light in the kitchen is shaded green-gold from the sunlight in the garden, as I linger over the salad I've made for lunch.

On the radio, people are talking about how to survive the heat—this is no day to be stuck in an office, they're joking, em-ployers can expect a record number of sickies. It doesn't make much difference to me, with no job to go to. But for the first time in a while I think, perhaps it's time to look into my options up here, seriously. And the thought doesn't fill me with horror.

I didn't go into the helpline on Saturday night. I'd finally heard from them: I had a voicemail saying I wouldn't be needed—not from Alma, but from someone higher up. She wasn't a volunteer, I could tell by her tone. It's best if I don't come in given the strain of recent events.

I know they're not happy that I went straight to the police about Sophie's call or tried to get them to trace it. But then it's an un-usual situation, taking a call from your own relative. I imagine that they're already arranging meetings about it, drawing up good practice guidelines for this eventuality, too.

Anyway, I've been busy these past few days, for me.

I've had to go back to the station again. Detective Sergeant Hopper, the woman officer who took my statement, rang, asking me to bring in handwriting samples, in case they're needed to verify the diary. I diligently dug out old exercise books, birthday cards I can't look at anymore. *Happy Birthday Mum. To the best mum in the world.* And the older ones, crayoned on folded card in careful childish letters: *Mummy. I love you. Sophie xxx.*

And, of course, the postcards home, carefully protected in a brown envelope.

"That's more than enough, Mrs. Harlow," she'd said, but with a smile. "Thanks for all this."

She's nicer than Nicholls. She said they don't even need to keep it all, that I could go and pick the stuff up later.

I ran this morning and yesterday, despite the heat, enjoying the feeling of my legs moving and my lungs pumping, before coming home sweaty and tired. I checked in on Lily. She was slow and sleepy, said I'd woken her up from another nap. She's not a complainer but even she doesn't like this heat.

And this afternoon I put music on loud, and started to tackle the pile of bills I've let pile up in the hall. I don't spend much, obviously, and Mark hasn't tried to get me out, yet—perhaps he feels too guilty—but I suppose this can't go on forever. I even replied to some emails, friends in London who are dutifully trying to keep in touch, despite my silence. Baby steps, back into the world.

Most of all, I have been trying not to dwell. To trust in the process. It sort of works, if I just keep moving. It was just bad luck that when I drove round this morning, to pick up the envelope from the front desk at the police station, Holly was there too. She was smoking a cigarette outside as I walked out of the building.

I didn't know whether to pretend I hadn't seen her, but she decided for me. She came straight up to me, too close, her breath warm in my face—nicotine and sweet mints. "You've got to stop this," she said. "You've got to make them understand. That they've got this all wrong."

"How've they got this wrong, Holly?"

"You need to tell them that I got mixed up. That it was my test, that I didn't mean it." She'd been crying, the skin red round her eyes. "Tell them it was mine. Please."

"I've got to tell the truth," I said gently.

I hesitated for a second, then walked on. I could hear her behind me, little hopeless sniffs. She didn't follow me.

So she's saying it was her pregnancy test, now. I suppose that's to be expected, to protect her boyfriend. I don't blame her, not really. He must be such a good liar. She probably believes him.

I don't think they've arrested Danny, anyway, I think it's just questioning—for now. I'm not sure how much they have to tell me, or they want to tell me, at this stage.

Even I could have sworn he was telling the truth, in the garage. But I called Dad again, this morning. He said I shouldn't worry about it, to try to keep my mind off it, for now. I've updated him on everything that's happened with the diary, the renewed police interest. I didn't tell him how I had started looking into things myself, he'd only warn me off, tell me to leave all that unpleasantness to the professionals. Besides, that's over now.

He wants to come and stay, or for me to promise to come and visit soon. They can both come, him and Charlotte, without the kids, he suggested.

"I worry about you, Kate, on your own there."

"I'm fine, Dad. You don't need to worry. I really am fine."

"But I do. Charlotte too, you know."

"I know, Dad."

But it's an old conversation, the two of us settling into its well-worn grooves. Almost reassuring. Things feel back to normal, almost. My normal.

I've nearly finished sorting through all my post and am sitting at the kitchen table, pleased with myself, when I notice the brown envelope in my bag on the side. The stuff back from the station. I should go through it now, rather than let it turn into something that I won't want to deal with for months on end.

Quickly, I go over and tear it open, pouring the contents back onto the table. Sophie's exercise books I'll put back where I keep them on her bookshelf, the birthday cards into my special keepsake box in the living room, and the postcards—the postcards I'll put back on the mantelpiece as usual. Done. This is the way to get things done, I tell myself, without turning everything into a Herculean task.

But instead I spread the postcards onto the table in front of me. All her familiar messages. I wish I had the diary, too. Maybe they'll let me have it soon. I try to remember the messages, the exact wording, he showed me—but it was all so quick, I barely had time to take it all in.

All I can picture is that frontispiece, her name and personal details. I'm remembering now: something about it, what was it, just seemed a little off. . . .

Name: Sophie Harlow
Age: 15
Address: Oakhurst, Park Road, Vale Dean, Cheshire.
Contact details: Sharlow90@yaymail.com

Something cold slithers down my spine. That wasn't her email address.

Not the one I know anyway, the one I've logged into so many times, the contents I know as well as my own. Now I get up and head to the study upstairs, taking the stairs two at a time. I switch on the computer and log into my email. The folder's called "Sophie," where I keep all the emails she sent me. There aren't that many of course, she didn't have much reason to email me. Just stuff she thought I'd enjoy: silly local news stories, funny animal videos.

Yes, I was right. Sharlow90@gogomail.com. They're all from this email address, the one we gave the police and the one they

WHERE THE MISSING GO 109

went through. She hadn't even bothered to close the window on her laptop, when they came to take it away.

Maybe she got it wrong, I think, she just filled in the wrong thing. Yaymail not gogomail. That's easy to do: there's so many of these email services about; this one comes with our broadband, I seem to remember. But even as I think that I'm shaking my head: she was sixteen years old when she left; if she knew anything, she knew what her email address was.

So. Maybe she had two.

Just so I'm sure, I log into her old email, the one that I know about.

It was never tricky: we'd found the password, "loopysophie," written on the jotter on her desk by her laptop, almost like she knew we'd look there first. The police took the computer itself too, to check the hard drive for anything alarming, before returning it: all clear. I'm trying to remember: did they ever say anything about a second email account? I'm sure I'd remember if they had.

I haven't checked in here for a while. I clear the few spam emails, reading each one carefully before deleting: an appeal for a male "performance enhancement" drug, a few fake software upgrades.

Sophie didn't email much. Teenagers were always all over their smartphones, so I read in the papers, plugged into a scary world we parents couldn't access. But Sophie was never desperate to be part of it, always leaving her phone around the house until the battery was dead, so we couldn't even ring it to find it. She seemed aloof in a way I never was, so self-contained.

I was glad of that, then. She didn't even complain when I told her not to post photos of herself all over the internet, she didn't know what sort of people might be looking or where they might end up. And what would happen in five years, when she was starting her career? Much better not to leave a trail.

But in the end, all I wanted were traces of Sophie, ways she might reach me. And I worried that it slowed us down, when she went. When her friends at school said Sophie hadn't replied to their messages that weekend, it didn't worry them: she was always a bit flaky getting back to them. When, eventually, she did get in touch with us back home, by that postcard of all things, that seemed to fit.

I suppose. It didn't really feel right and it still doesn't now. Now I sign out of that account, and log in again, using the email address she has in her diary with the yaymail.com ending.

You have signed in from a different device, the website tells me.

It asks me to type in those oddly shaped numbers and letters to check I'm not a robot.

Then I type in the password again: *loopysophie.*

Incorrect password.

I try again, various variations on it:

LoopySophie
loopiesophie
Sophieloopy

Nothing. I keep going.

Too many failed attempts, the screen tells me eventually. Now I have to go through the security questions.

The first flashes up. *What was the name of your first pet?*

Well that's easy. Morris, the cat we had when she was little. That cat was so patient, more doglike than feline, allowing Sophie to totter after him and give him clumsy hugs.

I type it in: *Morris.*

The error message flashes up.

Well it surely can't be King, the dog, but I type that in anyway. The error message appears again.

I try again with various different spellings, lowercase, uppercase, *Cat, Morristhecat, dog, Doggy,* and so on, until I'm locked out.

I go and make a cup of tea, frustrated. Think, just think. How would Sophie think?

Another hour passes. It probably was a mistake after all, she just filled in the wrong email address. Because I can't get past that security question and have got stuck in a loop of attempts, then locking myself out of the account for fifteen minutes.

I could be totally wrong. Maybe my memory's playing tricks,

she doesn't have a different email at all. But then I see it in my mind's eye again, so clearly: her familiar round writing on that lined paper.

I roll my chair away from the desk, fretful. All the doubts I've forced away are coming back—the things I don't understand. But this time I hold onto the feeling and let the thoughts come without pushing them down. Nicholls showing me the diary: "Do you recognize this as Sophie's handwriting?"

A new start, just until I'm feeling better about everything.

"Yes," I told him. "That's definitely her writing." A different answer appears to me now. *Yes. It's definitely her handwriting. But it's not her.*

It's not the Sophie I know. There's something so flat to me about the whole thing, her tone. Strange as it sounds but she's so . . . serious! I know my daughter. Sophie . . . dropping out?

So I've decided, I'm going to go. I want to live a different life. I've got a plan.

It's just like the postcards: so remote, so bland. So unlike her.

And then there's that other thing, that I have been resolutely not thinking about: that picture of Nancy. That hair, that sweet round face, the mischief in her smile. Just like Sophie. What happened to her?

Well, I can do something about that, at least. I get up.

CHAPTER 17

Vale Dean is the kind of place with no McDonald's, two card shops and four estate agents, three of them the big chains. I stop at the last and smallest, the local independent, and head in.

I recognize the man behind the desk from the "for sale" signs: Graham Hescott, a generation older than the eager young men in the other agents' offices. I tell him I am looking to downsize and keen to stay in the area. Yes, I'll be living alone. I don't need to say the word divorce. He's been working long enough to work it out.

He talks me through a few options, mostly flats in new developments, and the pricier apartments they've made by carving up the old Victorian mansions.

In the end I just ask. "And what about that big one, on Park Road—Parklands? Aren't they supposed to be turning that into flats?"

"Oh yes," he says. "Although they're taking long enough about it." We share a disapproving look. People aren't supposed to let houses go to rot round here. It's not good for property prices.

"So would it be worth me getting in touch, putting my name on a list?"

"If you buy in early you might be able to get a discounted price," he says, nodding. "We can put you in touch with the developers. Let me see. . . ." He clicks with his mouse.

I wait, the fan by his desk lifting the hair on the back of my neck. He must be boiling in that suit.

"Hm," he says doubtfully. "I'm just looking at our notes. Might be a bit tricky . . . building work seems to have stopped for a while." I know that, of course.

"Why's that?"

He shrugs. "Could be anything, really. Money running out, the bank getting nervous. Although the market is really picking up now." He shoots me a covert look. Don't scare a potential buyer. "Of course, inheritance tax can be very expensive."

"Inheritance tax?"

"People can get caught out. They don't always like to think of it."

"So—the owners died?"

He nods. "It went to their daughter, a few years ago now. Friend of mine was their solicitor, before he retired."

"Their daughter?" It can't be the Corrigans, Nancy's family. Surely they sold it well before then. They'll have moved long ago.

"I did my best to get in touch to see if she wanted to sell, but she was rather uncommunicative. But what a decision that turned out to be. The way the market's gone up round here, even before they turn it into flats—" He catches the look on my face, interpreting it as distaste for his professional enthusiasm. "But don't worry, Mrs. Harlow, there'll be plenty in your price range. I really do think you should have a look at this Carr Road development, it will be ready much sooner."

"Why don't I take a brochure." I give him my friendliest smile. It feels a little unnatural. "But you wouldn't have a contact for the Parklands owners, would you? I live next door, actually, and it would be very handy to be able to get in touch directly, about a few things. . . ." I raise my eyebrows meaningfully.

"Oh," he says, put out. "Oh, so you're next door, that place with the bay windows." I can see him trying to place me in his local map, wondering why something about that family rings a bell . . . in a second he'll remember. "You should have said. So are you planning on selling that house?"

"Probably. Yes, very likely," I say, as I see him perk up, "once my husband and I—Once my ex . . ." I trail off, mournfully. This is so hammy. But on the scent of a big sale, he's now eager to help.

"Just give me a second," he says, typing slowly, two-fingered. "Ah . . . yes. Just a phone number. American." He reels it off for me, carefully, as I scribble it onto the brochure. "Have you got that?"

"Got it." I smile again, a genuine one this time. "Thanks. Oh, and what's her name?"

"Sorry, I should have said. It's Corrigan. Olivia Corrigan."

At home I google the number, before I dial it. It's a Canadian dialing code, not American, but that's all I find out: there's no exact match in the search results. I search for "Olivia Corrigan" instead, but I lose patience as I click through the Olivia Corrigans who are too old, or too young or just unlikely: a former cheerleader in Oregon, a biochemist in Ireland. She might not still go by her maiden name over there.

What am I looking for, anyway? So they never actually sold the house, big deal. Before I talk myself out of it, I go to the phone and ring the number.

I've decided to be honest: I'm a neighbor and I'm trying to get in touch, to discuss the house. That could cover a lot of things. And then well, I'll see how it goes.

I just have to know what happened to Nancy. This way, her sister can tell me and I will then know, as of course will be the case, that there is nothing that connects Nancy's disappearance— departure, I correct myself—with my daughter's, and this nagging voice in my mind will shut up again.

But the number goes to voicemail, an automated machine message.

"Hello, my name's Kate Harlow." I put on my best, most amenable phone voice. "I live at Oakhurst, next door to Parklands in

Vale Dean. I believe you're the owner? I wonder if you could get in touch." I leave the house phone number, saying it carefully, twice. "Thanks very much."

Well, that's done. She might not even be there anymore. Maybe she's moved.

But I can't settle, moving about the rooms downstairs, flicking through the news programs for the reassuring drone of politicians. When they finish, I find they're rerunning *Jaws* on another channel and end up watching it again. I've always loved monster movies, it's reality that I can't stomach on the screen: gritty dramas about break-ups and babies and everyday sadness.

Afterward, I finally switch off the TV and admit what I've been waiting up for: for Nancy's sister to call me back. This is silly, I tell myself, go to bed.

The wind is picking up tonight, I can hear it streaming through the trees outside. A late summer storm must be on its way, soon.

Making my way up the stairs, I jump as I see movement out of the corner of my eye. My heart's racing even as I register the ginger fur: it's just Tom, making a mad dash to the landing. He freezes in front of me, his eyes fixed on mine. He still gets these kittenish bursts of energy, rocketing about the house when the mood takes him.

Annoyed at my fear, I go deliberately up the stairs and pause at the window to pick him up. I make a point not to rush. "What are you up to now?" I ask him. "You came out of nowhere, didn't you?"

I keep smoothing his soft fur and look out over the garden, all shades of violet and gray in the night. I don't know if I'll ever get used to how dark it gets out here. On the lawn, the light from the window forms a paler rectangle, my shadow framed within it, stretching out to where the rhododendron bushes blend together in one dark heavy mass. I need to get them cut back, they're getting overgrown.

Another gust of wind comes now, swaying their boughs, the whole wall of leaves suddenly lifting and moving as one. And I notice, almost idly, that one patch of shadows doesn't move in quite the same way, that one small corner of the mass isn't ruffled by the wind.

It's a shadow that, I see now, is not quite the right shape as the rest, a shape, pressed into the vegetation so you almost can't see it, that is just about human-sized.

I keep very still. There's nothing there. It's a trick of the eye. It must be. Or just something the gardener left when he used to come, a piece of trellis leant against the bushes, a shape that's just about to resolve itself into something entirely harmless, a bag of leaves propped on a dustbin.

And I keep telling myself that, that it's all fine, even as my hand reaches toward the lamp on the side table and, with a click, the landing's in darkness. There's a second as my eyes adjust.

The movement's quick—just a flicker, really. I almost miss it. It's just a small white blur in the night, a pale upturned oval tilted toward the window. In fact, the moment's almost over before I've time to catch up, to quite register what I'm looking at: what's out there in my garden.

Then the face dips down and the figure slips further into the shadows. Whoever it was is gone.

I call 999 from the kitchen phone. I don't care if it could wait till morning. Then I grab my mobile from where it's been charging in a corner and retreat up the stairs, to my bedroom, where the curtains are safely shut. But it feels like a long fifteen minutes before I hear the slow crunch of wheels on the gravel.

They're not officers I've seen before—both in their mid-twenties, the shorter one's beard not masking the roundness of his face—but they're confident and businesslike.

"There was a dark figure, not really moving . . . no, I couldn't describe him . . . no, I didn't see what he looked like. . . . I didn't see where he went."

They dutifully note it down, however scant the detail.

They have flashlights, and make a thorough show of looking all around the house and gardens, checking for unusual footprints in the flower beds.

"Does that look strange to you?" they keep asking me.

"I can't really tell," I say, examining yet another flattened patch of soil, trying to make out the tread of a shoe.

They've parked their patrol car in the drive. "There used to be a gate." I feel the need to acknowledge this. "But we didn't bother to get one . . . it's so safe round here."

More nods, and we make another loop round the house, the warm wind still whipping round corners. I tuck my hair into the collar of my jacket and try not to shiver. It's not the cold.

I've a sneaking feeling that I'm disappointing them, unable to proffer anything concrete.

Because we find nothing. There is nobody lurking in the undergrowth, no sinister rustles of foliage, no dark figure bursting out at us as their flashlights light up the pink flowers of the rhododendrons.

I feel faintly ridiculous as I make them tea back inside, their uniforms incongruous against my painted French gray chairs. They give me a leaflet about home security and tell me to lock my downstairs windows, even in this heat, people are opportunistic. I know all this, I have always been careful, but I nod.

Then a thought occurs to me: "My neighbor Lily, she's on her own. I don't think you should wake her up, but do you think you could check on her house, after? It's just up the other fork of the drive, the little cottage."

"We can have a look around," says the older one. Under the spotlights, his scalp gleams pink through his sandy hair. "Ten to one, if it was anything, it was some chancer passing through, checking if anyone's home. It's that time of year, with people still on holiday. These big houses round here . . ."

"There was a break-in not too far down the road about a month ago," says the one with a beard cheerily. I've forgotten their names almost immediately. "The owners were away, hadn't canceled their milk order, too, a dead giveaway. Might as well invite them in!"

He catches a slight warning look from his colleague. "And of course, it may have been nothing at all. It'd be easy in the dark to mistake . . ." He looks at me, too polite to say outright that I probably imagined it. "I wouldn't want my mum to be living in a big house like this all alone," he finishes.

I manage not to laugh. How old does he think I am? Then again, if he's in his mid-twenties, as he looks, perhaps it's not so preposterous after all.

"Maybe you're right," I say, wanting to be reassured. "I didn't get a clear look. Perhaps it was just the wind in the shadows, a trick of the light."

"It'd be easy to mistake," says the younger one, with a sympathetic smile.

But even as they start moving to go, the scene flashes in my mind again, and stays there, a picture I can't banish, as I wave them goodbye, and shut and lock the front door: that tall, still shape in the garden, tipped by a pale oval, against the dark.

A thought occurs to me now. When I switched the lamp off the shape moved, back into the bushes.

But until that moment, as I'd stared out of the window, the light framing me in my house as I looked out? Someone was looking right back at me.

CHAPTER 18

It's funny how different things can seem in the daytime. Morning has worked its usual magic, and I feel much better: even if there was someone there, and I wasn't mistaken, the police officers were surely right. It would just have been opportunistic, someone trying to find out if any of these houses have been left empty for the summer. Well, now they'll know mine isn't.

I checked all the locks before I went to bed, twice. It's a solid house, locks on the windows and double glazing, and bolts on the back door. And it still feels so safe up here, compared to London.

But I know this house could be a target, here on the fringes of the village, off a drive that could hide a car from the road. So I'm going to get an alarm sorted, soon, on top of all the locks. It'll be absolutely fine.

Still, it was a long night. I didn't fall asleep until the sky started to lighten through my window and I read, instead, resolutely not allowing my imagination to wander. I didn't want to take a pill. Just in case I didn't hear something.

This morning I woke up late, groggy and off balance, then I

remembered what had happened. Then my next thought came: Lily. Now I find myself hurrying to get ready.

I want to check on her myself. I'm sure she'll be fine, but I don't bother showering, just pull on my running kit, and take the shortcut through the bushes between the plots again, quick as I can.

There's an anxious minute after I knock and then let myself into Lily's house, stepping slowly through the hall.

"Lily? It's me. Are you there?"

It's quiet. Perhaps she can't hear me? I can feel my heartbeat quickening.

But she's in her sitting room as usual, in her comfortable chair, and my shoulders relax.

"Oh hello, dear," she says, turning toward me with a smile. "This is a bit early for you, isn't it?" I normally come in the afternoons.

"I just thought I'd pop by on the way to the supermarket, see if you needed anything." I've already decided I'm not going to mention last night. "I haven't seen you for a bit. How have you been?"

"I'm fine, dear. How are you?" No, she definitely wasn't disturbed in the night, I can tell.

I ask her what she's been up to these past few days: how was her coffee afternoon at the church last week? She makes me laugh at how another of the ladies, Violet, is pursuing the lone gentleman Sidney—she seems to be wearing him down.

But I've heard this story before, down to her withering verdict. "She's a trier, that one. I'll give her that." I wonder how much of the last gathering she actually remembers. She doesn't mention me coming round at the weekend, finding her sleepy and disorientated after her nap.

Yet she does seem more like the old Lily now, more alert and herself than she's been for a while. Younger, even. Perhaps she's better in the mornings.

We chat for a while, talking about her soaps, then there's a lull.

"I wanted to ask you something, Lily."

She tilts her head a little. "Yes?"

"About Nancy."

"Who, dear?

"Nancy. The girl you mentioned the other day, who looks like my Sophie?"

There's a beat, then she shakes her head, slowly. "I don't think I know a Nancy."

"Nancy Corrigan? You know, she used to live in the big house. Years ago, now."

"No, dear, I don't know." Her pause is almost unnoticeable. "I do hope I haven't forgotten again."

I decide to leave it, for now. I don't want to push it further, and upset her by chasing yet another thing that's slipped from her memory. Before I go, I head into her loo upstairs. I'm mulling over our conversation as I wash my hands.

So Lily doesn't remember mentioning Nancy. Well, maybe she wasn't even referring to the Nancy who used to live at Parklands. In fact, I ask myself, why would she even know about her? Nancy. Sophie. It could just be a coincidence; they don't sound too dissimilar—a slip of the tongue.

I shake my head in the mirror. No, I don't believe that. That's too neat. I think the thought of Sophie the other day jogged her memory in some way—she remembered another girl who went away.

So at some point, she must have heard about Nancy. That would make more sense, if she's lived here a while. People do talk. And then she forgot about it, I think, drying my hands on her embroidered white hand towel. Because she does forget things, all too often, nowadays.

But I feel cross that I've got no further. Frustrated. And now I feel the impulse, like an itch under my skin. I don't need to. I shouldn't. It would be an invasion of privacy. I don't—Before I can think about it any further, I just do it: I open the bathroom cabinet above the sink.

Yardley lavender scented moisturizer. Elizabeth Arden's Blue Grass scent. That face cream she's told me about, that Joanna Lumley uses. And her medicine bottles.

I pull out one of the brown glass bottles, filled with clear liquid. I don't know the brand name, I don't think—I squint at the smaller print label, wishing I had my glasses: ". . . contains morphine."

Jesus. I know what this stuff is. Liquid morphine, a powerful painkiller. I knew she had a bad hip but, wow. Poor Lily. She must be in real pain. And there's so much of it—at least half a dozen of these bottles, some already near empty. How much morphine does she need?

I glance down again at the label: Mrs. Lily Green, The Carriage House, Park Road, Vale Dean. It's hers, of course. "To take as and when, for pain."

There are pills too, I see, carefully easing out a packet: more of the same stuff in capsule form, with directions to take twice daily.

The doctors will know what you can take, of course they do. But even so . . . I frown. It's trusting her a lot, with this stuff, to keep on top of her dosage and timings and the rest. Should she really have so much of it? They might not realize how she's been, more recently. No wonder she's been so dopey and confused— and if I'm right that she's showing signs of dementia, as I fear, couldn't all this be making it worse?

I glance at the bottle in my hand again. I've still heard nothing back from the council. I can't ask Lily. She'll think I'm prying and just won't see the danger.

For a moment, a wave of hot emotion rises up over me: I feel so overwhelmed. I lean against the basin. I can cope, I can. But it's all coming at once. Sophie. Lily. Nancy.

Lily pretending not to know about Nancy.

Why do I think that? "I hope I haven't forgotten again."

Why is that worrying at me? She didn't seem distressed, like it touched a chord. Quite the opposite in fact: she was calm, re-signed even. Even though she'd forgotten something. Again.

And then I get it. That was it: this time, she wasn't the least upset.

Checking in on Lily as I leave, I see she's asleep in her chair, and pull the curtains closed, so the sun's not shining on her face. I'm not in a hurry now, so I'll walk down the drive—fewer insects, and branches—rather than the cut-through between our houses. And I am about to turn left, back down to my house, when I pause.

Instead I turn right, following the rest of the drive up to Parklands. Because what if there was someone in my garden, and they were heading this way? You hear all sorts about squatters. I've an idea that's normally in cities, not places like Vale Dean, but I just want to see for myself, in broad daylight.

It's just another fifty meters perhaps, but I feel almost like I'm trespassing as I walk up—I've never come up here before, close as it is. It's even quieter here than at my house; further back from the road, with the trees around blocking out the sound. You could be anywhere at all, really.

There's the iron gate, a big chain clasping the bars closed. But I simply walk over where the wooden fencing's collapsed to one side of it, and then back onto the driveway.

It's even bigger than it looks from further away: solid and imposing, the overgrown garden making its grand proportions look too big for its plot. It must be what: three, four stories? The front lawn's like a meadow now, the long grass brushing my hands.

I shiver. What am I doing here? What do I do if I find that there *is* somebody coming in here, a squatter or—what? Some confused junkie, jumpy and aggressive when he's disturbed? I don't know what I'd do. I should leave this to the police.

But still I keep going, my feet crunching up the path, stepping over a smashed purple-gray slate that's fallen from the roof. Up close I can see how old and tattered the plastic sheeting is up there, the remaining legs of scaffolding looking less like a support than some structure simply abandoned by builders. Someone probably stopped paying them. It's still beautiful though, the soft Cheshire brick banded with pale stonework that runs round the building, carved with rosettes. There are hundreds of these shapes—roses, not rosettes, I realize—spiraling over the brickwork.

And now I'm going closer still, up the stone step onto the roofed porch where the air is cooler, old leaves filling its tiled corners and piled up against the heavy double doors. It's still impressive up close: the stone door arch carved with more of the pretty floral motifs, each with its neat little inner ruff of petals. But the paint on the doors has bubbled and warped, the paler wood showing through in places.

I reach for the brass door knob on the right and twist gently, then harder. Of course it's locked. It doesn't look like anyone's been through for years, judging by the drifts of leaves everywhere, but I reach for the one on the left and—

I whirl around. "Oh!"

The man's a dark silhouette against the sunshine, black against the green of the trees and the yellow grass behind him. Then I place him: Nicholls, incongruous in his suit and tie.

"God, you scared me." I didn't hear anything, I don't know what made me turn round. I start to laugh nervously, my hand to my throat. "What are you doing here?"

"I wouldn't want to scare you." He's not smiling. "I heard there might have been an intruder round this way. Last night?"

"Oh, of course. That's quick." I didn't think a detective inspector would be that interested. The officers last night seemed much more junior. "Have you found anything?"

"There's no evidence of any break-in here. It seems secure. But all the same," he says, "I wouldn't suggest you start trying to find any trespassers yourself."

"Ah no. Of course not." I put my hands behind my back guiltily. A thought occurs to me. "Is your car down there on the road then?" I didn't pass it coming up.

He shakes his head. "Turns out you can park in the lane, that way," gesturing to behind Parklands. "There's a little path that cuts through to the road behind."

"Oh," I say uselessly. "I didn't know that."

"I can walk you out, if you like."

I bristle a little at being dismissed. "Actually, I wanted to ask you—what's happening now, with Danny, now you've got Sophie's diary? So, would he be out on bail now?"

"No, he's not out on bail." I close my eyes, relieved. "Because he hasn't been arrested, or charged with anything."

"He wasn't? I assumed from the way you were treating the diary that . . ." I trail off.

"We've no reason to do so, Mrs. Harlow. There's no suspicion of a crime."

"So are you even talking to him still?" I say sharply. "And what about the call, have you got anywhere with the charity?"

"When I've information I can share with you, I will of course do that." His face is a blank.

"I see." So Danny's out and about, to do what he wants. And they haven't traced the call, I'd put money on it.

Suddenly I want to go home again. "Right I'd better be off," I shake my keys, a meaningless gesture. "I'm just back down the drive. Bye."

"Goodbye, Mrs. Harlow."

I can feel his eyes on me as I walk away, my footsteps loud on the gravel. It's stupid, I know, but for some reason, I feel like I mustn't turn round, or hurry—like it would be a mistake, somehow. Just act normal. Everything is fine.

But my heart's still thumping in my chest as I get back into my house.

I don't know why I feel like I just escaped something.

CHAPTER 19

I spend the afternoon inside, with the study blind drawn against the sun, trying once more to get into the email account from Sophie's diary. I'm optimistic at first. Surely inspiration will strike, it can't be that hard.

But I still can't do it, locked in a cycle of getting the answer to her security question wrong and freezing the account. After that, I focus on trying different passwords, typing in different variations of her "loopysophie" password, before starting to randomly type in words that she might have chosen instead. Amberton, for her school. Charlotte, her middle name. Lilac, her favorite color. What bands did she like? Pop stars? I start typing in names, and then names with numbers—2000, for the year she was born. 99, just because. Eventually I break, my eyes gritty and tired.

I will sleep on it. And then if I can't get into it, I will tell the police.

I groan, my head in my hands. I can just imagine Nicholls, polite as ever: "And what exactly do you think it means if a teenage girl has more than one email address, Mrs. Harlow?" He'll think I'm looking for a way out. That I just can't accept that Sophie went

through all this alone. That she would rather run away than confide in me. Which is true, I suppose. I can't.

I'll sleep on it, I tell myself. And then I'll decide.

I'm winding down for the night, pottering about the kitchen and
wiping down surfaces that are already clean—there's less mess
with everyone gone—when the phone rings. I consider letting it
ring out.

"Who the hell's this?" I mutter to the cat. Charlotte and I used
to say this to each other if anyone rang after dinner, parroting our
favorite Peter Kay sketch. I check the oven clock: 9:35 p.m. Even
by my family's standards, I'm keeping old lady hours. I reach for
the phone.

"Hello?"

For a heartbeat, the faint crackle on the line catches at me, cast-
ing me back to the other night, at the charity. . . .

"Mrs. Harlow?" The woman's voice is soft, American vowels. I
relax, a little. It's not Sophie again.

"Yes, that's me."

"It's Olivia Marnell. I got your message, about the house." It
still takes me a second to place her, then I do. Not American, Canadian. "I used to be Olivia Corrigan."

She's very polite, apologetic even. I've explained who I am, and
talked—tactfully at first—about the state of Parklands. I got the
impression she doesn't realize in quite how bad a state it is. Eventually I tell her more bluntly: it's been pretty much derelict now,
at least since I've moved in. The trees are so big they could be
undermining the houses around it, let alone hers.

Finally she gets it. "Oh dear." She sighs. "I do apologize. My
parents—they didn't want to deal with it, really. For personal reasons. And now it's fallen to me, there's been a surprising amount
to take care of this end, in terms of arrangements, after my mother
died." She sounds tired. "But I'm going to get on top of the house
now. I'm going to decide what to do with it, in terms of selling or
getting it redeveloped. It shouldn't go to ruin."

"No," I say. "It could be a beautiful property again." How can I bring it up? I decide honesty is the best policy. "I can understand it must have been hard for your parents, though, if they were getting older. I heard"—I pause delicately—"I understand there was a family tragedy. In the past."

There's silence on the line.

"Sorry," I say hastily. "I shouldn't have mentioned it."

"No, that's OK," she says slowly. "I'm just not used to talking about it. My husband, my kids—they never knew my sister. And after we lost my dad, then Mom—well, nobody really knows."

"So—what happened? I read that she ran away."

"Yes," she says simply. "That's right."

"And after that you didn't ever hear from her?"

"No. We never heard from her," she echoes.

I'm shocked, somehow. For some reason I thought that there'd have been some sign, at least, some phone call or . . . I don't know, something they hadn't mentioned in the papers.

"But people don't just vanish, not now. . . ." I stop myself from saying anything else clumsy.

"I'm afraid they do. It was a different time then, too, no Facebook, nothing."

"Even so," I protest, feeling irritated. How can this woman sound so . . . resigned to it all? Suddenly, I realize that I was hoping to hear what I wanted to hear: Nancy had come back.

"What was Nancy like?" I ask. "If you don't mind." I just want to keep her on the line.

"What was she like?" She sighs again. "She was clever. She did well in school. She liked horses—she had a pony, Blossom, that she loved." She laughs. "He was vicious. He was sold, afterward."

"But what was she like to you?"

"To me? I don't know. She was my big sister. There were six years between us, so I looked up to her. She used to tease me sometimes, and I'd cry. But she'd braid my hair, sometimes, and let me play with her makeup. And she could make me laugh like no one else ever has."

"And what about, erm, boyfriends?"

I can hear the smile. "I don't really know. I was only ten when she went. But she was very pretty. She loved attention. I can't imagine anything got that serious."

"I read that he, Nancy's boyfriend, was questioned by the police, afterward." She doesn't bite, but I press on. "I don't suppose you remember his name?"

"No, I don't. They spoke to lots of her friends." Her voice hardens. "Are you a journalist?"

"No, absolutely not. Sorry. I don't want to pry. I just—I'm sorry."

But she's upset now. "This is exactly why my parents left, to escape all the curiosity. To protect me from all the questions. We came to Canada for a new start."

I feel bad: I can hear the quaver in her voice under the anger. "I really don't mean to upset you. It's just—my daughter's gone missing too. She ran away." I might as well admit it. "Your family's story struck a chord, that's all, being local, and I wondered what had happened."

"Oh," she says, mollified. "Well, you should have said. You don't meet many . . ." People like us, I fill in. The ones left behind. "I guess then I'm some years ahead of you." She doesn't offer any reassurance, or platitudes.

"So what do you think happened to Nancy?"

"I don't know," she says. "I don't know, and there's where I leave it. I leave it in the hands of God. Or whatever there is."

"Why do you think she went?"

"Well. They were going to send her to boarding school. My parents thought it would be best for her—they were traditional, you know? I've wondered if maybe that was why . . . she never seemed that upset. But you just don't know, do you?"

"But you do think she—that she's OK?"

She's silent. She's definitely going to hang up this time. And now, I don't want to know her answer. "Ignore that, I shouldn't have asked—" but she interrupts.

"Nancy's dead." She's almost casual. Like it's that obvious.

"Dead?"

"Of course she is," she says, more gently. "I've known that for a long time."

"You have?"

"Oh, I don't know what happened, what she might have got mixed up in. Who might have picked her up. But I do know that if Nancy was still alive, she would have come back. A very long time ago.

"They used to hitchhike, in those days, you know." She lets that hang in the air.

I wish, quite definitely, that I hadn't talked to her now.

"But why was everybody so sure that she'd run away then, that nothing else—God forbid—had happened to her? Didn't they search for her?" I sound angry: like they've let Nancy down.

"Well, they did, at first," she says, still infuriatingly calm. No, *resigned*. "But they didn't think anything that bad had happened. At first, they thought she'd still come back. You see, she left a note."

"A note. And that's what it all hung on?" At least with Sophie we knew, I think wildly, there was the CCTV at the bus station, her postcards home after—

"The housekeeper found it, on her bed, in the morning. She'd gone in the night. Although in a way," she continues, her tone thoughtful, "that was worse. Because it gave my parents hope."

I don't want to think about that. "What did the note say? I hope you don't mind me asking. It's only . . ." I trail off. I can't really conjure up a reason why I should know.

"That's OK. I can remember it, even now." Now that she's talking about Nancy she doesn't seem to want to stop. I suppose it's the same reason families called me at the helpline.

She recites it by rote, sing-song like a nursery rhyme: *"I'm sorry, but I've got to go away. Please don't worry about me, it will all be fine. But I need to get away. All my love, Nancy."*

"Oh," I say. "So short."

"She was never really a writer, Nancy. More of a doer."

Outside in the dimming light, Tom is stalking something,

slowly pacing forward across the grass. "Short like Sophie's," I say, watching the cat. He freezes, a paw suspended in the air. "And it was definitely her handwriting?" Another slow pace forward . . .

"Yes, we all knew that. There was never any doubt about that. . . ."

"No," I say. "Me neither."

There doesn't seem much to say after that. I thank her, before I hang up. And I mean it. She's been generous with her time, and her story.

I stay by the phone. I should get on. But I can't seem to move, a chill pooling at the bottom of my stomach.

It has to be a coincidence.

Brief little notes. No long explanations, no angry justifications, no recriminations. Just short, earnest goodbyes, in their own handwriting. So who could doubt, really, that they meant what they said?

And then, of course, there was the call from Sophie, I remind myself. Nancy never did that.

Yet a phrase plays in my mind again: "But I need to get away."

I don't need to pull out Sophie's note to know that it's the same, but I head into the living room and take it down from the mantelpiece anyway. There it is.

**I'm sorry everyone. But I need to get away.
Please try not to worry about me, I'm going to be
fine. I love you all, Sophie xxx ✿**

Just similar words, and that phrase, shared by two missing girls decades apart. Nothing really, for anyone to get alarmed about. Certainly nothing that couldn't be put down to simple coincidence—or the desperation of a mother to find what's not really there.

I know that, I do. But I can't stop myself asking the question.

Why does a runaway note that's nearly thirty years old sound like my daughter wrote it?

CHAPTER 20

The next day, I bring the computer from the study and set myself up on the table in the kitchen, where it's airier. It's too hot to be in that little cubbyhole any longer. I make proper coffee, in the French press, and I've my big jotter pad by my side, where I wrote down my notes from my call to Olivia. They're painfully brief, when I review them.

> Olivia Corrigan
> Nancy
> Left a note
> "But I need to get away"
> Was going to boarding school?

For something to add, I write now:

> Corrigans still own
> Parklands but sister says time to sell.

Now I'm ready to—what? I don't know what I'm supposed to do with that.

I stare out of the window, into the sunshine. My mind starts to wander. All I want to do right now is stop. To just stop thinking. And to go somewhere far away from here, where nobody knows who I am. For a second, just for a second, I can understand the impulse to run away. . . .

When the doorbell rings it takes me a second to come to.

"Oh. Hi!" I'm a still a beat behind as I look up into the friendly face in front of me, try to place the navy car in the drive. Then I recognize him . . . outside of his GP room.

"Dr. Heath, uh, hello."

"Hi, Kate, how are you?"

"Uh, I'm fine thanks, you?" I try to hide my surprise.

"I was in the area, doing some house calls, and I finished earlier than I planned. I thought I'd check in on you, too, before I go back to the surgery." I realize he's looking at me expectantly.

"Sorry, yes, of course. Come in." I step aside. I feel awkward and out of practice at having a guest. "Would you like a coffee? I've just made some."

"Please. I've just been at a patient's who gave me instant coffee in cold water, with milk that had gone off. I had to tip it into a plant pot." I laugh, relaxing a little, as he follows me into the kitchen. "So how've you been?"

"Oh good." I busy myself with the mugs, my back to him. "Well, you know. There's a lot going on." How ever to answer that question, when the asker knows things aren't well.

"And you're sleeping? Are you still relying on the pills?"

"Yes," I say instantly. "I do need them." I don't want to kick away that crutch. I just haven't taken them the last couple of nights, since the figure in the garden. And last night was OK, actually, now that I think about it. I was so tired from the lack of sleep the previous night that I just dropped off.

Maybe all the running helps. I went again, this morning, just in the fields round here. I can feel the ache in my calves, my body unused to the exercise. But it's a good ache.

"And how're you coping with . . ." I remember that I told him about Sophie's call last time. ". . . the investigation?"

"Oh, I don't know." I pour out the coffee. "I'm not sure where they're up to . . . I mean, they're not going to trace the call. Because of all the anonymity stuff. But they're looking into it."

"And what does that mean?"

"I don't know. The detective said they'd speak to the charity." What exactly are they doing, if anything? Nicholls has barely told me anything. It's still just me, with my pathetic attempts to take things forward myself. I clear my throat. "Would you like milk, Dr. Heath? I promise it's fresh."

"You can call me Nick, Kate. And I don't want to upset you. Are you finding the police helpful?"

I roll my eyes. "I don't know. This detective, Nicholls . . ."

"Nicholls?"

"Ben Nicholls, his name is. I'm not sure how much he's really doing. . . ." I turn round and hand him his coffee. I smile at him, his face is a picture of concern. But if he gives me any sympathy, I'll break down. "Actually, I did want to ask you something. My neighbor, Lily Green, just up the drive, in the little carriage house? Well, she must be in her eighties—I check in on her, every so often." He sips his coffee and nods. "She's been getting more confused, recently, and I'm a bit worried." How to phrase this? "I noticed that she's on some quite serious medication: painkillers. Morphine."

"So you noticed this?"

"Yeah."

"Where? In her bedroom? She had just left her prescription out? That might be something to worry about, if she has children round, but otherwise . . ."

"No, I saw it in her bathroom cabinet. When I was looking for something."

"So you were looking in her pill cabinet," he says.

I don't reply.

"Right. Kate, I have to say, as your doctor, that that does alarm me, a little. After what happened—"

"No, that's not it at all." I laugh, but it sounds forced. "You've got this wrong, honestly. I'm not—I wasn't looking for her pills. That was never—that was never my problem."

But he's not listening. "Last year, when it happened, I thought I was doing the right thing. I took you at your word. That you didn't understand how the pills interacted with alcohol—that you were being sensible. So I let you stay on them, it didn't need to go any further. Though your family were very upset."

"I know."

It was Charlotte who found me. Mark had left a few months earlier. I was very lucky, really.

That was back when the whole sleep thing had got really bad. Even the pills weren't working. Maybe I'd got used to them. I'd got into the habit of taking a few more than I should, just to get the effect. Then, one night, the April before last, I'd drunk a bottle of wine in front of the TV, and fallen asleep on the sofa. I didn't want to hurt myself, I really didn't. I just wanted to turn my brain off—I was so tired.

I'd woken up in a hospital bed.

Afterward, Charlotte had told me, crying, that my lips were blue when she found me. She'd known something was wrong, she said. It had been Sophie's birthday. So when I hadn't answered the phone that day, she'd driven round that evening and let herself in with the key I'd given her when we moved in. And I am so grateful to her, of course I am. It's just tricky sometimes, to be around someone who still treats you like an undetonated bomb.

"Kate?" Dr. Heath wants more from me. "You have to understand, it puts me in a difficult position when you tell me you've been looking through a neighbor's pill cabinet. That's a red flag. Can you understand that?"

"Yes." I feel like a child being told off. "But—"

"Your neighbor's medication is really her business, whatever her age."

And now I feel like I'm age-shaming my neighbor with dementia. "I know that, I do. But I'm not sure she's got enough support, let alone anyone checking if she's taking her pills at the right time.

I've been in touch with social services, through the council, and they haven't got back to me."

He sighs. "It's not a perfect system. But listen—why don't I check with the surgery, see if she's registered with any of my colleagues, I can ask them to take a look at her prescription."

"Would you?" I should have thought of that. Of course Lily will be registered there. Everyone goes to the Amberton GPs, from miles around.

"But really it's your health that you should be prioritizing."

He's looking behind me now, at the table. I follow his glance to my open jotter with my scrawling notes. A messy mind. I reach out and flip it closed, embarrassed.

"You're very alone here. Are you getting out much? Are you seeing friends and family?"

"Yes, a bit more." That's true, what with the running and the trips to the library and the garage, I've been out more than in, well, a long time. I'm not sure he'll count a chat with the local librarian as a budding new friendship, though. "And, I've got my family support." When I ring them back.

"Hm." He's unconvinced, but then he catches sight of the kitchen clock. "I've got to go. But why don't you make another appointment soon. Just to keep things on track."

It's probably a good idea. "I will, I promise. And thanks."

"Do. Thanks for the coffee."

I feel a bit flat after he's gone. It's nice to have company, even a professional. And his visit has reminded me of all sorts of things. My limitations. My mistakes.

But he's given me an idea. I'm going to further a relationship, I think, as I dial. Even if I'm not sure Nick Heath would quite approve of why I'm doing this.

David, the librarian from the other day, is surprised but pleased to hear from me as I remind him, as casually as I can manage, of his suggestion that I speak to his sister. When people know you want to know something, they can clam up. But he doesn't.

"Why don't I give you Vicky's number? I did mention you, but she's busy with the kids. And she's not the most organized person I know, I have to admit. . . ."

I don't know if I'll ever get over how helpful they are up here.

"Thanks very much, David. I'll do that, right away."

She doesn't pick up the first time, but she does ten minutes later.

"Hello?" She sounds harassed. "Jesse, no. No! Put it down!"

"Hi, Vicky?" I say. "My name's Kate. Your brother may have mentioned that I might call?"

"Hiya, yes. He did, didn't he? So how can I help?"

Quickly, I tell her that I'm doing a project on missing people, with a focus on the local area. "Social studies," I say, knowing it's a flimsy excuse. But like her brother, Vicky likes to chat.

"Nancy Corrigan." She sighs. "I thought she was so pretty." Nancy, she says, just had the best kind of hair. "Unlike my own frizzy mess! I had a perm back then, could I have picked anything that would have made it look worse? On top of my puppy fat, if I can call it that now I've still got it." She laughs, unbothered. "She was just one of those girls, you know. Someone you want to be."

But she's short on detail about how she left.

People said, in that random way that gossip goes around a school, that Nancy had gone to London. "God knows why she would, looking back now. What's she going to do there?" But it seemed she'd cut ties with her friends, as well as her family, and they weren't any better informed. She'd packed a bag, taken money—people said.

Soon, two policemen had come into school and, one by one, Nancy's friends had been called out of lessons to talk to them in the headmistress's office. But they couldn't tell the police what they wanted to know: where Nancy was. Eventually the police had gone away and the school had returned to normal routines, before lessons gave way to the long summer.

Nancy's year, upper fifth, hadn't all come back for sixth form anyway. They'd done, oh, cooking courses and things like that, and some had gone off to the sixth-form college in the next town, where you could wear your own clothes all the time. With Nancy's year dispersing, it didn't seem so strange, in a funny way, that one girl had gone so suddenly. Almost as if she'd just got a head start on everyone.

"Now it feels different," Vicky tells me. "I do think about her sometimes, even now. I must have been, what, fourteen then. I don't think I quite got it. Now I'm a mum, I look at my little boy and little girl—she's a baby, but she's so easy, honestly—and I think, those poor parents, what did they do?" I don't want to talk about the poor parents: I sense she could go on for a while.

"Yes, it was very sad," I say, knowing how heartless I sound. "And there was a boyfriend, I think, when she left? Who I'm trying to find out a bit more about. So I can speak to him."

I'm half-expecting her to say, no, like Olivia, she doesn't remember, but she chuckles.

"He was a bit of a hunk. Dark hair." Clearly, teenage Vicky was more informed about teenage romance than Nancy's ten-year-old sister.

"Oh?"

"They weren't my year though; he must have been a couple of years above, too."

"So what was his name?" I try not to sound impatient.

"Hm, let's see . . . James, Jack. J-something. Jay!" she crows. "That's it, Jay."

"And his surname?"

"Ooh, I couldn't tell you. He moved away. And the prices have gone up so much round here, I don't know how anyone could afford to move back!" she says happily, vindicated in her decision to stay. She lowers her voice a little. "People talked, of course."

"They did?"

"Oh, you know."

No, I don't know. "In what way?" Be nice, Kate.

"Well, teenagers argue, don't they? Some people said Nancy and Jay had broken up, that that was the real reason she'd gone. I mean, I couldn't be sure about that. Nothing concrete. But anyway, his family moved away, it must have been that summer. He didn't come back to school."

Half a name. "I see." Back to square one.

"But you know," she says, enthusiastic again. "I've got all my old school photos at my mum's. I could have a look next time I'm round, if you like. It might jog my memory."

"Could you? I'd be grateful." It sounds like a long shot.

"No bother at all. Thing is—Jesse! Careful with the baby! Put her down!—Thing is," she says confidingly, "they did have a leak in the garage that soaked all the boxes, all my old stuff." She laughs. "I should have sorted it all out years ago. So I don't want to get your hopes up."

"Well, thanks anyway." I make sure she's got my email, and my phone number, knowing I'm never going to hear from her.

"Don't mind at all. So, where's this going to end up? Will you write some kind of paper? I don't mind if you quote me, you know."

CHAPTER 21

I hang up when Jesse picks up on another handset and starts nonsense-talking down the line. I've got what I can from Vicky.

Back online, I'm methodical, searching for combinations of Jay with "Nancy Corrigan" and "Amberton Grammar" and whatever I can think of that might lead me to his full name; where he is now. I just want to know what happened: I want to know that he had nothing to do with Nancy's disappearance, that he ended up living a predictably normal, respectable existence in some anonymous suburb, his school girlfriend's disappearance now just a mournful episode from the past. Something that he thinks about at Christmas, or on her birthday. Just sad. Nothing more.

And that's as far as I'll let myself think about why I need to know this, now.

I spend a while looking at the updates they send to alumni, saved as PDFs online, to see if there's any mention of a Jay. There's not.

When the phone call comes I'm still in the kitchen, the sun lower now through the windows, making myself a cup of tea. Out of habit, I let the landline ring out. It's bound to be some cold caller, or Charlotte again. The man's voice breaks in on my thoughts, making me start.

"Mrs. Harlow, this is DI Nicholls. Please could you give me a call back—"

I'm across the room and seize the handset before he can finish. "Hello? I'm here."

He tells me he's got some news that would be better explained in person.

"Have you found her?" I hear myself saying, pitched too high.

"No. No, I'm sorry. I didn't mean to get your hopes up. Are you free now? I tried your mobile." I glance at it on the table—I've let it run out of battery once more.

"Yes, of course. Should I come to the station again?"

"No need for that. I'm in the area now and I'll explain face to face."

After I hang up, I bend to pick up the cat, burying my face in his fur. He mews in protest.

"Another visitor. It's quite the social whirl in here," I tell Tom.

But I'm nervous. Doubly so. Because sleeping on it hasn't offered any flash of inspiration to getting into Sophie's other email. I'm going to turn it over to the police.

Yet first I've got to make them understand how important this could be.

"Turns out we're not the only ones who've been interested in the charity's phone records. The Message in a Bottle helpline has had a bit of a pest problem. One caller in particular had been very nasty. Sexual stuff, whenever he got a woman on the phone. Threats. And he was persistent."

"Oh, right. You mean a pest caller." Nicholls has turned up, refused a cup of tea—"water, please"—and started talking. For a moment, I let myself feel the oddness of my life now: the suited detective sitting opposite me at my kitchen table, as I wait for him to get to the point. He's very calm, unhurried.

And what he's saying is true. Heavy breathers are the secret

bane of helplines, but they don't like to publicize it—it might en-
courage more of them. But annoy the volunteers too often and the
powers that be can, after a lot of soul-searching, block you. I just
don't yet see what this has to do with me.

"So," he begins, "it turns out that the charity had actually made
a police complaint about one caller in particular, via its headquarters in London. And they'd agreed police could access the
helpline's caller records for the last couple of months, to find him.
They were prepared for him to be charged."

I feel a little leap of hope. Could this be good news? He's got
Sophie's call details this way?

He continues: "My colleagues in the Met started looking at the
phone numbers that had been used to make repeated calls to the
helpline. It wasn't hard to find their guy: he didn't understand that
the confidentiality policy wouldn't cover a telecommunications
offense. This guy was making hundreds of calls from his house
landline—somewhere in the West Midlands—when his wife went
to work in the daytime."

So that's why I wouldn't have heard from this creep: I only do
nights.

"And we don't get a lot of repeat callers," I add. Not legitimate
ones. We get messages to loved ones, and we're supposed to refer
people elsewhere for longer-term support. "But I'm sorry, how's
this going to help in my situation? Sophie only rang me once."

"I do have a point," he says mildly. "Now, the charity wouldn't
agree to release the details of Sophie's call." So he did ask. "And
there wasn't any reason for us to try to force it." I nod. I don't
agree with it, but I understand. "So when I heard about this other
investigation, I took a look at the info they'd collected on the repeat caller numbers—call it professional curiosity—and I found
something a little unusual."

For a second I feel like he's waiting for me to say something,
then he goes on: "There were dozens of calls made to the helpline
from a number local to this area."

I'm confused. "Well, it's a national helpline—but anyone can
ring in."

"Yes, anyone can ring in. And with this one phone number, there wasn't any abuse, nothing like that. There was just a pattern: the caller rings, then hangs up a few moments after connection. We could see from the length of the call. My colleagues had already traced it, to a telephone box." He looks at me expectantly. "It's the telephone box at the end of Park Road. This road."

The one near the crossroads, not a hundred meters from my house, if that.

He rubs his chin. "Could you tell me why that might be, Mrs. Harlow?"

"No," I say, bewildered.

"Have you seen anyone hanging around that phone box, perhaps?"

"I can't see it from here." That's obvious. "You could try the people on the other side of the road, they're slightly nearer."

"Right." He's frowning slightly.

"I might have a mobile number for them if you want, there's an old neighborhood list somewhere that we were given when we moved in—" I start to get up.

"No, no, don't worry about that." But he's not moving from the table. "You must've been under an enormous amount of strain since she ran away," he says.

"I'm fine." I'm not. But I can feel this going somewhere I don't like.

He rubs the back of his head, a small gesture of discomfort. "I understand that there was an episode in your past. Mental health issues." I stare at him, my mouth a hard line. "An overdose. Benzodiazepines," he says it carefully, "and alcohol."

"It wasn't an overdose. Not how you mean, anyway. It was a mistake."

"Whoever made these calls from the phone box made them dozens and dozens of times. . . ."

Suddenly I understand. "Oh. You think I know something."

"Mrs. Harlow, no one's accusing you of anything, all I asked was—"

"You think I'm making prank calls," I say flatly. It's not a question.

"I didn't say that." He didn't need to. "And I wouldn't call them prank calls. Maybe"—he lifts his eyebrows, questioning—"calls for help, perhaps?" His eyes are kind. I can't stand it.

"Well, I'm not," I say. "Yes, I had some obsessive thoughts, over-anxious thought patterns." I won't shy away from this. "I couldn't move on from my daughter's—Sophie leaving. I didn't cope very well. And I couldn't sleep, so I took pills to help me. But I didn't make those calls.

"There *are* a lot of kids round here, they could be messing around." It sounds weak even to my ears. Who on earth would be calling from there? A thought crosses my mind: "And Sophie's call, you're not saying that was from that phone box, too, are you?"

"No." He shakes his head. "There was nothing from the phone box on the evening in question. Of course, you were working at the helpline then. Your colleague Alma Seddon, she's confirmed that."

Now I realize: in his eyes, I might well have just incriminated myself. Of course there wasn't a call made from near my house that evening. I was busy at the helpline. But the other times . . .

"Look, it's not a criminal matter to call a helpline and hang up," he says quietly, pulling something out of his jacket. "Regardless of whether . . . I just wanted you to know: there are some excellent resources available for families of the missing." He hands me a leaflet, one that I've seen before, and I keep my eyes on it as he starts talking about posttraumatic stress disorder, counseling, the various charities that specialize in these issues. He manages not to mention the one I volunteer for, I'll give him that.

"Thank you," I force it out. Be polite. Keep control. "I'm glad you're here, anyway. I wanted to talk to you about Sophie's diary, the email address in it. I've noticed some similarities with another case that I wanted to bring to your attention—" I look up, catch the expression on his face: I'm still not getting it.

My heart starts to pound. "What *is* happening with the investigation? After the diary—what Sophie wrote about Danny? You were speaking to him. And Holly Dixon, right? Is nothing happening with that?"

He speaks slowly, like he's working out how to put this. "Yes, we've spoken to both Danny and Holly. They don't necessarily quite agree with your version of things: of your conversations. Which is perhaps not surprising." I can imagine: I picture Holly in tears outside the police station, begging me to tell them the pregnancy test was hers. Danny insisting he didn't sleep with Sophie.

Nicholls leans forward, getting my attention. "And they say there was some tension between you and them. Before Sophie went away."

I can't deny it—I wasn't the biggest fan of either of them.

"When someone goes missing, it can be tempting to find someone to blame."

"That's not it," I insist. "I'm not saying that they . . . *did* anything, but I just know something's not right. Something's keeping her away. You've got the diary, you showed it to me!"

"The diary explains that she got pregnant, and her boyfriend wasn't happy about it. It doesn't change anything, not materially."

"But why didn't you say any of this before? You let me think . . ." But did he? I thought they were taking this seriously, that things were moving again. I try to remember what they've told me.

"I said that when I've information I can share with you, I would of course do that."

And with a sick plunge of my stomach, I realize that he just has: but it's information that suggests I might be unreliable, a little unbalanced. I feel the panic rising in me. "But Sophie was scared, on the phone." Oh God. "You do still believe that she called me. Don't you?"

He's as measured as ever, utterly professional. "You said the voice was a whisper. That the line was bad. Then you heard your and your ex-husband's names—your first names. And . . ."

"And I heard what I wanted to hear," I finish for him, dully.

"I'm not saying that, not at all, not necessarily." He doesn't say: it doesn't really matter. Not to the police.

I've had enough now. "I'm not losing it. I'm not." I stand up. "Thanks for coming, DI Nicholls."

"Mrs. Harlow—"

"Thanks for coming. I'll see you out."

*   *   *

I keep it together until I've shut the door after him and I hear his car engine start up.

I've still got the leaflet he gave me in my hand. I scrunch it up deliberately and drop it on the floor. I lean against the front door, shaking with anger. It feels better than despair, at least. How dare he suggest I've been making calls?

I push down the wobble of uncertainty, like my world's twisting around me. It couldn't have been me, could it? Fear clutches at my gut. Of course it wasn't me. I know that.

But if my family hear about this, what the police think. Mark. They'll think it's happening again, that I'm losing it. . . .

I go back into the kitchen and pour myself a large glass of water, then drink it down. I look at the computer and the closed jotter beside it. I need to face the facts.

I'm back where I started. No closer to finding my daughter. The police are not investigating.

No. I correct myself. It's worse. They don't trust me.

The email from the helpline is inevitable, I suppose. That's what I tell myself, when I read it that night.

"Dear Kate," it begins. "We'd like to take the opportunity to thank you for all you've done for Message in a Bottle."

That's the nice bit, obviously. The rest is not so pleasant. My services will no longer be required. They phrase it differently of course, stressing that the work of the charity can put high demands on its volunteers, and suggest that I might like to take some time out to reflect on how I might best put my skills to use.

I don't bother replying.

CHAPTER 22

I don't really know what to do with myself anymore. I made myself get up today, though I couldn't really see why, eating breakfast in front of the TV, losing hours there, my bad habit. I feel so tired and defeated. Then I started to tidy the living room uselessly, picking at dust that's barely there. After that I went into the kitchen and picked up the phone, twice, wondering.

Should I call Dad? Charlotte? For once, I just want some human contact. But what can I tell them that won't just make it worse? That won't make them think that I'm losing my grip?

Then I think: the one person who won't judge me.

I grab my keys and head out of the door.

Lily's in her usual spot, dozing in her armchair in a shaft of sunlight. Her head's lolled forward, that can't be comfortable.

"Lily," I say. "Lily." Her eyes open, blink into waking.

"Oh hello, dear," she says, lifting her face to mine slowly. "Has he gone then?" She must mean her care worker. I wonder if he's actually been though, or she's getting confused again.

"Yes, it's just me, Lil. Shall we have a cup of tea?"

"Lovely. Yes, please." I head to the kitchen, check the milk and make us a cup each. It all looks tidy and clean, I'm reassured to see.

I've two china mugs of tea in my hands, pretty things with violets splashed over them, when I see the scrap of newspaper on the sideboard, neatly folded on top of her telephone directory.

RAN AWAY?
Send a message to let them know you're safe
NO QUESTIONS ASKED
Just phone and give your message
We will pass it on
Send a MESSAGE IN A BOTTLE

I manage not to spill anything.

"Lily," I say, walking back into the sitting room, urgency in my voice. "Why've you got that bit of paper—the advert for the helpline?" I hear the sharp note and try to soften my tone. "You know I work there, don't you. That I volunteer there?" She doesn't reply.

I put our teas down on the little side table and try again. "Have you maybe tried to call me where I work? Maybe a few times?"

I'm not sure she's listening, but then she starts talking, surprisingly brisk.

"You said always to call, you know. You said: Lily, if you need anything, don't hesitate to call. Well, you know I told you I was perfectly fine, but you insisted. Well, I said, I don't need—"

"No, no, that's totally fine. I'm sorry. I just—I didn't know you knew I worked at the charity." My heart's sinking.

"Of course I do, I remember things." She's getting cross. A sign she's feeling vulnerable, I know now. Is she feeling a little guilty?

"Oh, Lily. I'm only next door. And you've got my phone numbers if there's anything." She must have been calling the charity number, trying to get hold of me. And then what—hanging up?

Asking for me? But from the phone box? I didn't realize she was in so bad a state, that she was so confused. What is going on in her head?

I have an idea now: I pull up the footstool in front of her. "Lily, how's your little boy?"

"My little boy . . ." Her brow creases.

"Yes," I say encouragingly. "Your little boy, you've told me all about him."

"I don't have a little boy," she says flatly.

"Oh. I thought—"

"I don't know what you're talking about."

"I'm sorry, Lily, I thought you liked talking about your little friend. You said he had blond curls like you had. Does he look like Bob, your husband, too?"

That's a mistake. "We didn't have any children." She looks upset. "You're a cruel girl."

I draw back, shocked. Lily's never angry with me. But then I've read that, on top of confusion and forgetfulness, mood changes can be a symptom of what I've feared: dementia.

"I'm sorry, Lily. I didn't mean to upset you."

"All right," she says fretfully. "But you ask too many questions. I don't like it." She sounds like a child.

"OK. We won't talk about it again." I take a deep breath. "I've got a few things to do but I'll come and see you again soon. Have a nice afternoon."

What the hell's going on with her? Back home I hurry to my computer, still on the kitchen table, and type in the name of the drug: the morphine I saw in her cabinet. I click on a website aimed at patients and start scanning: "It's a controlled medication. . . . Strict rules . . ."

One paragraph I read twice: "Don't break, crush, chew or suck morphine pills. If you do, the whole dose might get into your body in one go. This could cause a potentially fatal overdose."

Another note makes my stomach give a little flip: "What if I forget to take it?" There's a warning: never double up your dose to make up for a missed one.

Lily's so forgetful now. And she's got so much of it, bottles of pills and liquid. What are they all for?

That decides me. Lily isn't in a state to be managing this, not when the medicine itself could be making her more confused. The note on the bottle, to take when needed—she could be taking it around the clock.

I don't care if I'm interfering, I don't want to wait around for Dr. Heath to have a polite word with a colleague. Before I can think about it more, I call the surgery and give full force to the unsuspecting receptionist. She won't even confirm that Lily's a patient, which doesn't help my mood.

"It's dangerous," I finish. "Whoever's prescribing this stuff to Lily—I mean, Mrs. Green—could be in serious trouble. It's . . . it's negligent," I add, grasping for a legal-sounding word.

"Mrs. Harlow," says the receptionist, Valerie. "I do understand. Now, I've taken down all your details, and I'll pass your message on to the practice manager."

"OK. Good. And will they call me back? Because I'm going to keep calling you until they do."

"Yes," she says. I can swear I hear gritted teeth. "Someone will call you back." Hopefully not me, I can almost hear her add, before she hangs up.

I feel a little better once that's done. But it's not the receptionist's fault. I know I'm venting my frustration—at the police, at Nicholls, at my failure to get anywhere.

I get up, restless, and go to the window. How could I have made the conversation with Nicholls go better? I don't know if I could. Now I remember his comments, when he'd called me at the start, about how I came to pick up the phone call that night at the helpline:

"I guess it could have been anyone," I'd said then.

"Yes. Quite the coincidence, really," he replied, nice as pie. *"And is it always that quiet—just you on your own?"*

I should have known that's where he was going. That this is what they'd conclude: that maybe I didn't even get a call, not from Sophie anyway. That I was, at the least, unreliable.

Because it *was* weird that it was me who picked up.

I can admit that, now that I'm not trying to convince anyone else. Of all the times she could have called the helpline, for her to get through when it was just me.

I frown. For some reason, I felt like the caller was as surprised as I was . . . the line going dead, like she panicked.

But maybe she was just overwhelmed. What if she *had* been trying to reach me? What if she knew I was working there, somehow?

Think. If you search for me online . . . I go to the computer and do it quickly—yes, there I am. You have to scroll down a bit, to find it, but there's my name, mentioned in that newspaper article from last Christmas about the helpline. In the picture, I am standing in the back row of volunteers—and yes, my name's in the caption. She could have found me there.

So maybe it wasn't a coincidence. Maybe the call *was* meant for me: perhaps, Sophie understood how much I needed to hear her voice again, even as she asked me not to worry anymore—to let her go. And of course getting through to me at the helpline, not our home, has meant I've had no way of tracing the call: it keeps me at a safe distance. It keeps *her* at a safe distance.

It's just an awful lot of effort to go to to reach me, only to stay hidden. . . .

And now my mind's drifting to something else, because that isn't the only odd thing in all this. That diary was found by a dog walker, the police said. And for that to happen now, so soon after the call . . .

I picture the diary again, as Nicholls showed it to me in that little room: the frontispiece with an email address that looks right—it just doesn't match the one I know.

But, then again, who else would notice a detail like that, other than Sophie's mother?

My heart starts to hurry, just a little. I want to try something.

I pull up the page I've had open: the email account that I can't get into. Now, typing gibberish, I deliberately get the password wrong and get myself into the security process.

The question flashes up again. I've tried so many times to answer it, racking my brains as to what Sophie might answer: *What was the name of your first pet?*

This time, I type it in quickly: *Matilda.*

Matilda was the corgi I grew up with, a portly little dog with a strong sense of her own dignity. I used to tell stories about Matilda to Sophie when she was little, to make her laugh. . . .

The next question flashes up.

Where were you born?

I take a deep breath in and out again. I'm through to the next question. I was right. It *was* a question for me. Stay calm.

London, I type in. That's what Sophie would answer. We were living in a little flat there when she was born, south of the river.

Error. Of course.

But now I know. It gives me another try.

This time I type in *Manchester*, for me.

Correct. My eyes start to blur with tears, but I'm smiling as the third question comes up.

These are meant for me. Sophie pointed me to this email and left questions only I'd know. She knew I'd always come looking for her.

What's your mother's maiden name?

I was a Greenwood, but over time it just seemed easier to be a Harlow. Once we moved up here, and I wasn't working anymore, the shift seemed somehow definite.

But Mum was Rhodes, before she married Dad.

And yet I hesitate before I start to type again—I'm so close, I almost don't dare believe it. What if it doesn't work? What if the email account is empty or, worse, inactive now, and I'll never know what was in it. Please God . . . I type:

Rhodes.

And I'm in, the inbox laid out before me.

There is just one message, the subject line reading "FW," for a forwarded message. I click it open. I start reading.

Then I read it again, quickly. My mouth is dry, a beat starting to pulse in my eardrums. I swallow.

Oh, Sophie. Oh no. *What have you done?*

PART 2

CHAPTER 23

Sophie

They say going away is easy, that the hardest thing is coming home again. I read that somewhere, before I did it. I just didn't think it would all be quite so concrete, in my case.

I can't quite remember who came up with the idea in the first place. I felt like it was mine. Now, I'm not so sure. I knew people would be upset, of course. And I didn't want that to happen. They'll be OK, he'd tell me, you'll leave a note. I know the kind of thing you can say. And it won't be forever.

I didn't have to worry about what to bring, it was just what I should leave: my phone, my bank cards, things that they could trace. And I cleared out my account, though I knew I wouldn't need money. It had to look right.

Everything went to plan. I just got the bus from the station in Amberton and bought a ticket to London, on the coach coming from Manchester. And then three stops later, after the airport, I slipped off again with my bag, at the services, at the back of a group of students who wanted to smoke. I just didn't get back on with them.

He picked me up, like we arranged.

He didn't like it when he saw I'd turned up with my bag stuffed full, worried that someone might guess what I was up to, just from that. "Relax," I said. "No one thought anything. I told Dad I was going to Holly's."

"And did anyone see you leave school?"

"I don't think so. But even if they did, they'll just think I'm skipping class. Don't worry."

I thought it was beautiful when I arrived, the late afternoon sun throwing long shadows across the carpeted floor. The whole place looked warm and cozy.

"Oh look," I said. "It's all ready for me!"

"I didn't do much." He looked tense. I thought he was worried whether I liked it.

"I love it."

A big floor lamp stood in the corner, leaning over a tired green sofa. There was a rug, a small chest of drawers, an upturned box. "For the TV," he said. "I'm going to sort that for you." I walked over to the wall and ran a hand over the low wood paneling, smooth and warm to my touch, then traced a flower carved into the wood. I didn't know quite what to do, now I was here. Behind one of those old-fashioned screens was a mattress, made up with pillows, sheets and blanket. "Very posh." I smiled, wanting to show him I liked it all. There was even a fridge plugged into the wall.

I peered inside: milk, eggs, orange juice. "What, no mini-bar?"

"You're too young."

"Duh, I'm joking." The smell of paint tickled my nose. I sneezed.

In another corner, behind flimsy partition walls, was a simple sink and toilet, one of those old ones with a pull flush. He followed me in, his head nearly hitting the bare bulb above us, and turned the tap on and off.

"It all works. I checked it over."

I touched one white wall—it was still tacky to the touch. "You've been working hard," I said. "You've thought of everything."

"Of course I did," he said. I could hear the note of reproach at my surprise.

"It's nice," I said, to cover my sudden nerves. "And now it's all for me." I wanted to keep the mood light, for me as much as him; I wanted his excitement to match mine. "No bath," I added.

"I can maybe do something about that," he said. "It shouldn't be too difficult. For now, you'll have to heat up water in the kettle, and use the plastic basin."

"Seriously?" I laughed, and went to hug him. "Really, it's fine, I promise. And it won't be for that long." He stroked my hair.

Mum always said I was clever, and I try to tell myself the same, I do. But I feel so stupid.

That first night, he stayed with me. I felt OK, reassured.

In the morning, before he left, we'd talked again about what I'd do all day: read, make food, watch TV. I nodded. "Honestly, we talked about this—I understand. You can't be everywhere." But it still shocked me when I tried the door, after him, and found it locked: the metal handle refusing to turn in my hand. We fought about that, when he came back that evening. He used to come a lot, back then.

"It's for your own good," he kept saying. "It's not safe. For you, or me. Someone might see you, even here. It's not like you can go outside. So why do you need it unlocked?"

"But why do you need to lock me in?" I was frustrated, hot tears starting. "That's not fair!"

"Sophie," he said, his expression grave. "You've got to be responsible. It's my life at stake here, as well as yours."

I pulled a face. "Your livelihood," I corrected. "Not our lives."

"And when I've seen that I can trust you in this," he continued, "well, we'll see."

"But I won't go out, I promise. Don't you trust *me*?"

"Of course I do," he soothed. "It's just, you're impulsive. It's not fair to put that responsibility, for your safety and mine, on you. But you do understand, don't you? If it's locked, no one can get in, either. It's much safer. You're all alone in here. I'd hate to think, if you were asleep and . . ."

I hadn't thought about that. "OK, I get it." I took a deep breath. "I understand."

"Good girl." He kissed me on my forehead, and I smiled.

He's always made everything sound so reasonable. And he's so good at making me feel like I'm in the wrong. In the end, I let it go. It wasn't my first mistake.

CHAPTER 24

Kate

So she didn't run away. Not like we thought, anyway.

The message in front of me was sent from Sophie's other email account: *Sharlow90@gogomail.com*—the one we'd checked. She must have deleted it after she sent it; I know both her sent messages and her deleted file were examined.

I flex my hands; they've gone cold.

It took me a few seconds to realize what I was reading. It's an email conversation, a string of messages that she's forwarded to herself, to this secret email account.

Now I start reading them again, keeping my breathing controlled. There is no point panicking, not now. The messages are brief; I get the impression it's the continuation of an ongoing conversation:

10 May 2016 at 18:05, King Pluto <King_pluto@hotmail. com> wrote:
All set?

10 May 2016 at 18:09, Sophie Harlow <Sharlow90@ gogomail.com> wrote:
Yes! I'm ready x

That's Sophie's gogomail, the account we knew about. The replies come quickly:

King Pluto: Do you need to go over the plan
for Friday again?

Sophie: Only if you want to. Everything's fine with
me. I'm excited x

King Pluto: You know you've got to stay calm now. Don't act
too happy, or out of the ordinary.

Sophie: I know! I just started another row, coursework
this time. I feel bad :(

King Pluto: It's got to be done. Just a few days to go now.
Delete this conversation.

Sophie: You're such a worrier.
Don't I always?

King Pluto: I mean it. You know I'll
check. Delete it.

Sophie: All right, I
will. x

King Pluto: I can't wait until we can
be together.

Sophie: Me too. See
you soon x

King Pluto: See you
very soon.

So someone knew she was going to run away. Not just that, but someone was planning to go with her. And now one question is running through my head, on a loop: who? Because everyone she knew is still here.

I check the date of the forwarded messages—the whole exchange took place on 10 May 2016, between 6:05 p.m. and 6:17 p.m.— and pull up an online calendar. Like I thought: it was a Tuesday. Homework hours, when she'd be up in her bedroom, safely tucked away; me pottering around downstairs, upset after our latest clash; Mark still at work.

But she wasn't safe. She was making arrangements, three days before she went, with someone who wanted her to keep it a secret: "You know I'll check." How?

I think: if they knew her password too, they could just log in themselves. The confidence that she'd do what she was told chills me. No persuading, no endearments—just commands.

And I know when this was, I realize now. Just after that last argument, in the last week. I remember how it ended: Sophie slamming her way out of the kitchen. "Just let me go. I can't stand it! Don't you get it? I want some space!" To go up to her room, and talk to . . . whoever this was.

I've replayed that argument so many times. If I'd handled things differently that evening . . . it seemed to come from nowhere. Of course it did, I understand now. They were laying the ground to tell the familiar story: family strife, an unhappy teenager—a reason for going. But that wasn't it, was it?

And "See you soon." But when? The next day, at school? Or afterward—only after she'd gone?

But I just know.

The email shows that it was sent on 13 May, 02:35 a.m.—three days after their exchange. The day she ran away. Sophie forwarded this brief conversation to herself the night before she left, in the early hours, when we were all asleep—filing it away where no one could see.

This was a back-up plan, a just-in-case. She's her mother's daughter, after all: cautious. Oh, not enough to let me know where she was going. Not enough to tell me who she was going with. But just enough to leave a trace, in case . . . in case she ever wanted to?

Because wherever my daughter was headed, and whoever she trusted to know about it, a part of her—however small—didn't trust them. Not entirely.

I stay at the computer, trawling the internet for traces of this email address, the "king_pluto" one. I don't expect it to lead to a business card, but I hope that someone was stupid enough to slip up, just once, using that email or username to sign up for something or, forgetting they're still logged in, comment on some forum. To leave a footprint, somewhere.

There's nothing.

I lean back. Now it's happened I'm strangely calm.

I knew it. I knew it didn't make sense. Not how it was supposed to have happened. Not my Sophie.

I can't wait until we can be
together.

Then I do it before I can think about it anymore: I log in to my own email, the one I use for everything. I go to my drafts and pull up my standard inquiry email: "Have you seen this girl?" with her picture attached.

Within seconds I get a reply: I open it.

Your message couldn't be delivered . . . the recipient's
mailbox is unavailable.

The email's been shut down. Someone's already covered their tracks.

I prop my elbows on the table and rub my eyes. So who could she have been talking to? Be logical.

Danny? Or even a friend, in whom she's confided; someone who wants out too. OK. But then what? They just chickened out—and kept quiet all this time?

No. It's not just a friend. *I can't wait until we can be together.* But it's not Danny, either, I'm sure, after reading that diary, knowing how bad things were between them at the end. . . .

I jerk myself straight: I can't trust that diary, not anymore. Because it didn't make any mention of this—this person, sending secret emails to my daughter. For whatever reason, Sophie didn't want to write about him in her diary, even as she confided details of her pregnancy, her problems with her boyfriend, her unhappiness.

So the diary entries are . . . off. They're not telling the whole truth.

My heart starts to thud.

Was any of it true? All those new entries that I hadn't seen before, making it look like her leaving was all about a teenage pregnancy, getting the situation "fixed," and a hot-headed boyfriend reacting badly. Sophie running away had finally started to make sense.

But a little voice whispers: *and it gave you a scapegoat. Danny.*

It's all so much, I want to push the idea away.

How would I not know if Sophie was tangled up with someone else? She was sixteen, it's not possible.

But then there's the timing. After two years, for the diary to come now, and only now, when I'd found out about the pregnancy test, when I'd started asking questions . . . And what did Nicholls say? He said something about my raising concerns, that I'd done the right thing. "Because it meant that Sophie was on our radar again, when the diary got handed in." How lucky, I thought then. They might have missed it.

Now I think: it's too neat, the timing, for it to be anything but odd.

Jesus. If I've got Danny all wrong . . . what did he say, when I went to see him? I wish I'd taken notes; I've gone about this all the wrong way, so slapdash. He said that nothing ever happened between him and Sophie, he was adamant. And there was something else, surely. I'm missing something . . . no, it's gone.

But if there's a scapegoat, then there's someone else who's being protected: the emailer. The person who knows where Sophie is?

The person who really got her pregnant?

I get up, needing to move. Because why do all this, Sophie? Why lead me to the email messages? Why even bother with the diary if you're letting me know it's not telling the full truth? Why cover up for someone, and undercut it all at the same time? And why phone the helpline to say you're OK, then fill me with fear?

It doesn't make sense.

Until, with a sick lurch of my stomach, it does.

There's one logical answer, really, when you come down it.

Because it was all she *could* do. It was all he let her do.

CHAPTER 25

Sophie

At first, it was like playing house. Our own little world, just me and him—like I'd wanted. And it was exhilarating, after all the secrecy, to spend so much time together.

It was odd, though, at the same time. Sometimes we just didn't have that much to say to each other. I never had that much to tell him about how I'd spent my day, for obvious reasons. It was different to how I'd imagined it, if I'd thought about it all.

This is what it's like, I'd tell myself. *Being grown up. So grow up.*

A lot of the time, when he was there, we'd sit and watch TV, then later I'd clear up and take the dishes to the sink. It was a struggle really, to cook, but there was a microwave, toaster and, soon, a hot ring.

"And of course," he'd say, "you've got all day. You'll be a good cook yet."

"You must be joking," I remember saying.

My meals were more like camping: beans on toast, scrambled

eggs. Once he brought fish, which I tried to cook in the pan. The whole place stank within minutes—no ventilation.

So he didn't do that again. Pretty soon, he stopped eating the food I tried to make, he said he'd eat at home. It meant he didn't have to bring so much each time he came, too. Instead he brought cold stuff: bread, cereal, lots of fruit. "To keep healthy."

"I'll be fine." It was for my own good, I was putting on too much weight in here, he said.

But mostly, I was OK.

Then I started to notice some little things. Like his leaving trick.

The first few times I really did think he just missed me. That's what he said, after all, that he couldn't bear to leave me: I was flattered. He'd be gone only two hours, half an hour, even just fifteen minutes, once, before he'd burst through the door again, so eager to see me. It was different every time.

But I began to wonder. You see, normally when he visited, I'd hear his footsteps on the stairs. Yet whenever he came back sooner than I expected, the door would swing open and I'd jump. I wouldn't have heard him coming at all.

And though his words would be nice, just what I wanted to hear—"I've missed you, I couldn't wait to see you"—he'd always do the same thing as he came in: he'd take this quick, searching glance around the room. It was just with his eyes, he wouldn't move his head—like I wasn't supposed to notice.

Of course, he was checking what I'd been doing—trying to see if I'd already started to test the windows, or the floorboards, looking for ways out. And eventually I did.

Back then, I wasn't sure what it meant, not until that day he left the door unlocked. Whenever I'm in here on my own now, after he's gone I'll wait a bit and then I try the door—just to see. It's always locked now.

Only once, in the early days, it wasn't.

When the handle turned in my hand, I was so thrilled, I went straight down the stairs, two steps at a time, and pulled open the second door at the bottom of the stairs. That was unlocked too.

And he was there waiting. My heart leapt into my throat, even as I drank in the details: the hall in the light behind him, the same old wood paneling. Then he pushed me back in, silent, and shut the door behind him.

"You surprised me!" I said. "I forgot to tell you"—as he herded me up the stairs—"I wanted to ask . . . can you get me some more fruit? I think I need the vitamins."

I didn't really think I fooled him, not at all, but it's always been easier this way. To keep pretending.

So I chattered away, as he pushed me back in, his hand in the small of my back. He didn't say a word about it, not even when he returned the next day with the fruit I'd asked for. He knew.

I've failed him, I thought. *I shouldn't have done it. That's why he's angry.*

I know now, obviously. He didn't leave it open by mistake. He was testing me.

Still, it was weeks before I realized what the window meant. I'd spent ages trying to get the skylight open, standing on the chair under the blue patch of sky. Pushing upward weakly, just reaching it, I had no leverage.

"It must be painted shut," I told him, when he next turned up. "I can't see how it opens." I was already feeling claustrophobic. If I'd known what was ahead of me . . . "It's just too hot in here," I repeated grumpily.

"Don't worry about that," he said. "It must be jammed. I'll sort it."

The next time he came he brought me a fan, a proper standing one.

"But I want fresh air," I said. I remember feeling ungrateful.

"I want never gets," he said and laughed.

I hated it when he did that—when he acted like I was a child. Now, I don't. I welcome it. I just have a feeling that might be useful, if he thinks I don't quite get what's going on.

Because eventually I worked it out. I was examining the window closely, one bright summer morning, the fan whirring away in the corner. I'd piled a stack of magazines on top of the chair, got as close as I could to it. I felt like I was going to slip off, testing my weight before I went flying. But then I balanced, breathing carefully.

I ran my fingertips round the edges of the window, twice, above my head. It wasn't old, like so much of the rest of the place. He must have updated it for me. It definitely looked modern, the frame, painted white, made from something that wasn't wood. It was cooler, harder. Near to it, the glass looked thicker, my faint reflection slightly blurred. Double glazing?

A thought occurred to me.

I checked once more—I wasn't imagining it. It wasn't painted shut. It wasn't jammed. There wasn't a hidden way to swing it open. It didn't open at all.

After that, I started paying attention. I started looking at the place seriously: working out ways to get out. In case of an emergency, I told myself.

The low walls were solid, cool against my hands, as were the eaves, sloping up. They built these old houses sturdy. The skylight, set in the middle of the room, where the ceiling was at its highest—well, I'd tried that.

On another long afternoon, the high sun sliding into evening, I prized up the carpet in a few corners. Just to see. The wood beneath was thick and solid-looking.

"Oak," he announced, a few days later. "That's what this floor's made of." I froze, looking up from my magazine. There was some boring TV program on about renovating houses, that Mum would have liked. That had to be why he was saying it. "Tap it." Silently I reached a hand down and knocked on the floor through the carpet. "It's still pretty solid. It would be a shame to damage it."

I didn't say anything. I could feel my face heating up. Was he angry? Did he know? I couldn't tell.

It's my fault, I told myself. *I'm doubting him and I just need to trust him.* That's what he always said.

I don't know how far I would have gone, really. It's embarrassing to say, but it never really occurred to me then. That I'd what—start digging, scraping the walls with a spoon? Wait by the door, a bit of broken plate in my hand? I couldn't quite admit it, I suppose: my situation. And he was testing me, all the time, to see how far I'd go along with this. The point at which I'd start to resist—start to say no.

In the end, it didn't really matter, because soon everything would change.

And yet, we're still pretending, not admitting the full truth to each other, even now. Him? That this is OK, and that I could possibly be OK with this. And me—that I don't realize what this is: that I can't leave.

The thing is, I prefer this version of him, even if it's fake. I don't want to see the reality.

Because then I feel very afraid.

CHAPTER 26

Kate

I haven't moved, trying to decide what to do. I should tell the police.

But then I picture Nicholls at my kitchen table, explaining that calls had been made from the phone box near my house . . . I can't risk being dismissed again, facing the polite suggestion that I'm not quite reliable in this area; that it's all got a bit much. That even this, too, will have an explanation.

I can almost hear it: "So what you're saying, Mrs. Harlow, is that someone else knew Sophie planned to run away—but you can't think of anyone else who's missing. Well, now, that's to be welcomed, surely? And if Sophie didn't mention that in her diary . . . didn't you say that you'd found it, and read it before? Perhaps it's understandable. But, of course, we're happy to take a look. . . . If that will make you feel better."

No, surely they won't. Surely *this* they'll take seriously. They have to.

But I'm not confident, not totally certain.
I need someone to back me up.

Charlotte picks up on the third ring.
"I know it's been a while. But could you come and see me? Dad too? I've some things I need to talk about with you." I take a deep breath. "I need your help. It'd be better if I could explain face to face."
"OK. I just need to sort the kids out, check if Phil's around and—don't worry, it's fine, we'll be there. When?"
"How soon can you come?"

I feel relieved, just a little, when I hang up the phone. She's good in a crisis. Maybe it's time for me to share this with my family a little and let them help—I hope. She says she'll speak to Dad and drive them both over first thing in the morning, then I'm going to explain everything that's been happening, properly. I'll make them understand, then we can all go to the police together.

Those emails are more than two years old. How will one more night make a difference? But even so, I'm uneasy. I don't want to wait around.

Restless, I get up and go into the living room. Her postcards and note are still laid out on the glass table, untouched of course. That's a perk of living alone, I suppose.

Then I feel a jolt of excitement.

If Sophie's diary hid that email address, what could these messages be telling me?

I quickly go to fetch my jotter, feeling energized. I cracked the email; I got in there. There's got to be something here: a message hidden. I can do this.

After half an hour, I've reached the familiar conclusion. These words are random. No secret emails or words or puzzles. There's just nothing much to them.

Our address. A dutiful, bland message home, just enough to

reassure us all that she's still alive. Her writing unchanged, three kisses—xxx—always, that delicate little flower doodle by her looping signature.

I wonder when she'll grow out of that; I smile a little, flick a finger at the cards to scatter them. Maybe she has already. It was daisy-like, a child's idea of a flower, on the first card home, as usual, but then she mixed it up a little. That cheered me, when I noticed: was it a little sign that she was thawing toward me? Because they get more detailed, a little ruff of petals inside each one. It is supposed to be a rose, maybe?

Well, biology wasn't really her subject. I wonder if she is still drawing as much as she used to.

My smile fades. Perhaps if I'd focused less on academics she'd be here to give me proper flowers, not this sad little bouquet. Unexpectedly, tears spring to my eyes, the writing on the cards blurring. I'm tired, I tell myself, it's all been so much to take in. It's OK. It will be OK, it has to be. I can't get distracted.

So I'll just have to try something else. What else do I know?

They still remember me at the grammar school. Maureen, the secretary, comes out to have a chat with me on their nubby orange sofas, bright against the beige walls. She's the same, her pale blonde coif towering upward like a Mr. Whippy ice cream. The pupils haven't started back yet, so the place is quiet. She tells me they've been hosting summer schools over the holidays. "More trouble than they're worth sometimes, but needs must. And then we're back into term time! And . . . how have you been?" she inquires delicately.

I sense a bit of embarrassment about my unexpected appearance today. Sophie, however you look at it, has not been another one of the school's sterling academic success stories.

As I hoped, it was Maureen who called the police about the diary and she doesn't mind chatting. But it wasn't her who was handed the diary, but one of the cleaners, before the building had opened.

"We had the young artists in that week. Or was it the gymnastic summer school? Anyway, of course when I saw that it wasn't just one of our, um, current pupils' names written at the front, but Sophie Harlow's, I thought I must let the police know, just in case it was relevant, you see. Well, you never know."

"You were quite right," I say. "So, this cleaner, would they be about so I could have a quick chat, perhaps?"

"Oh. Well."

"Just to settle a few questions in my mind," I say hurriedly. "Nothing official." Whatever that means.

"I'm not sure . . . they come before school hours. They always seem to send different people"—she lowers her voice a little—"and I'm not sure how good their English is either. You *could* give the agency a ring. . . ." She looks doubtful: you *could* stick a pen in your eye, but why would you?

"If you wouldn't mind giving me the number . . ."

"I'd be happy to," she says, decisive now. "Just a moment," and she clicks away in her heels. That done, it will be my cue to leave, I sense: the grieving mother ticked off the list; now to sort the stationery order.

Perhaps that's unfair, she's trying to be helpful. But I'm gloomy now, imagining what lies ahead as I try to get past the company switchboard, the bemusement, then guardedness at the suggestion of something unsavory.

But what did I expect? "Yes, the man who handed it in seemed very suspicious, perhaps he knows something; I took down all his details"?

For something to do, I flick through the visitors' book in front of me. For all the hoo-hah after Sophie left, I can't see that they've updated their systems all that much; this is the book for guests to the school, more a relic of the school's traditions than any real security log.

I recognize the odd surname as I leaf through the pages, going back in time; that'll be the parent of a child Sophie must have mentioned. But schools renew themselves so quickly; Sophie's year will have left this summer, A levels done. I wonder if many of the pupils still here even remember her now. . . .

One name, neat caps in bright blue ink, catches my eye:

Nicholls, B.

I read across:

Greater Manchester Police

This is pages back; ages ago. I check the date:

2 October, 2017 IN: 2:30 p.m. OUT: 4:15 p.m.,

his tight scribble of a signature.

"Maureen," I say, as she emerges from the office, a piece of paper in hand, "I couldn't help but notice, this DI Nicholls, I didn't know that he . . ." what? ". . . had a relationship with the school."

"Oh, do you know him?" she says.

"Yes, he's been very helpful"—that's a push—"over Sophie's diary; it was him who let me know that they'd found it."

"He's very good," she agrees. "He gives talks to the students; safety and personal whatsit, part of the pastoral stuff. He's done it for a while, now. He's very popular with the teenage girls in particular. Tells them how to look after themselves." She laughs girlishly. "Of course it doesn't hurt that they've all got crushes on him, they'll all turn up to his talks." She's a little pink herself.

"Nicholls?" This doesn't really match the version of him I know; brusque at best, dour, if you're not so inclined to be nice. "But why does he bother?" I say bluntly.

She draws herself up a little. "Here at Amberton we take pride in maintaining alumni relationships, and we do think both sides get something quite important from—"

"So he went to the school? Here?"

"Of course he did," she says, mirroring my surprise. "Not while

I've worked here, I'm not quite that old, gracious me. He's quite the success story, he'll be a chief constable yet, you know, he . . ." I tune out, digesting this information. So Nicholls was new to Sophie's case. But not new to the area; not at all.

And I don't know why I assumed he wasn't local. Of course there's no reason for him to mention personal ties to the area, or to Sophie's school; he's a professional. Though he's had every chance. . . .

He gave the students talks. I wonder if Sophie ever went to one of them?

It's funny how your brain works. How something jogs your memory, a little nudge and some synapse sparks, a connection is made. It comes to me as I'm driving home: what Danny said, that was niggling at me.

He'd said sometimes Sophie's dad would pick her up. I'd corrected him, pettily. *"Sophie was a daddy's girl. But he didn't pick her up. I did, if she was late finishing. Mark was always at work."* And he'd shrugged.

I'd thought it meant that Danny had seen my car and assumed it was Mark's. But I'm racking my brains now: had he ever even met him? Mark was always working late and it wasn't like Danny was staying for dinner every night.

No, now I think of it, I don't think they had met, even briefly; there'd have been grumblings from Mark, if they had. I'm sure of it. So why did Danny assume it was her dad and not me?

The answer's inevitable, once I see it. He thought it was her dad because there *was* an older man in the driving seat. Someone he didn't know.

I've got to speak to Danny.

CHAPTER 27

Sophie

We still went out, in the early days. The first time he woke me one evening, I think I must have been dozing, curled up on the mattress. I was still dressed, so it can't have been that late. You wouldn't think you'd get so tired, when you've nothing to do. But I'd get cold quickly, when I wasn't moving around so much, so I'd crawl under the duvet even in the daytime.

"Come on," he said. "Quick." I didn't ask what the rush was about. Even then, I knew he didn't like me to ask so many questions.

I followed him through the door and down the stairs, off balance. I felt a spike of anticipation, even nerves, as he unlocked the second door, using the same set of keys. *I didn't know he kept that one locked, too.*

The blueish light from his phone barely pierced the shadows. It had been so rushed when I came here, I'd hardly paid attention. But again I had a sense of space, something in the sound our footsteps made. He led me down more stairs, then made me put a blanket over my head as we went out to the car, the same as when I arrived.

So no one could see me, he said. I couldn't even hear traffic.

His car was the same dark sedan. He told me to sit in the back seat.

I had a vivid flashback, to when he used to pick me up from school, before he said it was too risky. This time, he told me to lie down, so no one could see me.

I nearly fell asleep, lulled by the movement of the car, but after half an hour, or maybe it just seemed that long, he told me to sit up. I felt almost disappointed, stretching my stiff limbs. We were just driving through country lanes, the car lights picking out hedgerows and winding tarmac, nothing more.

"Can we stop somewhere, maybe?" I asked. "I want to walk around." I was desperate suddenly to run again, feeling the pent-up energy of weeks inside.

"Don't be silly," he said. "Someone might see us, then what would we do?"

I didn't think they would. But I didn't want to complain too much.

And it worked. Afterward he took me out again. I think he was already getting sick of our place, the stuffiness, the silence, the air thick with dust and neglect no matter how much I cleaned.

It was always the same routine. We never went far, just round the quiet back lanes, never where the street lights got closer together. And where was there for us to go? Sometimes, I found myself just falling asleep again. I felt safer in the car, almost back in the world again.

But then one time, bright lights woke me up. I kept still and peeked out under my lowered eyelids, my head lolling back against the headrest. We were at a petrol station. I listened to the noises: he filled the car up, paying for the petrol with his card in the keypad machine. The thought occurred to me then: I could just step out, hammer the window, scream for attention. There would be people in the station, or somebody. I remember my whole body tensed, poised, and then—he got back in and switched on the ignition.

We drove off. Shock flooded my body, at the strength of my reaction—just how much I wanted to *go*. I was fine. This was what I'd wanted. Wasn't it?

Still, I wonder: I don't know if I was as close as I thought, not really. Because a couple of times after that, I tested the handle when his attention was on turning a corner, or going through a junction, just to see. The child lock was always on.

Anyway, there were only a handful more night drives, two or three, if that.

I knew it would be the last time as soon as it happened. I had been quiet, that evening, not the cheerful girl he liked me to be. I was lonely, left alone all day. I'd actually told him that. Maybe that's why he did it—to punish me, a little. Or to test me, see how I'd react.

We pulled up by a house I hadn't seen before, a little cottage in a terraced row, with a smart dark green door. We must have driven half an hour, maybe more. He parked up across the street from it, away from the orange puddle of the street lamp and then waited, the engine off.

It was cold, but I knew better than to ask why we were there. His actions, I'd realized, didn't always seem entirely, well, reasonable. So I just sat on my hands to keep them warm, hunkering into my baggy sweatshirt. All the clothes he'd brought me were too-big castoffs. They'd last me, he said.

I turned my face to the window, breathed on it to make a cloud on the glass, drew a flower. Then I rubbed it off and peered into the darkness. There was movement in the cottage door opposite, a slow figure, carrying dark shapes—bin bags.

Something in the old man's shoulders, his tired slump, told me. I pressed my hand to the window, got as close as I could. Steadily, not too fast, without a trace of panic, the car pulled away.

"Was that my grandpa?" I remember saying. "Was that him?"

He didn't answer, just kept driving, as I tried to calm myself down.

He'd always ignored my questions, like he never even heard

me. He prefers to tell me things—to teach me. It was one of the things I liked about him, at first. I thought he was so clever, so certain about what everyone should do, and what everyone was getting wrong. The banks, politicians, teachers, my parents. Me.

But this time I kept talking: "Why did you do that? That was him, I know it." I was almost crying, my voice getting higher. "Is he OK? He looked so . . . so old."

He turned in his seat to look at me, his face furious.

"Shut up," he said. "I mean it."

I stared at him, open-mouthed. He never spoke to me like that.

"You knew what this would mean." Then his voice softened, as his eyes returned to the road. "We've both had to make sacrifices. But isn't this enough, what we've got together?"

I didn't know what to say. "It is," I stuttered. "More than enough." I just wanted him to go back to normal, like he'd been before. "Honestly, it was a shock, that's all."

He needed so much reassurance. I leant forward between the seats and put my hand over his, tense on his thigh, and felt it stiffen, then relax. "You're more than enough. I promise." After that, the trips outside stopped. Not forever, he said. Just until it was safe.

"Look what happened," he said. "It only upsets us both."

It's you who took me there, I thought. But of course I didn't say that.

CHAPTER 28

Kate

"Amberton Garage, how can I help?"

"Danny?"

"Who's this?"

In a rush I say: "Danny, it's Kate Harlow. Please don't hang up."

Silence, then: "Are you kidding me? What do you want?"

"Danny, I am so, so sorry you've got mixed up in all this—and I am trying to sort it out, really I am. But I need to know: that car that you saw picking Sophie up, when you thought it was her dad—"

"You're asking me about cars now?" His voice skitters higher. "Do you know the police had me in again, about Sophie? Holly got really upset. You've got to stop this, it's not fair, it's—"

"Danny, I *know*. And I believe you now, I do: you didn't get Sophie pregnant." As I say it I realize it's more than me trying to get him to stay on the line, I mean it. "And I know it sounds odd, but please. This thing about the car—I just, I need to know—why did you think that it was Sophie's dad?"

I'm waiting for him hang up. But he says, more calmly: "I don't know. Well, he was old. And when I asked her, she got embarrassed. Y'know, I teased her a little bit, about her dad still picking her up."

"I get it—and what did he look like?"

"I dunno. Old. Like a . . . dad. Like he could be *her* dad."

I roll my eyes—teenagers. "Anything else? Glasses? A beard? His hair color?"

"I don't know. I don't remember. I didn't go and say hello."

"And this car?"

"I don't remember."

I wince. Come on, Danny. "Maybe not the model, don't worry about that. But you know all about cars. What about the color, can you picture that?"

"Well," he says hesitantly. "Black, maybe, or navy. Dark. Yes, it was dark. Smart."

I lean against the wall. So it definitely wasn't Mark. Mark always goes for light colors, pale metallics—silver, beige, one year that horrible gold.

"Why?" Danny says now. "Do you think—this guy did something?" His voice is smaller now, fearful. He's not that old, I think. He's had a lot to deal with.

"I think he knows something. I've got to go now. And thank you, Danny. I mean it."

So some guy, someone older, not her dad, picked her up. And someone was emailing her secretly. Are they one and the same? *"I can't wait."*

An older man. Too old for Sophie, so they had to be a secret. A secret that he's managed to protect, until now. Until Holly told me about the pregnancy test, and I started asking questions.

I start walking, pacing up and down the kitchen, the nervous energy forcing me to move.

But what about Nancy? How does that play into this? Am I imagining it, seeing a link, when there's nothing there but a resemblance between two girls, separated by decades, and a chance stray phrase? Then there's this boyfriend of hers . . . Jay. The one they questioned, then he moved away.

He'd be old now too, to a teenager like Danny.

That's ridiculous. The whole Nancy thing.

The only reason I'm even thinking about Nancy, the only reason I even know about her, is because of Lily, who barely seems to know what day it is nowadays.

"Nancy was the other one, then. . . . I get a bit confused these days, don't I?"

I'm picturing her now: Lily pretending not to know about Nancy: *"No dear. I hope I haven't forgotten again."* Not seeming upset to have let that slip her memory, not at all.

I kick on my trainers and head out, swatting away the midges that are dancing under the trees. I'm thinking how to do this: I don't want her to clam up, she's been so touchy recently. Not herself. I can only try, I think, as I let myself in. "Lily?"

She's in her usual chair. But she looks frailer than I remember, dark blue shadows under her eyes.

"Hello, dear."

I pull up a chair, and ask her how she's been; what's been going on in her soaps. But she's a beat behind my questions; she can't remember what's happened in the last episodes. The room's a mess, too; saucers scattered around; old newspapers, the place too hot. I get up to open a window—it's so stuffy.

Another bad day: I must chase the surgery. But maybe that means . . .

Feeling guilty, I kneel down next to her. "Lily, I've something to ask you. Something important—about Nancy, who you mentioned the other day?"

"Nancy?"

"Yes, Nancy." I force myself to wait.

She looks blank, then: "She was a wild one. She got in trouble."

"Yes, you said that last time: she was trouble. But what happened to her? Do you know?"

"They were going to send her away to school—after she got in trouble."

Oh, I'm not going to get anywhere.

And then I realize: "She got *in* trouble." That old euphemism, from when it wasn't nice to talk about these things.

"Do you mean she was pregnant, Lily?"

"She was a one, Nancy. All that sneaking around, off in the deer park. That's where the young people used to go in those days, you know—"

"So did you know her?" I can't let her get off track. I think: how long has she been a housekeeper here? I didn't think her roots here went that far back. "Did you know her, Lily? Is that why Sophie's story reminded you of Nancy, the girl who used to live here?"

But she's tuning me out, her eyes looking beyond me. I lean in and grasp her hand.

"And do you know what happened to her boyfriend, Lily? Do you know? His name was Jay."

She turns her head to me and puts a soft hand over mine. "You mustn't look so worried. What's wrong?"

"I was asking you about Nancy, Lily, do you remember?" I try to keep the tension out of my voice.

"Nancy . . . no dear. I don't think I know that name. Should I?"

"Yes, you do know it; did you know Nancy? What happened to her?"

But it's too much, she's getting upset now: "Why? Where is she? Where's she gone?" She leans back in her chair. "Oh, I'm so tired."

I squeeze her hand. "Don't you worry about it, Lily. Everything's going to be OK. You have a nice nap, I'll come back later, when you're more yourself."

I stand up. Can it be possible?

In trouble.

If she meant what I think . . . pregnant. Nancy's little sister didn't breathe a word of this; neither did Vicky, her classmate—gossip like that would fly round a school. But only if people knew.

If her little sister wasn't told, say, or she didn't confide in her friends, they could hush it up.

So that's two of them.

Two girls who ran away. Two girls with secrets. Two girls who never came home.

CHAPTER 29

Sophie

There's lots of stuff I don't like to think about, these days. But you know what actually makes me pull a face when I remember? How I used to be.

I was so lonely in here, so starved of people, that I was so happy to see him whenever he turned up. Like some dog that still wags its tail when its master arrives to give it a kicking.

Even when he started to be different. He could be so short with me sometimes, like he never was on the outside. Sometimes he barely talked when he came round, only stopping to drop off the bags of food. He's just busy, I told myself, I've got to understand that.

But when he did stay he wasn't the same anymore. It felt like nothing about me was right.

"Why's this place such a mess?" and "Can't you brush your hair? You'd feel better if you did."

"I know, you're right, and I was meaning to." I just felt tired, all the time, falling asleep in the day. What was I going to do, anyway? I knew I shouldn't say that.

"I'm really sorry," I'd tell him, dissolving into tears all too easily now. "I'll try harder." But he didn't want to look at me, let alone touch me. Sometimes he said I was ungrateful.

I cried about that, too.

I suppose he was getting nervous, the longer I was in here. I was too.

This is my third summer. It's hard to keep track of the date. We don't do Christmas, or birthdays. I just got upset, so he stopped. I did ask for a calendar, a paper one, because now I didn't have a phone, but that never came. I know I've been here two winters. The days have been so long. But he doesn't like me to be bored. Correction: he doesn't like me to seem bored. Whether I'm about to cry with frustration at another day inside these walls, let's be honest, he doesn't care.

I've got the TV. It's just a little one, with a DVD player, and he brought me films. That was a relief. The silence was getting to me. Now I have it on nearly all the time, I just turn it down when I'm going to sleep. For a while I thought I might get a mention on the news, but it must have been too late: he didn't get it for me until a few weeks in. I don't know what that means. But it's nice to hear voices other than my own. I've got in the habit of chatting away to Teddy, telling him things about my family and my life at home, like he could understand. I suppose it's better than talking to myself. And I don't do it when *he*'s here, of course.

I read the stuff he gives me. The classics, "proper" books. Some of them I've liked though. *Jane Eyre*, I've read that again and again. She's like a friend now, Jane. And I exercise, press-ups and sit-ups and the rest, things that I make up. Sometimes I'll put on a music channel and dance around. I like feeling my muscles ache, the sweat cooling on me. It reminds me I'm still real. And it keeps me strong. I've never mentioned that to him. At first, I thought it sounded silly. Now I'm glad.

Some days I get a different itch, a funny urge just to fidget, to

fiddle, to do something with my hands. I drew, at first. I asked
him for paper, and pens, and pencils. And he gave me them: a
beautiful sketchbook, to start with; expensive chalks and waxy
crayons from a proper art shop. He got cross when he saw what I
did with them though. No beautiful landscapes, no glowing por-
traits of him. I like making things up. So now I'm careful, keeping
things out of sight.

I miss my mum. I miss everyone, of course, even the people I
thought I didn't like. I even miss school, can you believe it, all my
teachers, like nice Mrs. Vale and even grumpy old Mr. Kethrick.
But mostly, I miss Mum.

I'm OK really. When I can't bear it, when it almost gets too
much for me, I've got this trick. I'll close my eyes and imagine that
none of this ever happened. I'll just think, really hard, about how
it used to be. Not about people. That just upsets me.

I think about the boring stuff. Sitting on my bed, doing my
homework, the noise of the kitchen radio trickling up to me.
Curled up on the sofa watching TV, King snoring softly on the rug
in front of me, the rain slapping against the windows in big drops.
And I'll picture the scene, in my mind, so I don't forget.

I don't do it when he's around. He caught me once. He came in
when I was sitting propped against the wall, with my eyes closed
and my hands over my ears. He didn't like it. He wants all my attention. I still do it though, even when he thinks I'm right there
with him. When he wants to be together, I can go somewhere else
in my head.

A long time ago, it made me feel closer to him. He was always
so controlled, unknowable, despite all the nice things he used to
say. And I felt so special, chosen.

But now I don't want to be close to him, I don't want to be close
to him at all, though I try not to let it show.

Because I have realized something while I've been in here, something important. Trust can be a weapon.

I trusted him. He knew my secrets, my fears. How I felt about school, my parents, how much they argued, if Holly really did want to get with Danny. Just everyday, teenage stuff—good in a way I didn't understand then.

It all seemed so much at the time. Mum and Dad were arguing, more than usual. It didn't seem to have stopped them, moving up here, like they wanted. I wasn't doing well at school, my exams looming on the horizon like some horrible slow-motion disaster—a hurricane or a tsunami—inching closer. Just thinking about them, how behind I was getting with everything . . . I wasn't academic like Mum and Dad, not really. And then Holly and Danny—that was a mess, with her so jealous, it just got awkward. I couldn't keep everyone happy, anymore, so I was seeing less of him. It seemed such a big deal at the time.

And then he came along. I met him through school. I know now how bad that sounds. But it was just a crush, at first. I wonder, was that why I liked him, because it seemed so safe? Nothing was going to happen; I wouldn't get hurt. He seemed so gentle, and reassuring.

But then it did happen.

I was the one who made the first move. I just stood up on my tiptoes, my hand on his sleeve, and kissed him. I was blushing. He'd just told me, looking down into my face, that we couldn't do anything, that however much he wanted to, however much it felt we were meant to be together . . . I felt like it was up to me to show him that we could.

So he kept my secrets and, afterward, we had *our* secret. But now I've had time to think about all this, I'm not so sure, really, if it was me who started it, or if he just made me feel that way. In fact there's lots that I'm not so sure about now.

It's like I've finally woken up, and I can't believe how stupid I've been, and how messed up this all is, and if I go too far down that road I crumble and cry, and the panic rises up again, and I'll start shaking and choking, and that won't do at all, not while he's here, not in front of him.

So I don't, I just take big slow breaths and I fix my eyes wide open and make my face look sweet and pretty and all the time I'm thinking, this isn't over. I do my big wide-open eyes and smile and nod and don't say much—it's easier that way—and I think my thoughts behind my happy face.

Because now, I need him to trust me.

CHAPTER 30

Kate

I go from sleep to waking in an instant, no slow swimming to consciousness, the way you do sometimes. Suddenly my eyes are open, and I'm alert.

I sigh. I've been doing so well, I haven't had to take a pill for ages. I was going to tonight, I was so restless and cross, but in the end I forced myself to read, just a few chapters of *Pride and Prejudice*, my old comfort book. I poured my thoughts into its safer channels until, calmed, I could sleep.

But now I am wide awake, in the dead of the night. The room's dark, no bright moonlight tonight. But the birds are yet to start their dawn chorus: it's the quiet of the witching hour.

I must have kicked off the sheet in the night; I go to reach for it again. I always need something covering me, even when it's hot.

And then I go still, freezing in place mid-turn, propped up on one arm.

I wait. A beat, and then another. It's probably no more than fifteen seconds that pass in total, me straining so hard to catch the sound that I can hear the rush of blood in my ears, and I begin to relax just a little, realizing that I am holding my breath.

I hear it again. A creak. Just a small moan from old wood, so slight you might ignore it, or decide it was just an old house settling around you, if you didn't know what it was.

A slow pressure of weight on a floorboard, not so close, but not so far, either. Just outside my shut door, in the hallway. It's a familiar sound. There's a long runner of carpet there, but it doesn't stop that one board creaking, it never has, however slowly you tread.

I am sliding out of my bed now, my feet on the floor, before I form another thought: I take a step toward the closed door, oh so carefully. The boards in my room are solid, I know. Even Mark, who was big, could get up and leave me sleeping, putter around, without disturbing me.

But I can't make a sound. I take another step, moving with exaggerated slowness, and pause. In my white cotton nightie, like a statue in the air, I'm reminded of something so incongruous from childhood: playing Grandmother's footsteps. Take a step, and freeze.

There's not another sound from outside. I take another step, and then one more and I'm there, reaching for the door.

My hand is inches from the silver door knob now, reaching down, slow as a dream, then I stop. I could end this now, swing the door open and show my fears for the lie they are—the wild imaginings of someone under pressure, someone who's too much alone. I know I could and yet, I can't. I just wait.

At first I think it's just a trick of the light, the burnished gleam of the metal. Then I realize: the door knob is turning, slowly, so slowly you could almost miss it. By fractions of an inch, it's moving.

I hesitate, just for a beat. And then with a speed born of sheer instinct, something clicks into gear and I quickly turn the heavy iron key, the metal cold in my hand. The lock's stiff, I never turn it, why would I, but it closes now, the metal sliding into place with a solid clunk.

The door knob jumps back round, like whoever's turning it on the other side has let go.

Now I brace for the sound of footsteps, the panicked run of an intruder who's been surprised, heavy steps thudding down the stairs, two at a time, a shout to someone further down the house: "Go! Go! Let's go!"

Nothing. I keep listening, strangely calm, not thinking, just reacting.

"What do you want?" I say.

There's no reply, but I can sense the presence, every instinct, every fiber of my body, telling me that it's not just empty space behind the door. I put one hand on the wood, almost to steady myself. "What do you want?" My voice is high. "My cash is in my handbag, in the kitchen." And so is my phone, I never sleep with it.

I'm on one side of the door. And someone is on the other.

I'm weighing up the door: It's heavy, solid wood, the lock's an old-fashioned one but sturdy. It's the hinges I'm looking at, evaluating. It wouldn't be so hard for someone to bust off, all it would take is a couple of steps back and a few good tries, perhaps not even that. . . .

My hand on the door, I feel it more than hear it, the infinitesimal pressure of movement, a weight shifting outside.

I'm utterly still, waiting again. And then they come: footsteps, slow and unhurried, someone strolling down the corridor, avoiding that squeaking board—that lesson learned—and starting down the stairs, to the little landing by the window, and then down again, quickening slightly, as though a decision's been made.

I hear the front door open and shut, no effort to be quiet now, as casual as someone leaving for work. Then silence again.

I slide down by the wall, my legs giving way now; my chest's heaving, the tears about to come.

Once I got mugged, years ago; I know there's a moment, when you're torn between telling yourself that everything's OK, don't panic, and then oh, it's happening, they're actually following you, the whole gang of them, chatting between themselves, and now they're catching up: "Give me your bag or I'll break your fucking arm." I didn't start to cry until I walked into the Chinese half a minute away and they gave me sweet milky tea and pushed their phone over to me, so I could call the police. Then, only when I was safe, I let myself react.

So I can't lose it, not yet. I stay still, not daring to make a noise, though he knows I'm in here. What if it's a trick? The front door closing and opening, but no one going anywhere, me walking down the stairs, the figure stepping out of the darkness, where he's been waiting all this time. My voice wavering: "What do you want?"

In a burst of activity, I leap up and whirl round, I push my chest of drawers in front of the door, wedge my dressing-table chair on top too, my heart thudding. Then I open my window as wide as it will go. If I have to, I will climb outside; I will hang out by my arms and drop to the ground. I will push out my pillow and duvet, so I'm ready.

I listen; but I'm at the quiet side of the house, away from the road; all I can see is a sliver of garden and the trees between here and Lily's.

Should I scream? Lily won't hear. I can't hear cars; at this time of night the traffic slows to nothing. I shiver, the sweat now cold on my skin in the night air.

And what if it brings him back? I can't.

I'll have to wait.

CHAPTER 31

Sophie

He called me Nancy again, the last time. I didn't say anything.

It's almost funny, what I don't know about him. Who he is. Who he was. He never liked to talk about himself, or his family, or the past. We'd talk about me: school, my friends, my problems. I thought it showed how much he cared. But now we don't talk about me, and we don't talk about him. His visits are short, mostly. Oddly formal, in a way.

But I pay attention, squirreling away the scraps. It's not that I want to know more about him, not now. But I suppose it's proof he's not in control of everything. It's almost like a game I play, a one-sided game. To get through this. What will he let slip when . . .

It's like he goes somewhere else, as he moves over me. "Nancy," he said. "Nancy."

I turned my face away, as he finished. I don't know if he remembered what he'd said.

* * *

I almost didn't ask, the first time he did it. I must have only been here a few weeks, maybe a month, and I didn't want to rock the boat. I'd thought I'd feel closer to him, being in here, but sometimes I didn't, not really. In fact, quite the opposite. Sometimes he seemed so distant.

We were safe and we were together—all I'd ever hoped for us. And yet I was finding it harder and harder to ignore the feeling in my stomach, that gnawing cold in my guts.

You're homesick, I told myself. *That's natural. You just need to get used to this.*

But he wasn't helping. He wouldn't talk about what we'd do next, anymore: he kept telling me not to worry about it. All our plans, about where we'd go and what we could do—we'd never nailed them down, not totally. We'd have to react to the situation, he said before I came here, we just needed to make ourselves safe. But now I was in here, all his urgency seemed to have gone. . . .

Still, I made myself do it, afterward. I knew he'd be more relaxed, as we lay there in the darkness.

"Who's Nancy?" I just came out with it. He said nothing, his head on the pillow behind me. But I could hear the change in his breathing. I'm better at reading him than he thinks.

"What did you say?"

"You called me Nancy." I tried to make light of it, but I was annoyed, back then. More than annoyed. "You know, some girls would get jealous. . . ."

It didn't work.

"I think," he said slowly, "that it's time to establish some boundaries. . . ."

Then he'd switched on the overhead light, bright in my eyes, and made me sit up, still tangled in the duvet while he lectured me. He needed space, he said. I couldn't expect to know everything about him. I asked too many questions. Did I know what questions like that showed him? That I still didn't trust him. It hurt his feelings.

I didn't know what to say. I almost laughed, but I hid it. He was sitting me down like I was a clingy girlfriend. I might be young, like he always said, but I knew that our situation was so very far from that. He didn't seem to be able to see it.

But I didn't laugh. Something in his face told me that would be a mistake.

An old girlfriend, I decided privately. He was so jealous of my boyfriends, he'd once said, he couldn't bear to hear about them. It was only Danny, anyway.

It showed how much he loved me, I thought.

When he did it a second time, sometime that first winter, it was different. We'd been lying on the mattress, him stroking my hair. I was awake, my eyes fixed on the patch of starry night sky in the ceiling. It was cold—my breath made little puffs in the air, even though we were inside.

I couldn't sleep. I was feeling so different about everything, keyed up and awake. I was sleeping at odd times by then, we were out of sync. I just wanted him to leave now, so I could switch on the TV again, cuddle up in bed with Teddy, and be cozy.

Maybe he sensed it, me turning away from him—my impatience for him to go. I don't know why else he'd stayed. He'd already stopped sleeping over the whole night. He said it was best, the safest thing for us.

But maybe it was the idea of my waking up when he was asleep that he didn't like. I could tell he tried not to let me see where he kept his keys, always putting them away before he turned the handle and came in.

They had to be somewhere in his clothes, surely—he hadn't brought anything else with him tonight but the food bags. Maybe that little secret pocket that they put in men's suits, Dad used to keep change in there. . . .

I shifted, quietly, checking the weight behind me. He'd not moved for a few minutes now. He must have fallen asleep, after all. I could hear his breathing, slow and steady. I started to slide out from under the covers, carefully—

"Nancy," he said suddenly, too loud in the quiet room. He

wrapped an arm over me. "Nancy, stop it." I stilled, uncomfort-able. He was heavy. I've never liked that about him, the reality of him; the heat and sweat. So I'd moved, again, trying to shrug his arm off me.

His hands were round my throat before I knew it. "Nancy," he said, then mumbled other things, words I couldn't make out. Then loudly: "I said stop it!" I was pulling at his hands, shocked. I tried to twist away.

Then something changed in him: "You whore. You lying whore." I scrabbled under him, half off the mattress. But he was too heavy, his breath hot in my face. I was choking now, still trying to get his hands away from me. My bare feet were kicking on the carpet. Both hands pulling his thick forearm. *He's stronger than I thought, much stronger.* The blood thundered in my ears. The edges of my vision turned black, my sight shrinking.

I don't know what stopped him. Maybe he woke up, maybe he came to his senses. But his grip lessened, just for an instant, and with a shove, he was off me. I scrabbled off the mattress, my back against the wall, wheezing for breath. I wrapped my hands around my burning throat, keeping my eyes on him.

For a moment, we both just stayed there, looking at each other.

"Calm down," he said shakily. "Calm down. Don't look at me like that."

I couldn't speak. I couldn't pretend that this was OK.

"You called me Nancy again," I said eventually. My voice sounded strange, hoarse. "Who's Nancy?" I think a part of me, even then, was jealous. I know, I know. It was so messed up.

He didn't answer. He just started moving around the place, slowly and methodically, setting right the upturned table by the mattress, getting kitchen towels to mop up the beakerful of water we'd knocked over. I breathed in, and out, slowly, trying not to freak out. I didn't know what he'd do.

Afterward, he'd made us both a cup of tea, and had sat me down on the sofa, pale but cold-eyed. He held my hand. I think I thought he might say sorry.

Nope.

This was my fault. I'd panicked, I'd pushed him. He'd needed to shut me up. I was hysterical. It was my fault. I could feel myself teetering, wanting him to convince me: it wasn't a big deal.

But something steeled in me. I stayed silent, as he got up and left. He told me to get some sleep.

No, I thought. *This isn't fair. You're wrong. You are really wrong, something is very very wrong with you.*

And I've put our lives in your hands.

CHAPTER 32

Kate

No, nothing's gone, I tell the officers again, we've checked all over.

Yes, I'm absolutely sure. . . . No, I didn't actually see anyone, but I knew he was there. I felt him—yes, through the door—and I heard footsteps.

The look between them is less veiled this time. The second officer, the one with the pad, has already stopped taking notes.

It's all going wrong.

I stayed in my room until the birds started to sing and the sky lightened. I couldn't bring myself to unlock my door until I heard the engine and looked out of the window to see my sister's neat red car pull up. As ever she was early, thank goodness. I rushed down to them, barefoot on the gravel and hugged her, surprising us both.

"Your poor feet, Kate!" said Charlotte, shutting the door of her car in the drive; Dad was getting out the other side, moving stiffly after the journey. "These stones . . . and they trash your car if you're not careful."

"They're fine. I'm fine. I'm so glad you're here." They followed me in, talking about their drive—they'd made good time, coming early to avoid the rush hour. There isn't really a rush hour out here, we all knew that, but I was touched that they'd come so quickly—and relieved.

I didn't want to scare them, but once in the kitchen I turned round. "There was an intruder in the night; someone broke in. No, really don't panic"—as they started to ask questions—"I'm OK."

Dad called the police immediately, 999, as Charlotte got me to tell her everything; then we started looking through the house together, the three of us moving in a tight little group. Sophie's room was what I was most worried about, but it was untouched. The rest of the house seemed fine too.

"I don't *think* anything's gone," I kept saying, braced for a nasty surprise—drawers wrenched open; wires spilling from a wall where a TV had been ripped away; clothes and belongings strewn across the floor. Then I realized—I was remembering my dream the other night, searching through my ransacked house. But there was nothing wrong now. Everything seemed to be in its place.

I started to feel more and more uneasy.

The two officers arrived, uniformed in a patrol car; the man I recognized from last time, when I saw someone in the garden: the younger guy, with a round open face. I made sure to take in their names, this time—stay in control. He's Officer Kaur; his colleague, Officer Sweet, is compact and businesslike, her face carefully made up.

It's far too late, of course, for them to do anything, that much was soon obvious. I think that it must have happened about 2:30 a.m., I told them, but I didn't even think to check my alarm clock until later, when I took a break from my spot by the window to go over to the green digits and commit it to memory: 3:21.

It falls to Kaur to say it, as we're all gathered in the kitchen.

"Mrs. Harlow, how could someone have got in? There's no sign of forced entry. You said it yourself, there are two locks on the front door, and you unlocked them both as you went out."

I've been thinking this myself. As they've been looking inside and outside, checking the doors and windows, I've quietly checked something too, while Dad and Charlotte were putting on the kettle.

It's best if I show them. "Come and look at this," I say. "We can go out the back door."

We all file out through the utility room; the officers, then my family at the back. For a second it reminds me of something from my old life: a hostess guiding her guests out into the garden. What's happened to me?

Outside, I lead them around the side of the house and reach for the brick, hidden under a bush. Little things move, suddenly exposed to the bright light, wiggling back into the dark soil. The keys are still there: the Yale and the heavier one, for the deadlock.

"I checked a bit earlier," I explain now, "and saw them. I'd totally forgotten they were there. We used to leave them out for Sophie, my daughter, when she came home from school and I wasn't in. And when she—when she left, well, I suppose no one ever moved them." It's so safe round here anyway. Who'd ever find them? Then, when it was just me, they'd never crossed my mind.

There's a cough from behind me. "And these are the back door keys?" says PC Kaur.

"No, the front door."

Sweet now, her tone impressively neutral: "Mrs. Harlow, are you suggesting that someone used these keys, let themselves in round the front, and then put them back?"

"I don't think burglars behave like that, love," says Dad.

"I know they don't," I say, calmly. "But it's the only thing I can think of. And you know, even if I did put the chain on at night—"

"Kate!" Dad, of course.

". . . I know, I should, and maybe I did, I don't remember; anyway, the chain's so long, you can just reach a hand round and slip it off. I'll show you if you like." I look at the faces in front of me: the officers blank, professional; my family pinched with worry.

I fill in the silence. "I mean, I will get a new one of course; I'd better change the locks too."

"That'd be a—good idea," says Kaur. "Now, have you thought

about where you'll stay tonight, if you feel nervous again? Because there was the other night too, wasn't there." He's being too nice.

"Not yet. I mean, I've my family"—I gesture in their direction—"but what's going to happen now?"

A thought rises: do they know about the calls from the phone box? Would Nicholls have shared that information?

"Well, we've looked around, all over now," says the woman, Sweet, "there's no signs of entry, nothing's been taken, as you say. If that does change, of course, let us know."

"But aren't you going to dust the keys for prints?" I turn to Kaur. "And after that person in my garden, when you came, the other night . . ."

"I don't think that will be necessary, in this case, Mrs. Harlow," says Kaur. "We'll file a report, of course. So if you do find anything's gone, you'll have a crime reference number, and you can report that to your insurer."

Sweet starts talking again. It might be wise if I stayed with friends and family, perhaps tonight. Just for a night or two until I feel more . . . myself. Dad and Charlotte are chipping in now, and of course I can stay with them, maybe for a while; perhaps that would be best. I've stopped talking.

The two officers don't stick around long after that. I'm sure by now. They know. They know about the phone calls. I've shown up in a database, or someone's mentioned it. Something.

And they don't believe me about last night.

CHAPTER 33

Sophie

By the morning, I'd decided. It was time for me to say—no, tell him—that I was going to go away. It was time to leave. In the sunshine, the daylight coming through the skylight, I could squash down the terror of the night before. *It'll be OK*, I told myself, *I can sort this.*

But he didn't come. Not that night, nor the one after. My food stores got low. The milk went sour, so I poured orange juice on my muesli instead, and tried not to panic. When he turned up, early the following evening, it must have been straight from work, in his suit.

My heart actually leapt, I was so relieved to see someone. Then I remembered.

I was sensible about it, making us both cups of tea as I ran through what I was going to say in my head. Then I set out, as calmly as I could, both of us sitting on the sofa, why I thought it was time I should leave. That it was always the plan that I'd just hide for a while, give us some time to get things together. That there were all sorts of places we could go, now that they'd thought I'd run away, for months. No one would be looking for the two of us.

"Like we said, before," I reminded him. We had, only—only I wondered what had we actually planned, how concrete was it? There hadn't seemed to be any need to talk about dates, or time-lines, or when we'd definitely go away, just after it had all blown over. . . . I couldn't remember.

He listened to me, his face blank.

"No," he said, his tone almost mild. "No, you're not leaving."

"But why not?" I said. I made sure to keep my voice low. Reasonable. "I can look after myself, you can come and visit, wherever I am. A new start, like we talked about."

"No," he said. "It's not realistic, to move you and get you set up somewhere. Where, anyway? You'd only have to hide away there, too. Someone might recognize you, otherwise." He shook his head. "It's not an option."

"But you don't understand." I didn't mean to say it, but the truth spilled out. "I can't stand it in here anymore! I can't!"

His face hardened. "Sophie. This is what we agreed. It's what you wanted."

"But not like this. This was just until we got sorted, to give us some time. And I'm sixteen now, that's important, isn't it, even if they are still looking for me?" My voice rose. "I can't stay here forever!"

"It doesn't change anything." He looked at me, cold-eyed. "You were underage. In a court of law there's no doubt about it. I'm more than twenty years older than you. It'd be prison, the end of my career. And I can't go to prison."

I was shocked. He made it sound so horrible. He'd never spoken about us like this before.

"But there's no need—I'd make them understand . . . we were in love. We are."

I have a flash of inspiration. "I can go away, even if you can't yet. Like they thought I did."

"With no job? Or something cash in hand so you don't have to say who you are? You wouldn't like that, not in the long run. And then what would you do? No," he says, almost regretfully, "you'd crack eventually, go back to mummy and daddy. I've thought of this already. There's no alternative."

"But you could help me . . . you could give me some money. . . ."

The threat, when it came, was uttered so matter-of-factly, it took a moment to sink in. "I told you I couldn't live without you, Sophie. I'm not letting you go."

It felt unreal. *So this is us, for the first time, no pretending.*

"But I want to go," I said, pleading. "You can't keep me here forever. Please. You can't . . ." Anger swelled up in me, the weeks and months of not saying how I felt, just pushing it down. "It's not just up to you." I summoned my courage. "And I want to leave. Now. Give me the keys." I stood.

He looked at me from the couch, implacable. "Stop it, Sophie. I mean it."

"Give me the keys."

"This isn't funny."

"You're right, it isn't." In the corner of my eye, I could see his jacket: hung on the back of the chair. Near the door.

I know it was stupid, but I still didn't realize. I rushed for them, felt for the tell-tale weight, then wrestled them out of the pocket. Out of the corner of my eye, I could see him get up, walk round, like he wasn't even in a rush. He intercepted me before I'd even got them in the door. For a second we struggled, then he twisted them out of my hand.

"No," I screamed. "Let me go!"

Suddenly I froze, stunned.

And then his full weight was on me, the breath knocked out of my body, my back against the floor. He slapped me, once, round the face. Not a punch.

It wasn't even that hard, really. I suppose it was the shock, more than anything.

"It's all about you, isn't it. And what you want," he said. His voice sounded different, his accent slipping a little, somehow. "You little bitch."

I touched my tongue to my lip, tasted metal. I couldn't quite believe this was happening.

"I'm going to leave now, Sophie, until you've calmed down." His voice sounded back to normal again, smooth and ironed out like a TV presenter's. "And when I'm back, you'd better behave."

He got up, leaving me on the floor. "Things are going to change around here. I don't want any more of your whining, or complaining. I've had enough. Do you understand me?"

I wouldn't look at him.

"Do you understand me?"

"Yes," I said, in a whisper.

I was quiet as he left, waiting to hear the bolts slide into place.

Slowly, I got up. I touched the side of my face.

Then I pressed my ear to the door, listening for his tread down the stairs to the next one.

My legs were shaking.

I'm not hurt, not really. I shouldn't have pushed him.

But I knew. I knew this was different, a boundary breached. Even more than the other night, when he'd had his hands round my neck, his eyes unseeing.

This? This time he knew exactly what he was doing.

I waited a minute or two, till I thought he'd have gone. Something told me that he wouldn't be back, for a while. Then I rushed to the window, pulling the chair underneath it, piling up the magazines so I could reach.

I'll admit then, that was the moment. That I finally screamed. Almost just to see. If anyone would hear me, come and help. My throat still hurt from the night before. Still I felt silly, at first. Theatrical, like I was watching myself in a play. This couldn't be me, in this situation.

But that didn't last long.

And then I screamed, and screamed, and hammered on the window, my fists striking up against the glass. It didn't shatter, not a bit. Eventually I stopped, when my throat was sore and hurting.

I listened. I couldn't hear anything outside, not a murmur of a car engine or anything like that. Not even the birds through the thick glass.

And nobody came. Not then. Not later, when I tried again. So I climbed down. I picked up Teddy and cuddled him close. I know it might sound silly, but that always makes me feel better. It's almost like I've got a little friend in here. "It's OK," I told him, although of course I was really telling myself. "It's OK. He'll come around. It'll be fine. I'll work this out." But underneath it all, one thought kept repeating, running through my mind like a drum beat that I couldn't ignore.

I've made a very big mistake.

CHAPTER 34

Kate

"Would anyone like another cup of tea?" Dad makes himself busy again, after the officers have gone. He always does this when he's uncomfortable.

Charlotte shakes her head, folding her arms. "What else is going on, Kate? Why did you want us to come and see you, before all . . . before all this?"

She's like Mum, she doesn't go for the softly-softly approach. I don't feel ready to do this, not now.

"Look. I couldn't say this, not in front of them," I start. "And I know I've been a bit—off the radar. But I don't think this was just a burglary. There was someone in my garden the other night, too. And there's something else going on. I've found Sophie's emails—someone knew she was running away, was planning to go with her, I think."

There's a puzzled beat. "Well, who?" says Charlotte.

I shake my head. "I don't know yet, but I'm trying to find out.

But that's not the only thing either. Wait, let me explain properly. From the beginning."

And then I tell them: everything flooding out, like a dam's broken in me. I start with what they already know: the phone call from Sophie; how I think she sounded scared, that she didn't finish the call like she normally did; then I explain what Holly said about the pregnancy test, that it was really Sophie's; Danny denying anything had happened, and his comment about Sophie's dad picking her up.

"And you know Mark never did pick-ups, so now I'm thinking: who could that have been?"

"Uh-huh," says Charlotte, frowning in concentration.

Now I tell them the rest of it: the police finding Sophie's diary; the things inside it seeming to confirm that Sophie was pregnant, "and then," I say—I can't look at Dad—"she got it sorted," though Danny her boyfriend, wasn't happy. How it had me thinking we were really getting somewhere, that I was finding out why Sophie had left, painful as it was.

They're both quiet, listening to me.

"But then something really big happened: that's when I got into her emails—an account we didn't even know about, that she'd mentioned in her diary. And in it, there are these messages where she's talking to someone about running away.

"And then Nicholls—this policeman—I haven't told you about him." I explain how he said someone's making calls to the charity from the phone box near my house, how unhelpful I'm finding him. "He was at Sophie's school, years ago, and he didn't breathe a word to me. And I saw him at Nancy's house—"

"Wait, wait, who's Nancy?" says Charlotte, frowning.

"Right, I haven't even got to that; she used to live at Parklands, that big house over there"—I gesture to the garden—"and she ran away, oh, more than twenty years ago now, but she looks just like Sophie. And their runaway notes, they're so similar, I mean they're not identical, but there's a phrase that I found in both of them. Just let me go and get Sophie's. I'll show you, then you'll see. . . ." I'm heading off into the hall, and stop, turning round. "Aren't you coming? They're in the living room, it will make much more sense."

They're not moving.

"I'm sorry, I'm going too fast." Their faces are comically similar, eyes worried, mouths down-turned.

"It's OK," I say, more softly. I don't mean to shock them. "I'm really worried too, of course, it's a lot to take on—that finally, things are happening. But I really feel I could be getting somewhere." I've got to convince them. "She's out there, you know, and she's reaching out to me, to *us*, regardless of what she said about stopping contact. And I just feel once we've got some momentum, put more pressure on the police—oh, not the two who were just here. And definitely not Nicholls."

A thought occurs to me now. "You know, where's that number the police gave me. Because I did notice something was missing the other day. Sophie's old blanket, you know, her blankie she called it, and I thought, who would want that old thing, other than . . . And her Teddy's gone, too, isn't it? But if it's all tied together . . ." I stop stone-cold, my eyes fixed on nothing. "But that was before. My God, does that mean he has been here before. . . ."

"Kate, stop." Charlotte actually puts out her hands, both palms up. "We need to talk to you. About all this." She's right, I need to let them digest this, but—"You're completely manic, can you hear yourself?"

"What? No, I'm not, I just need to make you understand." The fear starts to rise in me again; if I can't reach them, Sophie's slipping away. . . .

"But, Kate, love," says Dad. "Please just think. Start at the beginning. If she's really scared, if she's in trouble—why ring the helpline? Why not just ring the police?"

"Maybe she doesn't want to, I don't know why," I say, realizing now that I can't tell them what I really think: that that call was meant for me, somehow. "Or maybe she's worried she'll be in trouble. . . ."

"Kate, I know this has been so hard for you," he says. "But . . .

"This isn't right." Charlotte interrupts. "What you've just said, do you realize how paranoid you sound? The police inspector is against you, acting oddly? What next, it's a cover-up?"

The realization's sinking in now, my hopeful energy dissipating. "You're not here to help me."

They eye each other warily. "We do want to help you, Kate, love, of course we do," says Dad. "But we really feel that you're not coping."

"Well, you're wrong," I say.

Charlotte shakes her shiny bob, her arms crossed. She always gets angry when she's upset. "I wish you could hear yourself. See yourself." I look down at my hoodie and bare feet; I know my hair's unbrushed. "I told you, Dad—"

He interrupts now: "You were right, it's history repeating. I'm so sorry, Kate, we should have done more; before, after Mark left, and you had all that trouble. Now"—he shifts on his feet—"we did hear he's got a new partner, so perhaps it's not surprising that you're finding things so hard right now. . . ."

"I don't care about that! I mean I do but not compared to *this*." I can feel the headache coming, the heaviness thudding behind my eyes. "That's why you've come to see me," I say dully. "But I don't need looking after. I need help, yes. To find my daughter. Why won't you listen to me?"

"Kate!" says Charlotte, frustrated. "This—this *story* you've just told us, and now? Someone's broken in, with no sign of anything gone?" I can see her trying to keep calm, never her strongest point. "I'm scared, honestly I am. You're delusional. You need help, serious help. He said—"

"Charlotte," Dad cuts in, a warning note in his voice.

"No, Dad, it's OK," says Charlotte. "Kate, when you didn't want us to take the overdose any further; I thought we were helping, but we weren't. We've allowed all this to get out of hand."

"How can you say that?" I am not letting her do this. "You know that was an accident, not a real—God—attempt to do anything. And I *am* OK: I don't have a problem with pills, I'm careful." Why is she being like this? "You know, I've only been using them to help me sleep, and not even that recently." A thought strikes me now, chilling me: "Why do you think I woke up in the night and heard whoever it was in my house?" And what if I *had* taken a pill, as so often I have in the past? And the creak of the floorboard hadn't woken me, instead the door knob had just kept turning silently, as I slept on. . . . I suppress a shudder. I can't think about this now. "Everything I've found out, everything that's happened: why won't you believe me?"

Charlotte looks at Dad, then back to me. "You should have been getting proper, professional help, Kate. A psychiatrist, not this grief coach who you never see anyway."

Finally my temper flares, the strain and fear of the night, the anger at the officers just now, spilling out. "I know why you're doing this. You've always been jealous of me and what I had. Now you've got a chance to cut me down, you just couldn't wait, could you?"

Charlotte takes a deep breath, her eyes filling with tears. "Maybe I was . . . jealous, once. But who would be now?" I flinch.

I can almost see her wresting back control of herself, as she becomes composed again. "I don't think it's healthy to do this; we need to sort this properly. Not here, not this way." She steps toward the hallway, grabbing her bag off the side. "Dad, I'm leaving. *Now.* I think you should come with me."

"Kate, I never meant . . ." He looks at me, appealing.

"We'll talk later," I manage to say. I can't bear him looking this upset. "We'll sort it out. Let's just—have a little break." I don't move as I hear the engine start up, then Charlotte roaring off, no care for the gravel scratching her paintwork this time. I went too far, I think, even as another part of me says, no: why wouldn't she believe me? What's got into her? I lean back against the counter-top, the headache pulsing behind my eyes.

So here I am again, alone.

No, worse than I was.

No police on my side. No family. It's all on me now.

To find her.

CHAPTER 35

Sophie

You'd think it would have changed everything: his hands around my neck; the slap to my face. And it did for me. But the next time he came round, he just acted like nothing had happened, setting down the bag of food and starting to unpack. So I went along with it, following his lead. I didn't want to. But it was easier.

Safer.

We pretended he didn't notice how nervous I was now, how jumpy.

And the days passed, lengthened into weeks, then months, then longer. I cried, when he wasn't here. Because he didn't like it when I cried. Through the skylight, I charted the passing of the seasons by that patch of sky: winter white; a green leaf blowing past, heralding spring; scattered clouds, then the long blue of summer, giving way to gray. Eventually, the dull white of winter again.

I couldn't forget what had happened, though. Now that I'd seen it, what lies underneath.

I knew he didn't either. He stayed away longer, leaving days between his visits. When he does come here now, it's never for long.

The really sick thing is, even now, we're still pretending: that this isn't what it is.

It was spring this year, when he'd turned up in the evening, looking pleased with himself. He had a plastic carrier bag in his hand, but it was too empty to be the usual food delivery.

He didn't say anything as he handed it to me, where I was sitting on the mattress. I knew by his air of expectation how I had to react—that it'd be a bad idea to be less than enthusiastic.

It was just a little puddle of fabric inside, fuzzy and pink. "My blankie," I said. "Isn't it?" I pulled it out to smell it. Home. I looked down so he couldn't see the tears welling up in my eyes.

"Thank you," I managed. "But how did you—how did you get this?"

"Don't you like it?" There was an edge in his voice, familiar by now.

"Yes, of course," I said. I tried to make my face happy. "I missed this."

That was the wrong thing to say. "Maybe this wasn't a good idea, after all. I try to do these nice things for you." He sighed heavily. "Your parents spoiled you, that's the problem." I hate it when he starts like this. I think he genuinely believes what he's saying.

I was shocked the first time: "A spoiled little princess," he'd called me. I forget why, I hadn't kept the place tidy enough, or got up quickly enough when he came in.

"But you said . . ." I'd trailed off at the look on his face, even as I thought of all the times before, when he'd told me the opposite: how it wasn't fair how my parents treated me, that I needed looking after properly.

"Thank you, really. It's so clever of you to get it," I said carefully. I wanted to cringe at how transparent I was, but his shoulders relaxed. "I'd never have dared it." He liked that too. "I'd have thought it would be hard for you to get in. . . ." I wasn't going to ask how.

"It wasn't too difficult." He picked up the remote and changed the channel.

So did someone let him into the house? I couldn't think what excuse he'd use. But then what's the alternative—that he waited until everyone had gone and . . . what? Let himself in?

A little chill ran down my spine then, as I remembered.

Once, he'd walked me back to the house, not just leaving me at the end of the road as usual. Mum and Dad must have been out, their cars weren't in the drive. Still, he wouldn't walk all the way up to the house, seeing the security lights clicking on for me. I'd giggled, knowing he was behind me in the shadows, as I'd rummaged for the key under the old brick round the side. At the front door, I'd waved out at the darkness, confident that he was watching.

All the years later, is he still watching my house—my family?

I knew one thing, anyway. This wasn't a gift. It was a threat.

Yet a lot of the time he's sweet, even now. He likes to act as if we're just like any other normal couple. So long as I'm doing what he wants.

"You are happy, aren't you, darling, just us?" he asked me the other night, sitting next to me on the sofa. He likes us to watch TV, his fingers running through my long hair.

I stopped asking him for scissors a long while ago. He's not stupid.

Tell him what he wants to hear.

"Oh yes," I'd said. I caught the flat note in my voice, and tried again. "So happy." I almost left it there. "The thing is, I really feel that now, with time passing, maybe we can think about—what happens next. Where we can go, together. From here." My voice sounded weak, defeated, even to me. But I can't give up trying.

"Mm," he said, and put his arm along the back of the sofa. I made myself not flinch. "You know," he began, his voice soft in my ear. "You know . . . it really is just us now, isn't it. No one knows you're here, after all.

"If anything were to keep me away, anything at all . . ." He was stroking my shoulder, drawing little circles on my skin. "No one would know you were here. And what would you do then?"

He's said it all before. Still, I was cold, staring at the flickering screen.

"Of course," I echoed. "We must stick together."

Because it's the only option open to me. He has to trust me.

CHAPTER 36

Kate

Now they've gone, I am wired and exhausted, ready to crash. But there's nothing to do now but sleep, for a little bit, dozing on the sofa.

When I wake up, the house is quiet, the sun telling me it's already the afternoon. Too quiet, it feels now, just the wind in the trees, the odd distant hum of a car on the road.

I want to get out. Quickly I shower, the hot water waking me up a little; downstairs, I can hear the landline going. I pull on jeans and a T-shirt. I need to think about what to do next. But I can't stay here. My head's killing me: I can feel the pressure in the air, the sky not blue but that heavy, blank pallor—surely, finally, it's going to rain soon.

Before I go I remember to pull out my mobile from the pocket of the hoodie I had on earlier. I've two missed calls from Charlotte already, and a voicemail. I play it as I grab my handbag, snatching my car keys.

"Kate, are you still screening my calls? Even after this morning?"

My sister is seriously rattled; the drive home hasn't quietened her down. "We need to make some changes, Katherine. We can help you with this, I promise. But you need to let us. Phone me, soon, or I'm coming right back over. Bye."

I didn't think she'd be on my back again quite so quickly.

And then another message: it takes me a second to place the male voice.

"Kate, it's Dr. Heath. Nick. Now, I've had your family on the phone—they're rather concerned about you. We think it would be a good idea if I came and checked on you, nothing to worry about. Are you in today? Why don't you call me." He reels off his mobile number. "I'm doing my rounds today, anyway, so I'll see if you're in."

I swear under my breath. So this is why Charlotte's calling me, so soon after she and Dad left. They've already got my doctor involved. Can they even do this? I know I gave them permission to speak to him, when they were so worried—but shouldn't that expire at some point? I don't know. They can't do anything, can they? Make me go somewhere. And then I couldn't do anything for Sophie.

That decides me—I'm not waiting around for them to turn up and talk at me—and I hurry out of the house, heading for my car. I barely see the road as I turn right out of the drive, my windows down, and then stop at the crossroads, turning it all over in my mind again.

The faceless man. Sophie. Nancy. What's connecting them all? This boyfriend, Jay, so maybe he got Nancy pregnant. Then what? And now—thirty years later, history repeats itself? It can't be him. It can't be possible. But I've got to find him, somehow. . . . Nancy has to hold the key.

A honk behind me. I lift up my head—the lights have turned green. I press down on the accelerator, lurching forward. I need to get off the road, I'm so distracted that this is dangerous.

When I get to the village I turn in at the supermarket: I'm thirsty, I realize suddenly. I'll buy a bottle of water.

Once inside the place, I think, as I always do, that it's far too big for its village setting. And yet you can always be sure to bump into someone you don't want to—

"Katie! Is that you?" I turn round. It takes a second to place the two sleek blondes in their leggings and bright trainers: Ellen Fraser, a basket on her arm, and with her Lisa Brookland, my husband's girlfriend.

I don't want this, not today.

"Kate, how are you?" says Ellen, glancing at Lisa next to her. But Lisa's chin is up just a fraction, to tell me she's nothing to be embarrassed about. "Are you OK? You look . . ."

Lisa interrupts: "Actually, Kate, I was going to call you. But as you never answer your phone . . ."—taller than me, she takes a step closer—". . . we may as well do this now. Now, Mark's very worried, everyone's worried, you're clearly falling apart. But it's really time you moved on now and I—" She stops as I give her trolley a little nudge toward her, so she has to take a step back.

"No. Stop it, please," I say politely but firmly.

Lisa flushes with anger: "But have you even given any thought to getting a lawyer yet, or moving out of that house—"

"I said, stop it." Something in my voice seems to make her pause. "You go your way," I say, "and I'm going mine." And I give the trolley a push, so it bumps against her knees.

They get out of my way.

"Can you believe . . ." I hear Ellen say quietly, as I walk off. The thing is, I realize all of a sudden, I really don't care anymore, not about them—but my worry renews itself. Everyone is concerned for me, about what I might do next. But what should I do next? I feel like everything is closing in on me. Fragments of conversation reach my ears as I pass through the aisles, oddly disembodied.

". . . y'know why they're diet crisps? Because you only get seven in a bag! It's a joke, it really is. . . ."

"Apples, milk, kitchen roll. Apples, milk, kitchen roll. I'm sure there was something else. . . ."

"Mummy, look at these ones, can we try them, please can we, Mum-mee. . . ."

"No, I'm still here." A pause. "Why would I go without telling you? No, I'm still here." A girl's voice, a teenager. "You'll have to come back and get me. . . ."

I stop. "No, I'm still here." Why does that tug at something in my brain?

I turn round and see the girl, her phone in her hand, loping off to the exits, all long hair and high dudgeon, clearly outraged at being forgotten.

"I'm still here. . . ." Sophie said that on the phone, in that call, that triggered all this. "I'm still here."

She meant she was still on the phone, of course. Not like this girl.

This girl is still here. She hadn't gone anywhere. . . .

Suddenly, I feel off balance, like the floor's twisting under my feet. I lean against the shelves behind me, dislodging tins.

"Careful!" One of the assistants is already hurrying up. He stops: "Are you all right, madam? You look a bit peaky. . . ." I nod, slowly righting myself. "Sorry. I'm fine, yes." I start walking again.

Of course Sophie went away. That's what everyone knows. There's no doubt about it, it was clear from the start. There's been so much: her note, the sighting at the bus station, the postcards home. The call to the Message in a Bottle helpline, a helpline for runaways, for God's sake.

Although she sounded scared; no "Love you, Mo" for me. Just "I'm still here. . . ."

And then the diary, pointing to why she'd really gone. Just in case, say, someone started asking questions. Because in the end, the diary wasn't what it seemed, was it?

"I'm still here. . . ."

I stop. Behind me, the automatic doors open and shut, sensing I've not moved.

I know. I know what those postcards were telling me. It was there, all the time, under my nose: you just have to read them properly. It's so simple I hear myself laugh out loud, then stop, shocked at myself.

No wonder I couldn't see it. Sophie was never into crosswords, word games, all that stuff I liked. She was visual, she loved art, her drawing. And that's how she's been trying to communicate with me, even now.

Sophie wasn't just doodling flowers on her messages home. Oh, she was, but that's not all they are.

I know them. I know what they are now.

Stylized and symmetrical, they're not much like real roses. But that's because she's not drawing roses, but carvings of roses, the kind you might see etched into antique stonework. Pretty, carved stone roses that might run round the sides of a big Victorian mansion house, say, with a little ruff inside of each one, the sort of detail we don't bother to build into our homes nowadays.

Slowly I break into a jog, heading to my car, then pick up my pace. Because I recognize them now—I am absolutely certain where I saw them.

I was outside Parklands. Sophie's been drawing the roses that cover Parklands, sending me the house's motif. I bet you'd find roses inside that place, too—inside Parklands, the house where Nancy grew up.

Because Nancy was always the answer.

CHAPTER 37

Sophie

There was nothing I could do, not at first. I couldn't see any way out: I just had to get through it, I told myself, wait it out. I didn't let myself think about what I was waiting for. I couldn't break down. If I lost control . . . something told me that would be a bad idea. I just had to wait, for an opportunity. Be patient.

And then one day, that first winter, the opportunity came: he said it was time for another postcard.

The first one had been my idea, something we'd discussed before I went. We'd been planning how we could be together, without people coming after us. We never used the word police.

"I just need to get a message home, don't I?" It seemed so simple to me. "So they don't worry."

"How?" We'd been in his car as usual, he'd picked me up to snatch some minutes together. It was easier than you'd think, when no one's looking to catch you.

"Well, I could phone."

"They'd trace it. You couldn't phone home, not straight after anyway. There'll be too much attention."

I felt silly. "A letter then," I said. "In my handwriting, so they know it's real."

He was silent, so I knew he was thinking about it.

But I didn't like it when he showed me the postcards. It must have been a fortnight into me being here. Still the early days. Even then, they didn't sit right. I don't know where he'd got them, he must have ordered them off some collectors' website or something. They were so anonymous. Spain! read the one on the top.

So this is where they might think I was, sunning myself on sandy beaches? It seemed like such a slap in the face, for everyone I'd left behind.

"There're a lot of them," I remember saying, uncertainly. He was wearing plastic gloves, so he didn't get his fingerprints on them. The hair on his wrists showed through the rubber. I didn't want to look at it for some reason. It made it all too real, silly as that sounds—given how far things had already gone.

But I did it, as we'd agreed. I wrote the message he told me to say, word by word—"We can't take any risks, or let any detail slip, you need to say exactly what I want"—then signed my name, with my little daisy flower as normal. It was such a short, cold little message, I couldn't imagine what Mum would think.

I hoped she wouldn't worry too much.

I didn't know he'd ask me to do it again. The days were so short by then, we must have been well into winter. I couldn't quite believe I was still in there, if I actually let myself consider how much time was passing. I didn't know what was happening outside, and he didn't tell me—or wouldn't tell me.

Like before, he dictated it to me.

"You know," I said, "I'm not sure that's a word I'd use." Because I'd thought about this, in case he said I had to do it again. I'd had a lot of time to think.

I was going to send a little message of my own somehow. With the first letter of each line, I'd spell out a word down the side of the card: Help. Or maybe SOS. Whatever I could get past him, I wasn't sure. So I kept making mistakes—not all of them deliberate—trying to get in the odd word that I'd chosen. But he would just make me start again, and he was getting frustrated. "I'm sorry," I said, tears in my eyes. "I keep getting it wrong." I wasn't just acting. These postcards, these messages home—they scared me, hiding our tracks even more. How would they ever find me?

But he was getting angry, which was worse. Which is why, in the end, I did what he said. I wrote down just what he wanted, his bland, careful message.

"Is that all of it?" I said, about to sign it. I was cross-legged on the mattress, writing propped on a book. And it was then that I saw it, one of the little flowers on the wall paneling behind his head, where he was sitting on the sofa. I'd always liked them. I just drew it, the rose, with its little inner frill of petals, instead of my usual daisy. It was a quick sketch, little more than a doodle.

My stomach fluttered and squeezed as I handed the card over to him.

He didn't say a thing. He read it carefully, holding it in his gloved hand. I hadn't taken much of a risk, really. "It'll do," he said, slipping it in his jacket pocket, before he left.

"We're going to be OK, aren't we," I whispered in Teddy's ear, after he'd gone. "We are, we are, we are." For the first time in ages, I felt full of lightness.

Of course, nothing happened. No one came. But it made me feel good to know that I was doing something that he didn't know about.

So the next time, I did it again, and the next, copying just how they were carved on the wall: the rounded, identical flowers running around the room in a row, their petals arranged in their centers, so they looked like double rosettes.

I didn't really dare hope it would do anything. And the longer I stayed here, the harder it got to imagine that anyone was even looking for me. Who'd even recognize them? I knew no one came round here anymore, that much was obvious. I felt like someone in a fairytale, leaving a trail of breadcrumbs that the mice gobble up. But it stopped me despairing, every time he made me send one of those postcards home, lying that I was OK.

And it was more than that: I was doing something he didn't know about. Rebelling. It was like using a little muscle, that I hadn't tried for a long time. Practice, maybe. I'm still not sure for what.

CHAPTER 38

Kate

I'll find a window. They can't be that secure, it's just wood, old now, warped by rain and heat. I'll get a hammer if I have to. But first I try the main door to make sure I'm right.

With a trembling finger, I trace the outline of one carved flower. There they are, like I thought: roses. A whole arch of them, dozens, if not a hundred of these stylized flower motifs carved into the stone at Parklands.

Just like on her postcards home.

Sophie put her signature daisy on the first one, just like she always did. When she started changing them, I didn't understand.

But now I see the roses clearly, understanding her message at last. They're stamped in the brickwork of the building, too, marching round the boarded-up windows, matching the tiles under my feet; a riot of geometric blooms, everywhere, now that I know. I know they will be inside, too.

I don't have time to stop, fear urging me on. I push against the double doors with my shoulder, hard. They're solid, but these hinges are old, metal could rust—the right door gives, just a little. Not that much, but . . .

I reach out a hand for the door knob and twist. It wasn't locked.

I step over the piled-up letters, leaving the door open behind me, and stop, waiting for my eyesight to adjust from the brightness of the late summer afternoon outside. The hall is big, paneled in dark wood. The air is cold, that chill that you get in houses that have been closed up too long. The envelopes under my feet spill across the floor, years of circulars, now covered in dust; the postman must have stopped visiting long ago. I smell old paper and dirt. It's so still.

I walk further in.

Doors circle round this dim central hallway; the stairs to my right, grandly curving round and up to an open landing. I'll start with the door on my left, standing just slightly ajar, the old-fashioned key still in the lock under the handle; I remember Lily saying they let the rooms, individually.

I push on the heavy dark wood and enter slowly.

There's a flicker in the corner of the room: a dark shadow creeping forward.

Adrenaline shoots through me. I jerk back, recoiling, and freeze. The movement stops.

Then I realize, suddenly releasing my hands from my throat: it's just a mirror, propped in a corner, reflecting my own cautious entrance into the bare room.

I find the light switch now, and flick it on. The bulb flickers on, then with that electric ting, goes off again—it's blown.

But already I can see better in the darkness. The furniture's long gone, packed up, or sold; even the wallpaper's been stripped. Just the plaster detail on the high ceiling hints at the old grandeur of the house. A huge crack running across the mirror, fracturing my reflection, tells me why it wasn't taken with the rest.

My heart's still pounding, my body processing the shock. I can't lie to myself: I'm scared.

I work clockwise around the ground floor: more empty rooms,

bare wires poking out of the walls where telephones or lamps have been unplugged, faint oblongs on the walls where pictures once hung. The boarded windows, high on the walls, let chinks of light in round their edges, enough to see. I've a mad impulse to tear the boards down, to let fresh air and sunshine into the stale rooms. But it's easy enough to get into them—the doors are just standing open, the keys still in the locks, like whoever cleared the house out didn't bother to shut up the emptied rooms behind them.

What was the kitchen is at the back of the house, down some steps: it's gutted already, the units gone, bare pipes spilling out of the wall. And there's a little hall, with more doors off it. I keep going, quicker now, exploring the rooms in this part of the house— servants' quarters once, perhaps; small and plain and mean. There's nothing to suggest people have been here in years, not even trespassers.

I head back to the main hall and take a breath, steadying myself on the paneling. It takes me a second to realize: I feel them under my hand, first, then I look. Little wooden flowers. The floral motifs are repeated here too, running around in a band at waist-height, repeating up the side of the stairs.

Slowly, with the inevitability of a dream, I take the first step.

CHAPTER 39

Sophie

Everything's changing. For so long, I've been desperate for something to happen, but now it is and it's too fast. And it's all because of the phone call, I'm sure of it.

He told me maybe a week or two ago: we wouldn't be doing a postcard this time. I'd make a phone call instead. My heart leapt. *It's working, he's trusting me.* I'd been trying so hard. . . .

And then he said we'd practice first. He was going to coach me in what to say.

"What?" he said. He must have seen the disappointment I tried to hide. "You think I'm going to let you slip a message out, to tell them whatever you like?" It was so near the truth that I froze.

But he stayed calm, almost reasonable. "Sophie. If you were ever to do anything stupid or dangerous"—I realized I was holding my breath—"you know, it wouldn't take me more than a moment. Before anyone got here, police or otherwise." He wasn't even looking at me. "You understand that I'd have to, for my own safety. I couldn't let someone jeopardize all I've worked for." He managed to sound almost sad. "Even you."

And then he told me what he needed me to say.

Finally, one night, he decided it was the moment. He went out briefly and when he came back he got out a clunky mobile phone. He made me wait for a bit: made a call, then hung up.

"Come here," he said at last, and I went to the sofa next to him. "Now, are you going to be sensible?"

I nodded.

"Whatever happens?"

I couldn't think what he meant. "Whatever happens."

He dialed in a number, and put the phone between us, clicking it onto loudspeaker.

"Hello," the voice said. "Message in a Bottle."

I parroted what I had to say. The reception was terrible: it kept cutting out, it must have been the thick walls. The woman was older, friendly-sounding. And I was so relieved, just to hear a grown-up's voice other than his, after so long.

"I've got to be quick," I told her. "I need you to tell them not to worry anymore about their daughter—that she . . . that *I'm* fine, really I am. . . ."

The line started skipping, yet again, then her voice cut through: "What? Who? Who do you want me to tell?"

"They're not to worry if they don't hear from me after this, it only hurts us all." I hated that. "I'm Sophie Harlow," I said, at his nod. "My parents are Kate and Mark Harlow. Hello? Hello?"

"Sophie," the woman said, almost thoughtfully. Then calmly, really: "Sophie, is that you?"

There was that moment of confusion, just before you realize something, like a cartoon character windmilling in the air before he falls off the cliff.

This wasn't in the plan—I looked at him: there was not a trace of surprise in his face. He nodded.

My stomach dropped.

Of course. Of course it's her. He planned it, all along. Letting me talk to her, so she'll think I'm fine. . . .

"Are you still there, Sophie?" Tears filled my eyes. Stick to the script. I couldn't risk veering from it. "Are you still there?"

It was then the fear hit me in full. *This is it. He's covering his tracks.*

"Yes, yes, I'm here." And as I said it, I realized: that was my cue—my only option. Trust her. I gave the phrase every bit of meaning I could, like I was stamping on the words.

Slowly, deliberately, I said: "I'm still here." I didn't dare look at him.

But she just replied: "Love you, So." She sounded so sad. Defeated. Not like Mum.

The line went dead.

"Love you, Mo," I whispered. I always have to finish, it's what we do.

I lifted my head, slowly. His hand kept pressing down the button on the phone for another beat, just to be sure, and then he picked it up and took out the battery, his movements deft.

He didn't explain why he'd arranged that—and I know better than to ask. But if he's trying to convince her that I'm OK, even though she won't be hearing from me again . . . what's he planning to do next?

The diary shook me, when he showed it to me. I'd brought it here when I left, and never wrote in it again. I couldn't write what I really felt about him. But he must have found it, and taken it away.

It wasn't like I'd been telling it everything anyway. *Took the dog for the walk,* things like that, just little reminders that only I'd understand, if anyone looked, because I couldn't write the truth— *Took the dog out and he picked me up in his car at the end of the road.* And I was right to, because Mum did find it. I was so angry— scared I'd slipped up. But I'd been careful enough.

This time he had it written down in advance what he wanted me to say, and I had to copy it, him watching over my shoulder.

And I realized, as I wrote. This stuff he was making me say, this load of lies, about me and Danny, him scaring me after I did the test . . . Someone had worked out I'd got pregnant.

But these cruel things I was writing, would people believe them? They'd hide me even further away, like piling branches on top of a body in the woods. I don't know why I had to think of a nasty thing like that.

So I went as slowly as I could, trying to think of what I could do. Finally I was done, flicking back through the diary before I handed it back—and then I saw the title page.

"But it doesn't have my name in it," I said.

"What do you suggest, that I post it to the police with a covering letter?"

"No, of course not," I say. "It's just—like you always say. People have forgotten about me."

He couldn't admit I was right. But he leafed through it, irritated, and then handed it back to me. "Fill in your details then. Don't make a mistake."

That's when I did it—I wrote down my email address, only it was the wrong one.

You see, I've had a lot of time to think in here—about what I might do, if I ever get the chance.

He'd told me to delete our last email conversation, and I had. But just before that, I'd pressed "forward," saving it to my drafts. I don't know why, really. He was so thorough. Maybe the finality of it all scared me a bit.

I wasn't going to do anything with it. But I couldn't sleep that last night. I stayed up, quiet in my room, just messing around. Not thinking about what I had to do. Everything was ready. Almost everything, I remembered, and I got up and went to the computer.

Even then I was going to delete the draft. But I didn't, not properly. Instead, I found myself setting up another email account, to hide it in. It wasn't a plan, really, so much as a . . . souvenir. I think I just wanted to leave a trace, even if it was only for me. Proof that all this had really happened.

Of course, it asked me security questions. Well, he knew all my answers. So I set them up as if it were my mum answering. I told myself it was kind of a dig. I was still annoyed about the diary. But maybe part of me knew: you can trust your mum.

Even as I handed the diary back to him the other day, I could feel the grayness coming over me again. *Who am I kidding? Who's even going to see that?* Not for the first time, I wanted to go back in time and shake myself, scream in my own face.

I am so desperately, totally over my head. But maybe . . . just maybe . . .

If anyone can find me, she can.

CHAPTER 40

Kate

The stairs are a broad sweep toward the landing, passing under tall leaded windows, more boards blocking out their light. This must have been expensive carpet once, too, but now the thick weave is dirty and worn bare in places. Here upstairs, someone's covered the wood paneling in shiny white gloss in the bedrooms, in some misguided attempt to lighten the place. But it's the bathrooms more than anything else that show their age against the classic bones of the house: there's one very eighties avocado suite, rust stains under the taps.

From the main landing, overlooking the entrance hall, short twisting corridors lead to more rooms, shabbier, strewn with the detritus of their former inhabitants: a flimsy folding table; an old sun lounger that can't have been intended for inside; piled-up magazines, *National Geographics*. I pick up one and open it, and see the small insect body. I put it down quickly. Silverfish.

I start edging around the half-open doors after that, unwilling to touch anything else. I don't know why empty houses get so dirty—heavy gray clumps of dust fill the corners.

I'm nearly done now. I must have covered most of the house, moving quickly, and I'm about to head downstairs for a final look, when I realize I've missed a door, in a corner I thought I'd checked. It's shut. But the old iron key turns smoothly in its lock, the door opening into a small set of stairs, and I start climbing, my head close to the ceiling.

I must be under the roof now, in a little hallway under slanting eaves. I explore; the rooms here are smaller, oddly shaped, light coming through the boarded-up windows close to the floor. Servants' quarters, once upon a time? *No,* I think, *they're too nice.* The outer, original walls, have the same wooden paneling, the rose decoration, as the showier rooms on the lower floors. Perhaps this was a nursery, or some quiet living space for the lady of the house, that's since been sectioned off. My footsteps sound on the threadbare carpet as I emerge at the end of the hallway.

I'm at the last door, now. This one's shut too, but the key's still in it.

There's a light coming from under the door. And there's a bolt at the top, and the bottom.

Heavy steel bolts, I can see. Locking only from the outside.

The skin on my arms is prickling. I look down: I've goosebumps, I notice absently.

I bend to unslide the bottom bolt, then the top. I turn the key, feel the gears of the lock shifting.

I open the door.

The room's empty, one glance tells me that. Now I see why it's lighter in here, even before I flick the switch to turn the bulb on. The modern partition walls have cut off the room from the attic's original windows, so they've put in a modern skylight overhead, through which the sky is a dark violet square. No one's bothered to board it up—I suppose it'd be hard to climb in from the roof.

I check around with care, anyway, my last hope dwindling. The wooden roses run around the wall panels, below the sloping eaves. Behind a door in the corner is a small loo and sink; old-fashioned black and white with a hanging flush. Maybe they put it in when this was a place to send the kids—a den, or games room. But that's it.

And that's the house done.

There's nothing here.

Fantasist, my mind whispers. *Paranoid*.

She's not here.

I've looked everywhere now. This house gives me the creeps. And no wonder, with its sad history. I suppose Nancy and her sister could have played in this room. But Sophie's not here.

I go over to the window, and look up: fat drops starting to hit the glass, one by one. Rain, finally. Of course she's not here. What did I think; she'd just be cowering behind some door? So I thought she was telling me it's all to do with Nancy. Or Nancy's house. That didn't mean she'd actually be in here. She meant something else, maybe, that I've misunderstood.

And now it's time to go home. Face the reality. Sophie left. I'll talk to my family then, maybe Dad—if I can get the police to . . . Exhaustion overwhelms me. I don't know what to do now. I'm failing her. Again. She's leaving me these messages, and I'm failing. Wearily, I walk to the doorway.

I start to pull the door closed behind me, just as I left it.

The pain's like a bite. I snatch my hand away—a splinter. "Ow!"

In the dim light the bead of liquid swells up on my fingertip. I suck it automatically, and wanting to see what I cut it on, swing the door round.

Someone's forgotten to take these down. That's my first thought, when I see the drawings pinned to the back of the door.

There must be dozens of sheets of paper tacked to the wood, stuck on with Scotch Tape, and they're all covered in crayon scribbles—blue, green, purple, yellow. On one sheet, there's a wobbly red spiral—a snail? Or perhaps it's just a shape that's fun to draw, if you've little fingers and a bright red crayon. On another, a rainbow splodge. Whoever did them can't manage stick people yet—and there are no trees or flowers or farmyard animals. But someone's bothered to keep them, all the same. Just like I did, with Sophie's first drawings.

Another drawing catches my eye now, and I step closer to look at the big buck teeth and cartoon eyes—it's a bunny character to color in, drawn in pencil by a skilled adult hand. Colorful scrawls burst out of the lines. The artist's initialed her character—SH for Sophie Harlow, just like she always did—but I've already recognized her confident, easy style.

And I almost missed seeing them. It'd be easy, with the door open like that. You might forget the drawings were there, if you were clearing a room, say. Taking everything out, removing any sign that someone was ever here. Perhaps rushing a little, for whatever reason. You might not remember to check behind the open door, flat against the wall. You might walk straight out, if you had other things to think about.

Like he did. He missed them. He's forgotten to take these down.

I'm on the floor now. My legs gave way, I register in a corner of my brain, as both my hands reach out to the door. This is it. Sophie. I know it, I can touch it. Here she is.

My beautiful girl. *And her baby.*

CHAPTER 41

Sophie

It wasn't a lie, what I wrote in my leaving letter. Runaway note. I don't like the sound of that. Runaway sounds cowardly, like you couldn't face the music. I thought what I was doing was brave. But who am I kidding.

I got Holly to do the test with me. And at the last minute, some instinct told me to go into the bathroom alone. I don't know why, not really. She would walk around without a top on, would chat away with the toilet door open, but I'd never been like that. And he'd always warned me that we needed to be careful, to keep this just between us.

So she believed me. Somehow, I'd walked out of there with a smile. "Negative," I'd said, then taken a deep breath. I'd wrapped the wand in tissue, quietly slipped it into my bag to get rid of later. I wouldn't leave it in the house.

I don't know how I forgot about the packaging; I was flustered, I suppose. Holly took the blame. She was a good friend to me. I wish I could talk to her now. But I felt like he would know what to do. He was always so reassuring, always so capable.

I remember when I told him. I said to Mum and Dad that I was taking the dog for a walk, then slipped out to the end of the road. They always believed me. I ran to his car, the rain pelting down, pushed King into the back seat and climbed in the front, my heart racing.

Afterward, he was so quiet.

"Because they're not always reliable," I said. "They can tear, I read, and you might not notice. . . ." I trailed off. Of course he knew that. But I needed to fill the silence.

"I know. Don't worry. It's OK."

I was so relieved. He didn't even seem that surprised.

And I told him I wanted to keep it. I didn't even say the word—abortion. It might make the idea more real, the only way forward.

"I'm sixteen soon," I kept saying, as he stared ahead, over the steering wheel. "It's OK. We'll be OK." We spent so much time in that car. There weren't many places that were safe for us.

When he turned to face me, his face stayed in shadow. "No." He was shaking his head. "You don't understand. You were fifteen at the time. And they'll be able to work that out." For a moment, it was strange. I had a funny feeling like—like I didn't know him, not really. He seemed so distant. I couldn't imagine what he was thinking.

Then I'd reached out, touched his arm softly. "Let's go away," I'd said. "Like we've talked about." It was like breaking a spell.

"You'd do that for me?" His voice came out of the darkness. I wished I could see his face.

"Yes." I had no doubts. "For you I would." I couldn't lose him.

"Let me think," he said. But he sounded pleased, speculative. He'd leaned forward to kiss me then, his eyes dark. *Dark with emotion*, I thought. It was so romantic, how much he cared. The things he'd say, so lovely and surprising from someone like him. *I can't live without you. I'll do whatever it takes. I'm not letting you go.*

Now? Now I know better—he reminds me of something else. I couldn't get it out of my head, once I realized. It was a nature program I'd seen at Grandpa's on TV, when I was little, so it scared me, when the big fish swam past too close to the camera. That's what he reminds me of, funny as it sounds. He's got shark's eyes. Alive but dead, at the same time.

I suppose I panicked. My stomach was still flat, but somehow hard now. Alone in my bed, before I went to sleep, I'd press a hand to it, feeling its solidity. In the end his idea seemed like . . . not just the best option. The only option. There would be much less upset, he said, if they were only looking for me. Then we could explain things in our own time—when we were ready.

"We'll have to go to a hospital," I'd kept saying. We could go out of the county, he'd said when we made our plans, it would be fine.

"Don't worry about that. It's all under control. Don't you trust me?"

I never knew how to answer that. So I tried not to worry, once I was in here. I ate the vegetables he brought. I read the books he gave me. My belly felt like it wasn't part of me, huge and swelling and marbled with blue. I couldn't quite accept it, even then. It was like a dream.

When it started, that cool autumn evening when the pains got really bad, he was there. He was checking up on me all the time back then. He talked me through the breathing and the rest of it.

"We need to go," I said. I knew I needed to stay calm. "Soon."

"Not yet."

"Soon."

And at some point, as the day turned to night, it dawned on me—I'm not going anywhere, not at this stage. I think I must have said as much. It was all blurry by then. Maybe a part of me, the bit that I'd buried deep down, knew that this would happen all along.

"Keep going," he kept saying. I didn't want to hold his hand. I was fine. I made it through it, anyway. He gave me something that made the pain less. Far away, I could hear someone whimpering, then I realized it was me. Then I must have slept.

* * *

Eventually, I woke up. It was daytime again. He wasn't there. The baby was sleeping in a cot by the mattress. I propped myself up on one arm, carefully, and looked at his tiny eyelashes, his little fists. I stroked one with a finger. His skin was incredibly soft. Slowly, very gently, I picked him up.

He'd told me I could pick the baby's name. I knew he wouldn't like family names: Mark for my dad, or Harlow for me. And suddenly I knew: those button eyes and so cuddly. Teddy.

"You know, that's the beauty of having a baby young," he told me when he came back. "You'll bounce back quickly."

I said nothing. I felt . . . so different. He'd said we'd go to the hospital. He'd promised me.

You lied. I couldn't stop thinking that—*you lied to me*—as I watched the tall figure moving around at the bottom of the mattress, tidying up the wet towels and other things. *Who are you? What am I dealing with?*

Then I looked down. Little starfish hands, dark eyes. I knew the baby couldn't really see anything, not just yet, but it felt like he was peeping at me. I held him close and sniffed his baby smell. And that's when I felt it. Totally silent, nothing you'd ever notice from the outside. I know *he* didn't. But my whole world shifted. *You come first now, little Teddy.*

Suddenly, now it was all over, I felt it. A wave of pure fear. So strong, I almost couldn't breathe. Later I couldn't understand why it hit me then, after I'd come through it, but I do now.

Some part of me realized what I couldn't fully face back then: what I now had to lose.

There's only been the one time I forgot, just for a second. That evening soon after he'd strangled me, when I rushed for the door, was almost through it—and then I heard that small cry from the corner. That's when I froze, stunned I'd ever forgotten. *Teddy—*

And then his full weight was on me. I'd missed my chance. But I'd never really had one. I couldn't leave without the baby. And now I couldn't risk doing anything that might hurt him.

* * *

244   *Emma Rowley*

I wasn't the only one who was different after the baby. Even when he made me put the cot in the corner, away from the mattress, we could still hear Teddy cry to be fed, so he stopped staying over all night, and when he did stay it was less often. I slept a lot in the day, like Teddy. That annoyed him too, when he'd find me dozing.

But it was more than that. Once, I'd just finished feeding the baby. He'd been sharp since he came in, annoyed that I hadn't got up.

"Do you have to hold him all the time?" he said tightly. "You're spoiling him."

"Spoiling him? But he's just a little baby," I said, and snuggled Teddy to me.

The way he looked then—so calculating, like he'd just worked something out.

So I played it down, and I still do, when he's around—how much I love the baby, his brown eyes smiling half moons above his pudgy cheeks. Now, he's bigger, he'll toddle over to me unsteadily, wrap his chubby little arms round my neck and give me a clumsy kiss. I have to ignore it, if he's here with us. Watching.

It's ridiculous, really. I could almost laugh. Except I don't.

In fact, if I think about it, it's all I can do not to panic. Especially when he changes our routine.

It was this last winter, my second in here. Teddy and I would wake up to see ice on the inside of the window, and know the darkness would set in early. Teddy was so pale. I've done my best, making sure he plays in the light of the window, but it's not enough. I knew he was more than a year old by then, but I didn't know if he was as big as he should be.

So I tried to say it as gently as I could.

I'm worried, I told him. It's not healthy for a little boy to be inside all the time. Your boy. Your son.

He'd seemed to want him so much, on the outside, but he never seemed to engage with him. *Maybe it was more about what a baby represented*, I thought. *Or a way to get me in here*, I thought later.

He's been so careful since then that it couldn't happen again.

But he did start paying more attention to Teddy after that, as he chattered and crawled.

Then one night, he started talking. "I've been thinking about Teddy."

I was facing away from him, on the edge of the mattress. I think it must have been one of the very last times we were together. I can't be sorry about that. The thought has crossed my mind: *I might be getting too old for him*, but that's yet another thing I've tried not to think about. Not until I get out of here.

I stirred uneasily. "Oh?"

He shifted over to me and put a heavy arm over my waist. "He's a big boy now, getting bigger."

"Yes," I said, too eager. "You're so right, he's growing, so he needs fresh air, sunshine—"

"So that's why," he interrupted, "I'll be taking him with me, when I leave."

I went stiff. "You're—you're taking him away from me?"

"Isn't that what you wanted?" He said it so lightly. "Fresh air for him, a break for you."

And he did it, too, as I sat up under the duvet, my heart racing. He woke up Teddy, confused and sleepy, and carried him outside, in the dead of the night. They didn't take long, that time, me pacing about the place until they came back in a gust of cold air, Teddy's cheeks chilled.

He wouldn't tell me much about what they'd done. "We were outside. He seemed to like the plants." And of course Teddy couldn't say, though he seemed to be fine, even to enjoy his trips, after a while.

That's how we made the call. He took Teddy out, handing him a bit of chocolate to keep him quiet. Within minutes he was back again, without him. He read my fear correctly.

"Don't worry, you'll have him back," he said.

The words hung between us, unspoken. *So long as you say what I told you.*

*   *   *

But I can't think about the past anymore. Despite the heat, I can tell this summer's nearing its end: it's been getting darker earlier, the shadows lengthening across the floor. I don't think I could bear another winter here, yet when he told me I wouldn't have to, I didn't feel anything but afraid.

"We'll be leaving soon." His back was to me so I couldn't see his face. "Well," he said, turning round. "Aren't you pleased? Isn't this what you wanted?"

"Of course." I got up, trying to inject my voice with excitement. "That's wonderful. Can you tell me where?"

He shook his head then, surveying the room, like he was thinking about what to take. "You'll like it." There's this new air about him—it's almost anticipation. He's upbeat, nearly cheerful.

Now, he's left me bin bags to get all my stuff together. There's not much to pack, just some clothes and toiletries. I just need to stop and focus, to work out what I should do, but it's all so rushed.

Something's going right for me, at last. Or something's going very wrong.

Because I try to tell myself it's a positive thing, that we're leaving at last. I've been so good, or at least he seems to think so. I just have to keep waiting, and watching, for my chance.

But then the thoughts come back again.

He's had enough of you. He could get rid of you.

The hairs prickle on my arms.

No, don't be silly, you'll get through this.

I've got through it so far.

But I can't stop thinking about what all this could mean. Him keeping Teddy away from me, getting the baby used to him. Making me end that tiny bit of contact with my family, the cover-up that he'd kept going. This sudden hurry to clear this place.

Because I can't see how it can mean anything else.

That he's going to do something. That no one is going to find me.

That this is the way it's going to end, for me.

PART 3

PART 2

CHAPTER 42

Kate

Here she was. Here they were. And I'm too late.

I've lost her. I've failed her. And I've now lost her again, forever.
The thoughts loop ceaselessly through my brain, as I wander back
downstairs. Through the outside door, it's raining properly now;
the raindrops falling with the pent-up force of a summer storm. I
stay in the hall, sheltered. The picture's still in my hand, Sophie's
drawing, the child's coloring in. My face is numb. Dimly, I wonder
if I'm in shock. But I've got to keep going. I pull out my phone
to call. Who? Dad. No, Charlotte. No, the police, I've got to . . .
Evidence. I shouldn't have touched this, should I? But then I see
I've got a text.

> Hello! Have you got it? Tell me what you think. What a find!
> Vicky x

It takes me a second, and then I place her. Vicky, the librarian's sister. What's she talking about? On autopilot, I pull open my

email and scroll down; I don't see it. So I check my junk folder, wait for it to load—and there it is: an email sent last night.

> Hiya Kate
> You'll never guess. After we spoke, you
> got me thinking: maybe I still have it.
> So I went round to Mum's and, guess
> what, I found it. It was to mark the
> centenary, they got all of us out on the
> playing field. Back row, right on the
> end—next to Nancy. Told you he was
> a bit of a hunk! Vx

Jay. It feels like an age ago: she was going to try to find his surname somehow. I feel like I'm a swimmer, coming up from the bottom of a pool—rising back to reality. But a part of me's still in that room. It was so small. Just that tiny skylight, set into the roof.

I click on the attachment. My phone freezes, the digital egg-timer telling me it's slow to load: blurry black and white shapes. Vicky must have taken a picture of this on her phone—it's loading sideways, I think—rows hinting at . . . what? I turn my phone around to understand what I'm looking at.

Yes, it goes this way, the detail now appearing. It's part of a school photo. She hasn't bothered to try to get the whole thing in, she's just got the end of the student body; three dozen or so little figures, stacked in four rows, a green stretch of lawn behind them.

The faces are tiny, just smudges above the blue of their uniforms. I pull at the photo to zoom in on the back row. I misjudge it and go too far—a face fills the screen.

Nancy. Smiling, her shoulders back.

I wonder if it was the same day they took the portrait that ended up in the paper, her fair hair's pulled back the same way. I pore over it for clues, traces of what happened to her, but of course there's no sign—nothing to say, "This is the girl"—that marks her out. She's a pretty teenager, nothing more, nothing less, and oh, so young. . . .

Carefully, I nudge the photo to the right again, just one place, and wait for my phone to catch up with the boy on the end.

A shock of dark hair, pale skin, sleepy eyes. He looks younger than I imagined.

I suppose I'd always pictured him as just a little older than me, aging in the same way. But he was, of course, a teenager then, just sixteen.

Here he is. Jay. No, this isn't right.

I scroll down to where the names are listed in tiny print along the bottom. It's almost impossible to read—out of focus and the camera's captured the shine of the photographic paper, a pale streak wiping out the lettering in places. I read across to find the right name, scanning the row . . . Billingsley, E—I squint—Elisabeth. Curran, Helena. I skip across: Corrigan, Nancy; there she is. And next to her, Nicholls—I scroll in closer, trying to make out the blurred lettering. Nicholls, Benjamin.

That's him, to Nancy's right, at the end of the line. Benjamin Nicholls.

I think: she's got confused. Vicky's got this wrong. Because this isn't Jay.

Then: it's been a long time, no wonder she's got mixed up after all these years. And I knew Nicholls grew up round here, I knew that already, didn't I? DI Ben Nicholls, alumnus, who still comes back to the school, like Maureen the secretary told me so proudly.

And at the same time another part of my brain is running over the sums. Jay would be what, sixteen back then, add twenty-six years, so, early forties now? Like me. Like Nicholls. So yes, they could well have been in the same year. Friends, even.

I scroll back up again, my sweating fingers leaving faint smears against the glass. I pull at the image to expand it, so the whole face fills the screens, the picture grainy this close up.

Chin up, confident, staring across the decades. I can see the likeness to the man he'd become so clearly now. Those curtains of hair, all the boys had that style then. Now he's got that short, professional crop. And he's filled out—his face is weathered, of course. What is it again, more than twenty-five years? That will do that to someone.

And then finally, I know, my thoughts coalescing into some kind of sense.

I've no doubt now, no doubt at all.

DI Nicholls. Benjamin Nicholls. Benji.

Jay, for short.

OK. Don't panic. Think.

It can't be. Not a policeman.

Someone touched by an old tragedy, they might well choose to start afresh, to drop an old name. And there's no reason he'd tell me about his past, about a missing girl from nearly three decades ago.

But now images start to flash through my mind, disjointed scenes. Maureen, at the school. "He gives talks to the students. . . . He's very popular with the teenage girls in particular. . . ." Nicholls, when I first encountered him: "I'm up to speed on the case, I've read through the files." Yet from the start, somehow . . . off. Reluctant for me to get too involved.

And then telling me about those strange calls, from near my house, that made me look crazy. Did anyone else even know about them? Did they even happen?

Say he saw Sophie, at school. Did seeing her, the spit of Nancy, dislodge something in him, an old obsession reigniting? He saw a chance, to what—repeat the past?

And that phone call when I told him what Holly said about the pregnancy test. "I would suggest, Mrs. Harlow, that you don't take investigations into your own hands. That's rarely—helpful." He was warning me off.

And I saw him here. That black silhouette against the sunshine when I saw him here, right here at the house. "I wouldn't suggest you start trying to find any trespassers yourself." And me wondering why I hadn't seen his car. "You can park in the lane, that way"—gesturing to behind Parklands. "There's a little path that cuts through."

My stomach is churning. I wonder, distantly, if I actually will be sick. I was so focused on being caught here, I felt guilty. He said he was checking up on the house. Was he? Or was it him the night before in my garden, checking on me? Curious, maybe. Before he went back—back to Parklands. Back to Sophie. A policeman wouldn't struggle to find a reason to look around an empty house. And he'd know how to get in.

I'm absorbed in my thoughts, riveted to the spot. So maybe that's why I don't hear the sound, so faint, just a soft footstep on the tiles of the porch. It must be just the light that changes, the pale slice into the hallway dimming as I stare at the phone screen in my hand.

Something, anyway, makes me look up.

The figure in the doorway is blocking out the light.

CHAPTER 43

My mind goes blank. I take a step back, looking around for somewhere to run.

And then my eyes adjust and I realize: it's only Dr. Heath—Nick—looking around curiously.

"Oh thank God, I thought . . ." My knees feel weak, watery. He looks a little embarrassed, the scribbled Post-it that I'd left on my front door still in his hand. "Uh, sorry to intrude. I found the note at your house—we can do this another time, if this is a bad moment. . . ."

Incongruously, I feel the urge to laugh, a relief reflex after the scare he gave me.

"I left that note for my sister"—I didn't want her to freak out even more if I didn't answer immediately—"I forgot you said you were coming round too—but never mind that now." I take a breath, trying to make sense. "You've got to help me. She was here, right in this house, in the attic, all this time. I've realized now, I saw the pictures that she drew. Do you see? This is where she's been, all this time. This is where he was keeping her."

His expression is wary, like I'm really losing it now. "OK, slow down. Who was keeping who here?"

"It's Jay. Nancy's boyfriend, the boyfriend of the girl who used to live here, DI Nicholls—it's the same person, he's the detective on the case. I saw it. I've got a photo! Do you understand?"

He looks baffled. "Kate. I just came by to check on you, to check everything's OK, and I find you here, inside this derelict house. This is *trespassing*...." Like that's the worst thing you could do.

I clutch at his arm. "I know it looks bad, but you have to listen. She was right here—my daughter, Sophie—"

"*Sophie* was here?" He looks around me, like he might see her behind me. "What do you mean—have you called the police?"

"No, I—I can't. There is something really weird going on, and I think it's him. The policeman, he's behind it all." I thrust my phone at him blindly. "Look, this is him, I'm sure of it, he looks just the same."

He looks down at the screen, then back at me, frowning, like he's trying to put the pieces together.

"And this is the detective who's looking into your daughter?"

"Yes, that's him."

"But he was just here."

"What?"

"I saw him, as I was turning into your drive—he was coming out of here, in his car. I passed him just a few minutes ago."

We take Dr. Heath's car. His was behind mine in my drive, blocking me in. "It'll be quicker," he said. He seems bemused, treating this like an unusual episode in his working day, but he's humoring me, he's coming with me. He didn't have much choice, me half dragging him over the threshold and pulling him away from Parklands. "Please, if I'm wrong I'm wrong, but if I'm right—please trust me, just for now. I can explain later but please ..." There was no point trying; I let go, went to brush past him—

"Fine, I'll go on my own."

"No, it's OK, I'll help you. Just—Just slow down."

Now he pulls out of the drive carefully, looking both ways. I want to scream; hurry up, hurry up, my right knee is jiggling with anxiety. "So he was definitely going this way?" I ask again.

He's turning left out of the drive onto the road, thoughtful. "Yes, this way, along to the park."

"Maybe he's gone there? There's places you can go in the deer park, it's so big. . . ." What did Lily say? They used to go to the park, the young people.

"It's a straight road," he says, "no turn-offs, so we'll just see him parked up, if that's where he's gone. Or if he's coming back this way, we'll see him too. Keep your eyes peeled."

He sounds so reassuring. But my mind's racing. The door to the house was left open, I walked in. Does that mean Nicholls was just here? Moving her, rushing maybe, so he didn't lock up? Should I just call 999 now, try to tell them their detective on my case has been deliberately muddying the truth?

"If I call the police, will Nicholls hear it on his radio?" I don't know how it works. "I don't know what to do," I say, my voice half a sob.

"Tell me what you know." His calmness calms me. Now I try to explain, as quickly as I can, what I know. It's a relief to unburden myself of the load of my knowledge, what led me to that empty attic, where I found the drawings on the back of the door. "And it's all connected, this Jay, I mean Nicholls, I think he did something to Nancy and then hid Sophie away, persuaded her somehow to do what he wanted. He grew up here, it's all tied into that."

I keep my eyes ahead, not wanting to catch a look of disbelief. "Do you believe me?" I turn my head, at last.

His face is grim. "Yes. Yes, I do. I shouldn't, but I do. At least— something's not right, at the very least."

I lean back in my seat. "The police—I don't know, I don't know how he's got so involved in this, in the investigation, but he's everywhere. I can't wait for them to wake up. If he's moved her—it can't have been far. . . ." If he's done something else—if I've scared him into doing something stupid—no, don't think like that. "If we catch him up—if he's gone to the park—then we'll know what he's up to."

"Yes," he says. "I think that would be wise. We'll just see where he's gone, for now, to make sure. Then we can call the police." I'm so relieved that someone is taking me seriously—no exclamations, no incredulous questions, just acceptance.

For a moment I'm spent; exhausted. We fall silent. The rain's coming heavier now, lashing down against the windscreen, the wipers going. It's almost cozy in the car, and I'm struck by the scene's complete normality. We could be a couple on the way to the supermarket, were it not for the speed he's going at; the hedges brush against my side of the car. He's concentrating as we bomb along on the winding country road. My pocket's buzzing against my thigh—I slip out my phone and glance down: a voicemail. Automatically, I click to listen and put it to my ear, my arm against the window.

"Hello," says the woman's friendly voice. "This is Valerie from Amberton Surgery. With regard to your inquiry about Mrs. Green's prescription." Lily. I hear papers shuffled. "Now, her records all appear to be absolutely fine"—so it's nothing urgent, I'm about to hang up—"but the surgery manager does ask could you give us a call when you've a mo. Dr. Heath shouldn't really have her on his register, if he's next of kin, so she just wants to check—oh"—a little laugh—"that's a note for me, not for you, sorry. But do give us a call when you can. Bye!"

I click to hang up—and catch his eyes darting to mine. "Who're you on the phone to? I thought you wanted to wait to call the police, together?"

"I do, it was just a voicemail." I drop the phone back to my lap. So she's fine, her records are fine, well they would say that, that doesn't answer anything at all, typical. But next of kin. With Dr. Heath? What relationship could they have? She's an aunt maybe, a cousin? They're so cautious, doctors, all this confidentiality about records and the most mundane of things. Don't get distracted.

"So when we get there," I start. "So when we get there . . ." and I can't finish my thought.

There's no reason Lily would know he's my doctor. But he's had every chance to tell me that he was hers, I asked him outright. I told him about Lily's pills, that I was worried, and he said he'd look into it.

I glance at him, intent on the road. In profile his face loses its open friendliness.

I don't really know him. The thought crosses my mind, out of nowhere.

But I don't. All his concern for my family, solicitous inquiries after my well-being, my health, have helped create a sense of intimacy, of history, since we moved here. And yet. He knows a lot about me. I don't know him, only that he came here after time away, abroad. But where was he before that?

I stare at the wet road ahead.

Dr. Nick is related to Lily. And so he's the person who has been giving her medicine that is making her confused. Forgetful. Unsure of what's going on near her. In the house she once looked after.

And Lily knew Nancy. She's been looking after that house, much longer than I first thought. So did Dr. Heath know Nancy too? He's about Jay's—I mean Nicholls's—age, too.

And then there is Sophie's older man, picking her up from school. Someone who she'd trust. Someone we all trusted, maybe. The dark car, that Danny saw Sophie getting into. The bonnet in front of me is blue, navy blue, and we're slowing now, so we don't miss the entrance to the deer park—it's a sharp turn into the car park. And I'm thinking, Dr. Heath must be what, early forties? So he's about Nancy's age too.

It's too incredible.

And now we're here, turning into the car park to the entrance to the deer park, it's nearly empty now, just the odd car at the far end.

My phone's still in my lap.

I keep my head up, like I'm still watching the road, and cast down my eyes. And I start tapping in numbers, not moving; surreptitiously. Like I don't know; like there's no reason I can't make a call, I'm not entertaining this ridiculous idea—

"Who are you calling?" His voice is flat.

"I just want to let my sister know where I've gone; she'll be looking for me, you know, and you took the note I left—"

"Give it to me."

"Just one second—"

"I said, give it to me," and my fingers are shaking now, I can't get the buttons right, *it's him it's him it's him*—

The blow throws my skull against the side window, the glass smacking against the side of my head. I slump forward over my seatbelt, black spots jumping before my eyes. I can hear myself wheezing. The phone's slipping out of my hands, now slack, my eyes closing, so I feel, not see him, scrabble at my lap to grab it. And then too quickly it all recedes, the world going dark.

CHAPTER 44

My head hurts. I open my eyes. The floor is flat and brown. A dirt floor, gritty against my cheek, covered in a slurry of gray and white. Bird droppings, years and years of them. They must have been nesting in here. There is something wet on my bottom lip, warm and metallic.

Nausea wells up from my stomach. Should I shut my eyes, pretend that I am still out? But then I wouldn't see him coming. No, keep them slitted, like I can hardly open them.

There are feet in front of me now—shiny leather shoes. I can just focus on the tips.

"I know you're awake." He crouches down and puts a cool hand on the pulse in my wrist. "You're fine, Kate." He straightens up, and walks away. "Stop it. I mean it."

My eyes track up now, from his shoes, to what he is holding. I lift my head, a couple of inches from the floor, then slowly fold myself round and lean against the wall, feeling it rough through my clothes. My face is still throbbing, my cheekbone is hot. I put one hand to it, checking myself.

The knife is silver and vicious. It doesn't fit in the hand of this man, in his shirt and tie, his smart work clothes.

I keep my eyes on him, but widen my field of vision to take in the rough walls and the dirt floor, the door behind him. It's cold, a damp chill coming up from the ground, and the bare light overhead is dirty with cobwebs. I'm in an outhouse, not much more than a room with a roof. I've seen them in the deer park, buildings from its farming past.

I need to say it out loud now. I want to scream it to the rooftops. "It was you." My voice is cracked, like I've woken from sleep. "You had her, all this time."

He smiles, showing his teeth. "Bit late, but you got there in the end"—the knife moves in his hand, a silver gleam under the light—"though I'm afraid it is too late, for you."

Dr. Heath. Nick Heath, here, in front of me. I still can't compute it. My doctor, the man I told my fears to, who prescribed my pills, gave me an ear, so sympathetic. But now his energy's different; the mild façade gone, something keyed up and sharp about him. The person underneath finally showing.

And that knife . . . it's a kitchen knife, long and pointed. But I know, absolutely, that he would use it.

Unsteadily, I get up, using the wall as a support. The park empties at dusk, even the dog walkers clearing out. He must have left the car nearby, then carried me the short distance to this place.

"They're coming, you know," I say, some instinct kicking in. "They'll be looking for me, even now. They'll have noticed, they'll be worried. You should let me go, we can still sort this out. . . ." But the panic rises as I remember: even if anyone was looking, we didn't take my car. He said we should take his.

"Oh, really? Who's looking, then? The police?" He tilts his head, his expression almost sympathetic. I am back in the surgery: him listening to me, his professional face on. "Your family? Because I don't think so, Kate. I don't think anybody is looking for you."

Behind him, a faint light is showing under the closed wooden door. The lock's a simple latch. If I can make it past him—past that knife. Or there's that smaller one, to my left, standing ajar— no, that must be to another room, or cupboard, I'd just be trapped.

So it's the door behind him. My whole body is tensing now, ready to run, to fight—

"Don't try it." He lifts his arm just a little.

I freeze. Keep him talking, I tell myself, play for time. Wait for my moment.

"They're going to know though. They'll work it out; you're right under their noses. You can't do—anything to me." But my words ring hollow.

"Oh? But they haven't worked it out so far, have they?" he says gently. "And I don't think you're going to be telling anyone else." He looks strangely relaxed now, easier in himself than he normally does.

"What have you done to Sophie?"

"When I saw the note you'd left I was a little alarmed, it's true," he continues, like I hadn't spoken. "It was such a rush. Having to move . . . everything. But it was feeling rather uncomfortable, being close to you. And I was surprised to see you actually in-side Parklands; I'd left the front door open, in my hurry. Unlucky." He raises his eyebrows. "Or lucky, as it turns out. Because here we are."

"You don't need to do anything," I say wildly. "You don't need to hurt me. You can go away, start again." I've got to reach him. "You don't want to hurt me. We've always got on well, haven't we?"

"Oh, please don't be stupid, Kate," he says, his tone impatient. "I know you're not stupid. It's not personal. But I can't go any-where. I don't *need* to go anywhere. I just need to carry on, like I did before."

Of course. I remember my confusion when I read Sophie's se-cret emails: someone was planning to go with her. But everyone she knew was still here. *He* was still here.

"Because that's what you've done, all this time—just carried on." Hiding in plain sight. Anger rises up in me now. "And you'd—

what? Visit her? All the time, keeping her locked away, in that horrible room?"

He frowns. "It was what we planned, to be together. And, later, it was what had to be done. It was the only way to keep us safe. She was too young to understand that."

I shake my head, thinking of that lonely attic. "Whatever Sophie thought she was going to, you know she didn't want a prison. You know that." And where is she now? Where's he put her?

"We were happy," he says. "But you wouldn't just let it go." His voice grows harsh. "It's your fault, all of this. The postcards home, they weren't enough. And they were a risk. What if one day I slipped, left a fingerprint, or some tiny trace for investigators. So I let her phone you, in a way that would never be followed back to us. A kindness, to you both, to say goodbye. But you spoiled it. You couldn't let it go. . . ."

Not a kindness, I think. It was control. You have to be the puppet master, cleverer than everyone else. You could get addicted to that feeling; take risks. I swallow, my mouth is dry. "And it was you. In my garden. In my house at night. Because I was getting closer."

"The first time, I was . . . looking. No harm in that. It's good to be prepared. The second?" He looks almost gleeful. "Let's just say, there are ways to make things look not quite what they are."

But I woke up and disturbed him: stopping him. What's to stop him now?

I start talking again, babbling. "You can't hide this, not this time, they'll find you. They'll find me. You can't—"

"Can't I?"

"No. There's no way," I say. "There are all sorts nowadays, the DNA, forensics, they'll work it out. If you do anything to me . . ." I wish I sounded less scared.

"You're right," he says, so reasonably it silences me. "I can't do it. It's too big a risk."

And he pulls something out of his suit pocket, tosses it toward me. Reflexively, I catch it: I can't quite make sense of the small bottle until I read the name. Kate Harlow.

He says: "You're going to do it."

"Where did you get this?" They look just like mine.

"I'm a doctor. It's not hard." He nods at the pills in my hands. "And you're going to take them."

"What?"

"It's a very sad situation. A mother who just couldn't cope with the loss of her daughter. She'd tried once before, didn't succeed. This time, however . . ."

And now I get it: an overdose. But there'll be no help for me this time, no one to find me and wake me up. "You're deranged. This wouldn't work—"

He talks over me: "A history of erratic behavior. Medical records that testify to that. A family who will agree, however sad they are, that they, too, have been worried recently. Police concerns, after reported incidents—a trespass, a break-in—but no signs of any intruders. Odd phone calls, to a helpline."

My head jerks up. "That *was* you. You were calling the charity, from the phone box."

"Well I wasn't going to call from the surgery or my mobile, was I? I needed to know when you were there, when you took your breaks, when your colleague did; when you'd be on your own. Your patterns."

"And then you put the helpline advert in Lily's kitchen." I see now. "I thought it was her making the calls."

"No one was supposed to check those phone records," he says reprovingly. Like I've broken a rule of the game. "It's supposed to be anonymous, as you well know, and there was no reason to. And I had a special phone for Sophie, of course. But I had to . . . react, when you started pushing.

"And it worked better than I could have hoped. The police just thought it was you making the calls. Kate was cracking up again." He's pleased with himself, I can hear it in his voice. Proud.

But his boast tells me something: he's not infallible. Because he had to change his plan, react to what I was doing. Something small opens up in me. Not hope, not yet; just a glimmer of possibility.

"So maybe you did cover that up, and they believed you. But

you can't just keep going. You had to do the diary too, didn't you—get Sophie to write those new entries, once I knew about the pregnancy test. To explain that away and put the blame on her boyfriend. You had to keep covering up your tracks. And I was asking about Lily's medicine too, they know at the surgery that you're giving her medicine and you're related—"

"I can explain it," he says, angry now. "They'll believe me." He opens his eyes wide, innocent.

And then I see it: something in the way his blue eyes are placed in that pleasant face.

"You're Lily's son. That's why you were there, that's how you knew Nancy. Living in the shadow of the big house that your parents looked after."

"No," he says, irritated. I wait. "Bob was my stepfather. She remarried after my father died."

"And you didn't take his name. So you kept that quiet. What, did you not like to mention it at school, what your parents did?" I'm guessing, but his mouth tenses. "And what about this, now?" I fill my voice with as much conviction as I can muster. "You know this is the end for you. They won't believe it."

"Oh, they'll believe it." He laughs. "You'll be surprised what people will believe."

He's so assured, he's not even worried.

Yes, I think, because you've done this before.

Sophie, a runaway who wasn't a runaway. Now me, a suicide that isn't a suicide. And—

"Nancy," I say. "She didn't run away either, did she?" He doesn't reply. "So what did happen? Did you do the same as with Sophie, trick her, hide her somewhere?" I'm throwing words at him, trying to get him off balance; to get under his skin. The door behind him, it'd be what; eight, nine steps?

"And then what? Did you get bored of her, decide to get rid of her? To *murder* her—"

"No!" His voice is loud. "Shut up." His top lip is glistening now, he's sweating despite the chill. "Nancy was an accident. It was her fault—it was all her fault."

"How? Because she got pregnant? With Jay's baby? Is that why you did it? Because the girl you wanted was with someone else. That's it, isn't it. She was pregnant with his baby."

"It wasn't his," he bursts out.

I stay silent.

"It was ours. They'd broken up. I comforted her. She didn't want anyone to know. I understood: we were . . . different." I can imagine: the housekeepers' boy, still no one you'd notice; Nancy, a teenage princess. Him infatuated, totally. "And then she got pregnant. She was so upset, but I knew what to do. We were going to go away, until we were older, until her family couldn't bully her." His mouth twists. "We'd even written our notes, decided what we'd say. But she let me down." There's a whining note in his voice now.

"That night, when we'd planned to go, she came to me. She told me it was *fine*." His voice breaks on the word. "She wasn't pregnant anymore, because she'd told her parents. They'd sorted it, that's what she told me, and now she was going away. It was going to be smoothed over, like nothing had happened."

"She was going to boarding school." Just like Lily told me.

"She didn't even mind. She said she wanted a fresh start. I said, we could still go. We could still be a family. I'd always wanted that. She said it was madness, she was far too young to have a baby. I got angry, I called her—names. And she said she never wanted to be with me, not really. Look at you, she said. Look at me. And then she—she laughed at me."

The room is very still. I can smell the damp earth.

"So you lost control," I say slowly. I see it now. Not planned. Opportunistic. A teenage boy rejected, reacting in blind fury. "What did you do? Did you stab her? Did you hide her?" Suddenly, rage is filling me; I want to hurt him, like he's hurt so many people. "Is that it? You stabbed her?"

The knife in his hand flashes again, and I shrink back against the wall.

"She provoked me."

"But then why did she leave a runaway note. . . ." I can see the answer in the sly curve of his mouth: just the hint of a smile. "No, *you* left the note." He went into Parklands, into Nancy's house, and left the note she'd written on her bedspread. That's what they found, when everyone woke up the next day. "But Sophie? Why did you have to do this to her, too?" There's despair in my voice. "Just to hurt someone?"

"No. No, this is why I knew people would never understand. It wasn't to hurt—it was love. When I saw her, I knew. They could have been sisters. She even lived next door to Nancy's house." His voice softens. "It was like it was meant to be; my second chance. *Our* chance—to repair the past."

So it wasn't a mistake: Sophie getting pregnant. *A baby.*

"But you couldn't run away with her, this time, you'd have been discovered. You hid her, instead."

"No one would have understood. But we were in love."

"But you know now, don't you?" I have to make him realize. "This is the end—it's over."

He shakes his head slowly. "Not yet. I can fix this. I've done it before." He points the knife at the bottle in my hand. "Because you're going to take those pills."

"I'm not." He won't be able to cover this up, not again, even if I don't get through this—his skin under my nails, scratches on his face, whatever it takes, I will leave traces that they will find, if something happens to me, leading them to Sophie. "You're not going to cover this up. I won't do it."

"Oh, but you will do it." His certainty shakes me. "You'll see." He takes a step back, the knife still in his hand, and now he's beckoning through the smaller door, through to the next room. "You can come out now."

At first I hear nothing. Then the rustling, just faint. The footsteps are slow, tired-sounding.

She walks in.

CHAPTER 45

Her hair's grown. Of course it has. And she's so pale, under the grime. She's no shoes on, just graying socks, a big T-shirt under her jumper and old tracksuit bottoms. She is taller, too.

My eyes fill with tears. Sophie. She's alive. She really is. Wild joy fills me—and then fear. "Sophie—" I take a step toward her, my hands reaching out.

"Don't move another inch." He points the knife right at me and I freeze.

Above the masking tape, her eyes are full of fear, like a cornered animal. The tape's round her wrists too: her hands twisted awkwardly in front of her; back to back.

"So that's why you're going to take the pills," he says. "Or I'll hurt her." He says it so calmly, so matter-of-fact.

I understand now. "You don't need to do this. You can go away. You don't need to. I won't tell anyone. Just let us go and—"

He gestures impatiently. "Stop it, Kate." He sighs, like I'm an annoyance. "Of course you'll tell someone. Look what you've done so far."

"I was just trying to find out what happened," I say now, keeping my voice steady.

"We wanted to be together. Didn't we, Sophie?" She nods. *He's broken her*, I think, *my poor girl*. "But you wouldn't let her go. And yet you couldn't find her either, could you? Right by you, and you never realized.

"You've failed her, until now. You told me that. But now here's your chance: your chance to save her. To make it right, like you wanted."

To save her . . . and I stop. Then what? A half-life with him, hidden away. Or worse?

Make it right. I wasn't perfect. But this wasn't my fault.

I stare at him; the hatred radiating off me. It wasn't my fault. Sophie didn't leave me, not forever; she just made a mistake. She wanted to come home. I'm not a bad mother.

It was him. He did this to me—to us. To my daughter. He ripped our lives apart.

"So that's why," he says, "you're going to do what you're supposed to do now. Take the pills."

"You wouldn't." My mouth is so dry with fear my tongue sticks to the roof. "You don't want to hurt her. Nancy was an accident." No. I can't be this close, only to lose now. He takes a step toward Sophie and lifts his hand. "You wouldn't hurt . . ."

"No, I don't want to. I never want to. But she's been a bad girl, haven't you? A disappointment. And I didn't even know, until your mother told me, the full extent of all your little tricks, to get away from me." Her eyes are shiny, wet with tears, above the ugly silver tape covering her mouth.

"So that's why," he says to me. "That's why you're going to do it. And then we can start again. Things will have to be quite different, I think.

"Now." He steps close to her, puts the knife just against her cheekbone, near her eye, and presses almost delicately. A small red bead swells up under the point and then rolls down, like a tear.

"Stop," I say. "It's OK, Sophie." No more playing for time. At least this way she's got a chance. I unscrew the cap, my hands fumbling with the safety lock. I can make myself vomit, I think. Or I'll spit them out; I will keep them in my cheek—

"I'm going to watch you do it. Let me see your hands." He's always been clever.

"How do I know though?" I say, lifting my head. "How do I know you're not going to hurt her?"

"You don't. But Sophie's going to be a good girl. She knows what happens if she's not. Don't you?" he says to her.

She nods quickly.

I look at her at last: "Just survive, sweetie. Do what you have to do to survive, that's all I ask."

I do it as slowly as I can. Maybe I could pull through this, I'm calculating, I did last time. But I can see: there must be what, fifty pills in here? Far more than before. That would do it, no doubt about it. And I'll be here, won't I, quietly falling asleep in a dirty corner of an empty building, where no one will find me.

I hold the first pill in my mouth and swallow. I start choking, tears coming to my eyes. I cough once, harshly, then hiccup it up again, holding it in my mouth.

His eyes are wide, showing the whites. "I told you not to try anything. If you try to—"

I shake my head. Tears are starting to spill down Sophie's cheeks, following the track of the blood.

"I'm not trying anything. I can't swallow it down."

"Do it. Try again."

So I do. But the same thing happens, I can't even get the pill down my throat; I hunch forward, cough it up again, my body racked. He's agitated now, shifting on his feet.

"It's OK. It's OK." Keep him calm. "I just need some water."

"Water?"

"I'm serious." I need some water. If he's distracted, if he leaves the room . . .

But he looks from me to Sophie, uncertain. She looks back, her eyes big, and he decides. "So get some." She doesn't move for a second. "Get. A bottle. Of water. From the pile."

"I can get it," I say.

"Stay where you are." He points the blade back at me. How strong is he? But I can't risk anything, not while he's so close to my daughter.

She steps back through the door slowly, and disappears from my view. From the other room, there's a dull thud, like something was knocked over. She'll be struggling, with her hands bound.

"Hurry up!" he says, his voice raised. But she's already back now, something crooked in her arms. One of those big bottles of water, plastic. How long does he plan to have her here? It's sliding through her arms, like she's going to drop it again.

Impatiently, he wrests it off her and walks over to me. I tense, bracing myself against the wall, one foot against the cool bricks, and he stretches out an arm to hand me the bottle. "Take it." He's too close now; he wants to watch what I'm doing. "No tricks. No pills down your sleeve, or on the floor." His eyes are intent, almost hungry.

This can't happen. But it is, I can't stop it.

I take the bottle off him, using two hands, finding it awkward with the pills to hold too. Everything seems to be unfolding in slow motion. It's going to happen.

He's so near I can smell his aftershave, woody, mixed with the smell of the dirt floor. I feel the weight of the water bottle in my hands. I see Sophie, behind him, her eyes intent on mine. I feel the chill in the damp air. The pressure behind the plastic, under my hand, and Sophie, her gaze not wavering. We're doing what he wants. I see her gaze shift to the bottle in my hands, then back to meet my eyes.

And I do what he wants. I hold it against my body; position it just right; I turn the cap. The water bursts out, a white stream, spattering against his glasses; shaken after Sophie dropped it. He recoils, putting his hands up reflexively to wipe the lenses, only for a second, before he recovers.

But it's enough, just enough, as I've already let the bottle fall and am throwing myself at the hand holding the knife, grappling for it, my whole weight on his arm, pulling him down with me, and now we're both on the floor, his arm's under me, my bodyweight on it. And suddenly I've got the knife, my nails digging into his skin, I've actually got it loose and in my hand, and I throw it, as far as I can, skittering across the floor away from us, but he's strong, like I thought, of course he is, "You bitch, you stupid bitch," he says, and he flips me back under him, his glasses hanging half off, his expression contorted with fury, and he has got me.

I throw one arm up, my elbow connecting with something with a crunch; but he gets it down again, he's so much stronger than me, pinning both my arms under his knees, and now his hands are on my throat, he's crouching over me, his heaviness crushing me, his eyes blind with rage. I feel his fingers, hard and strong, all his force behind them. And now I see Sophie behind him, too close, she needs to get away, she's trying to help, but her hands are still tied, I can hear her muffled screams, her face red under the silver tape; she's trying to pull him away, her hands on one shoulder, slipping; she can't grip properly, and he stops for a second and backhands her; he sends her flying back, down to the dirt.

I take one big heaving breath in while his hand's off my throat, filling my roaring lungs, but I still can't move, my legs kicking uselessly, trying to find purchase in the loose dirt surface. Then he's back on me, both hands pressing, harder than before, his intent clear; and Sophie's up again, further away now. But I can see, there's nothing between her and the door, the path is clear, and yet she's turned back, she's scared, her eyes fixed on mine. I can't form words, I try to tell her with my eyes, *just go*, but she's not, she's coming a step closer, the wrong way, she's got to get out of here, before he realizes what's happening and I'm so afraid for her, *go go go*.

And then she decides, I can see it in her face, she's nodding, her face a grimace under the tape, and she's unsteady from the blow, but she's moving now, backing away from us. His fingers are still tighter now, around my throat, he's silent and calm above me: he's going to do this, *just like he did it to Nancy*, and my vision is narrowing, going dark round the edges. And I'm so scared but

I'm singing inside too, because she's gone, I can't see her now, as the blood drums louder in my ears. If it gets her away, she can go, she'll be free.

But I've got to keep him here, as long as I can, or he'll be after her, *it will all be for nothing*—the thought courses through me, as he hunches over me, he's so close to me now, his breath hot in my face, and *yes*—I jerk my head up, hard against his nose, I feel something breaking. There is something hot and wet spilling out over my face, and I twist underneath him, getting one arm free, just for a second, and I throw it out, grasping, my fingers reaching blindly for a rock, something, anything, but there's nothing, just the cold, bare floor. He's silent, his eyes staring, his fingers back round my throat, even tighter. . . .

And suddenly it's there, the knife, I don't know where it comes from, I threw it away with no thought of using it. But it's here now, and I can't believe this is happening, it's almost like I'm removed, watching it from outside myself, but I see it slide in, between his ribs, before he knows it.

He groans. And now the liquid heat is spreading between our bodies, shockingly warm. He's so heavy, and his fingers are still at my throat, but easing now, the pressure weakening. And then suddenly I can roll him, I can push him off me entirely; I can scrabble up from under him.

His eyes are glazed with shock, as he looks up, still not understanding what's happened, until he slowly puts his hand where the knife went in, close to his heart.

The blood is dark on the floor, already soaking into the earth.

CHAPTER 46

We're outside. From far away I hear the wail of a siren. It's dark now, the rain a drizzle, washing me clean. I've never felt more free. I feel fine, more than fine, untethered from the world, probably better than I should, still riding a wave of adrenaline and energy. *She's here, she's here*, my whole body is thrilling with the knowledge, but she's in a bad way, I can see. My daughter is twisting her hands beside me, the tape bunching into rope but holding strong, and I know what I must do. I go back inside, and I pick up the knife, I wipe it on my jeans, then I cut the tape open, so carefully, making sure not to touch her skin. "Shh, it's OK. It's OK." Gently as I can, I pull the tape off her mouth, her hands fluttering over mine. The skin is raw underneath, her lips dry.

"Mum." Her voice is thin with fear. I hug her. The siren's closer now, the pitch getting higher.

"Sophie. It's OK, Sophie. It's going to be OK. Let's go." I start walking, propping her up, still hugging her—and holding her. I can feel her weight, solid in my arms, I can smell her hair, but she's shaking and then she pulls back, her eyes wild, her mouth an open scream.

She manages to get it out: "Mum. He's got Teddy. He's got Teddy."

For a moment I can't understand. He's got Teddy, she's saying, over and over. And I just can't get it, I'm imagining her stuffed toy. "Teddy? But that's all right, Sophie, we'll get you another one. . . ." She's in shock, I think she must be, after what's happened. She's like a child again, wanting her teddy.

But she stops me, grabs me, surprisingly strong.

"No, Mum, *no*. He took him, Teddy. He took my baby. My baby." Her voice is rising, desperate and thin. "What's he done with him? What's he done with Teddy?"

I'm stunned for a moment, before the understanding comes in a rush. And then it's like the knowledge is already there.

"Sophie, I know. I know where Teddy will be."

We take his car, the keys still in the ignition.

"He hasn't taken him anywhere," I say. "If he's—safe, I know where he'll be."

The journey there takes just minutes, but it feels like longer. I start to pray, holding Sophie's hand as I drive. We don't talk: there are no words now. Dear God, please please . . . I can't shape the thoughts, until we pull up outside the cottage. I run in.

"Lily," I call, pushing the door open. "Lily!" There's no answer.

Maybe I got this wrong. I rush through to the back, to her living room. Sophie's behind me already, breathing too fast, half-sobbing. Maybe I—

And there's Lily, bending over, in the corner, by the window. She straightens up and smiles, a big, beaming smile.

"Oh, Kate," she says. "Just in time for tea."

She drops a hand, a gentle pat on the head of the small figure clutching at her skirt. "Now careful of those sticky hands, darling. Oh, I'm so glad you're here. Kate, meet my lovely little boy."

CHAPTER 47

Sophie

So now you know. When he told me about the house, that he knew somewhere I could go, so they wouldn't split us up, it felt like it was meant to be. And the situation had just got so . . . big, so terrifying, so quickly.

He'd come to give a talk at school, about careers in medicine, at the beginning of the school year. I only went because Holly was interested. But I stayed behind afterward, just to say hello. And then he suggested I come see him at the surgery one time, on my own. Reception didn't think anything of it when I said I wanted to book in with him myself. I didn't tell anyone. He was my doctor, after all.

But I liked him. And very soon he went from Dr. Heath, to just Nick. He wasn't like my parents or any of their friends, or like any of the teachers. He didn't talk to me in the same way at all. He talked to me like a grown-up. It was exciting.

And then . . . I suppose in the end, that is what happened. That was the problem. I grew up.

CHAPTER 48

Kate

They found Nancy.

It was Nicholls who decided to dig in the building we'd been in—I heard Kirstie mentioning it to another officer. She's back, helping us again. It was a hunch, but a correct one: to check what was under that compacted earth floor, why Heath had thought to pick that place to take Sophie, after he emptied the attic. And it was the way Heath operated, repeating himself, retracing his steps—trying to make the present fix his past.

I feel so sorry for Nancy's sister, Olivia. It's one thing to suspect that someone you love is never coming back, but to know, for sure . . .

She wasn't buried deep. They couldn't be sure how he'd done it, but from what we know of him—he'd strangled her. They think she just went to meet him there in the park, after everyone was asleep. They'd probably met there before. Teenagers looking for somewhere to go.

But this time, only he came back.

He could have taken either his step-dad's keys or his mum's—Lily's—to get into Nancy's house. They'd both have had a set, working there all the time. No one knew about him and Nancy: it seems it would have been awkward, to say the least, if her parents had found out she was seeing the son of the help. I wonder, perhaps, if she liked it a little bit—the excitement of a secret.

Afterward, he just kept on as he always had, fading into the background, unnoticed. Maybe he helped the rumors about Jay along, we can't really know. I think, given what he did to me, that he did.

But I'm getting ahead of myself. So much has happened since then. Since Sophie came back.

My house was very full. There were lights in the drive as more cars pulled up, people swarming around, asking so many questions. Someone had put a blanket over me. I found I was shivering as the summer night drew in, my hands shaking visibly.

I had, finally, silenced Charlotte. She couldn't get a full sentence out. "Kate, I was so worried. . . ." She crouched down in front of me to pass me another cup of tea. Her face was pale. "You weren't here, but your car was here. I thought . . ."

"I know. I'm OK. We're OK." But I almost couldn't believe it either.

And there, in the middle of it all, the sun that we were all revolving around, was Sophie, right next to me on the sofa in our living room. Even the police felt it—I could hear it in their voices: something like awe. Teddy was in her lap, the little boy wide-eyed at all these people. She'd given him the remote control to play with—he loves pushing buttons—while I did the talking, Sophie quiet by my side. At one point, amid all the bustle, she fell asleep. She must have been exhausted.

Two years, three months and eleven days, she'd played that waiting game, seizing her chances, finding chinks in his armor. The message on the call to me. The email address in the diary. The drawings on the postcards. And then her last rebellion before the end came, so simple it looked like stupidity. It *was* stupid, so clumsy, so risky, it still scares me to think of it—her dropping the bottle of sparkling water, hoping that it would be ready to explode, shaking his concentration just for a second.

Her eyes telling me to do it—to take our last chance.

They had an officer with Lily, I'd checked.

It had fitted together like pieces of a jigsaw. "My little boy." She hadn't been imagining things; she was muddled, yes, but it was more than that: those drugs, keeping her more confused than she should be, dulling her natural sharpness.

And then there were my dreams, where I'd heard that childish laughter that sounded just like Sophie. Of course it did. It was Sophie's baby. "He took him out, sometimes," she told us. "At night."

But Heath hadn't always been outside. He'd taken Teddy to Lily's, too. It let him control Sophie, allowing him to do things without a little boy around. And it got Teddy used to being looked after by someone else. So that's where Heath had decided to leave him, in the end. Before he . . .

To break my thoughts, I leant forward and gave Charlotte a squeeze. "Really, I'm OK. Have you got hold of Dad yet, to let him know?" I wanted to distract her from her fretting.

Because she came through for me, in the end. She'd come round that afternoon, as she'd told me she would, only to see my car in the drive, and me not answering the door. She let herself in, and found the place empty. She probably missed us by just a few minutes.

Next she tried to get through to my phone, ringing unanswered in the footwell of his car. Charlotte had panicked: at what I might have done. "Something stupid," is all she'll say. So she'd called 999, and they'd sent round two officers in a patrol car. But that wasn't enough for her; she'd gone into the kitchen and seen Nicholls's card, tucked by the phone. She called him too.

So they were already looking for us, a patrol car parked in my drive, when we drove up in Heath's car and ran into Lily's cottage. It was PC Kaur, the officer who'd been round to check after the intruder in my house, who found us there. His mouth dropped open when he saw me, covered in blood; it got wider still when he took in Sophie behind me, her ghostly pallor, and the little boy in her arms, his blond curls too long.

"There is a body in the park," I told Kaur, "in the outhouse nearest the car park. It's Dr. Heath."

And I just kept repeating it, throughout, as more people arrived, gathering in the drive. "Dr. Heath," I keep saying, "he did it. He took Sophie."

Then I saw Nicholls, coming out of my house, his suit crumpled.

"And he killed Nancy," I said, over their heads. He stopped right there. He looked young for a second, just like his school picture. He really didn't know, I realized.

"I'm sorry," I said more softly. "She's dead. And he did it. Nick Heath."

CHAPTER 49

I'm not going to go to court. Nicholls told me the other morning, sitting at my kitchen table in his suit, after driving round on his own. He'd heard through people he'd worked with at the Crown Prosecution Service: no one wants to prosecute a mother acting in clear self-defense. There's a lot of attention on them, of course. Everyone from the broadsheets to breakfast shows wants to talk to me.

I have already talked until I am hoarse. The police have been polite but thorough, running through my story again and again. But they believed me from the start—I could see it in their eyes. Sophie and Teddy have been treated with kid gloves, of course, assigned social workers and "given time to heal," as they put it. In time, if she wants, she can tell their story to the world.

That morning, I thought Nicholls would go after passing on the news and asking after them both. They were playing in the garden and we'd watched them for a moment through the window, while we drank our coffees. But he didn't seem in a rush to leave, so I just brought it up. A lot had become clear to me by then, from the police officers who interviewed me and what was written in the papers, but I wanted to hear it from him. It was the first chance I'd had to speak to him properly—he'd had to step away from the case, once it became clear that what happened to Nancy and Sophie fell under one investigation.

"You know, for a moment, I thought it was you who took Sophie," I said. "I saw that school photo, of you and Nancy, and realized—you're Jay."

He didn't speak for a second. "I *was* Jay," he said slowly. "After we left—my family moved down south—no one called me that anymore. It was supposed to be a fresh start. But I always liked it here." He turned to me. "Heath would have been in that photo too, if you'd had time to look at it. He probably realized that."

"If I'd had time . . ." I remembered, again, that wary look on Heath's face when I told him it was Jay—Nicholls—who'd been keeping Sophie at Parklands, revealing that I didn't suspect him. I think it was then that he changed his mind about what he was about to do to me. "I suppose it was safer to get me to that isolated building, rather than do anything there."

But I did get one thing right: it wasn't entirely coincidental that Nicholls was looking into Sophie's case.

"It struck a chord, I suppose. That was partly why I got into policing. I felt like no one was looking out for her after she left." He grimaced a little. "I mean Nancy, of course."

"Though I didn't exactly advertise that part of my past. They said we'd argued—we hadn't. But people talk." I nodded. And I wondered if Heath, unnoticed, didn't help it along a little.

"I transferred forces, back up here, a few years ago. I was on major investigations, working nearer the city center. I hadn't really heard about Sophie, until all this. I moved to this division about a year ago now, working closer to Amberton and, well, where I grew up.

"So when Sophie's call came through"—he rubbed the back of his head—"it felt close to home, in a lot of ways. I wanted to make sure there was nothing more we could do. But it seemed quite clear cut. And when the diary emerged, suggesting it was her pregnancy and her crappy boyfriend"—I smiled to hear him sound less than perfectly professional—"I thought, no wonder this kid doesn't want to come home."

"I could tell."

He frowned. "I shouldn't have communicated that. But I had wondered if something like that had happened to Nancy. That she was scared of what her parents might do, or say."

"That's what Heath wanted everyone to think. That we'd failed Sophie."

"Yes. But still . . . something about it—it was too neat, that diary emerging when it did. So I kept an eye on it all. When you said someone had been in your garden, and I realized where you lived, I came and looked round Nancy's house—"

"Where I saw you," I interrupted. "I thought you seemed . . ."

"Shifty," he fills in for me. "Maybe. I told myself I was just doing my job, but it was more than that. It made me think—what could I have done differently, after Nancy disappeared? Because it had never made sense to me. Anyway, I kept paying attention. When I saw the repeat caller records, it seemed like you were . . ."

"Losing it," I said bluntly. "And you knew about my past."

"Your husband had mentioned it, when he came in to discuss the diary." He looked down. I could imagine the spin Mark put on all that. It's easier to blame someone else than to look at your own failings.

And of course there was Heath, all the time, pouring poison in my family's ears.

That's another thing that's come out. After I'd overdosed, I'd given permission for him, as my GP, to liaise with my family. He'd said it was a good idea. And I'd never rescinded it, I had never even thought. So he'd been hiding behind a veil of concern, updating them on my mental health, encouraging them to check in with me and him—in case, say, I reacted badly to Mark's new girlfriend, had they heard about that, actually? Not to alarm them, oh, not at all, but he did have a few worries. . . .

He was finding out what I was up to and, later, laying the ground. So if something were ever to happen to me . . .

Everyone trusts a doctor, after all.

People have suggested, tactfully, that I might have been mistaken: that I could be reading too much into my dreams. And maybe I'll never know for sure. That dark figure I'd dream about, leaning over my bed . . . The police said that it would have been very unlikely, that it was too big a risk for him to take, to enter my house more than once.

But I know. I remember that night I woke up to find that presence, waiting, breathing, on the other side of my bedroom door—expecting me to be asleep. He'd told me to keep taking the pills.

Heath used to park up on that back road behind Parklands, they think, to go and see Sophie, using that cut-through that Nicholls mentioned that time I saw him outside. And if anyone did see the doctor's car parked in a road nearby, well, nothing to worry about, GPs do house calls at odd times.

They think he cut himself a copy of the keys to Parklands long ago. Perhaps even when Nancy lived there: a teenage boy lifting his mum or step-dad's keys from the dish in the hall one quiet afternoon.

"It was a strong cover," said Nicholls, bringing me back to the bright morning. "But when I learned that you'd reported another break-in, I kept going—I told you I'd look into it. Finally, we got the phone records. It takes weeks, you see."

"And?"

"And the call *was* untraceable, as I expected. It was just a mobile number that called you at the helpline, at the time that you said. The phone wasn't registered to anyone, but that's not surprising, if it's just pay as you go. It had been used fairly locally—the call had gone through a mobile phone tower not too far from here. But they cover a wide area."

"The coverage is bad out here," I added.

"Still, something just felt wrong. You see, the phone had only ever been used that night: two calls, just a few moments apart."

"The test call, to check I was there—"

"And then Sophie was on the line. I was thinking about it, actually, when your sister called me to say she couldn't find you, and I came straight round. But I'm sorry. I was almost too late."

"I felt like you were always warning me off," I said.

"A bit. It's easier to investigate without . . ." He trailed off. "But it wasn't just that. I was uneasy about this one. It reminded me too much of the past. But I thought I was letting it distract me from the task at hand."

I changed the subject. "And you hadn't seen him—Heath—since school?"

"No. Even then I could barely have told you his name, to be honest, let alone where he grew up. I didn't know about him and Nancy. No one did."

Other stuff has started to come out now, sometimes in the papers, sometimes the police let me know. After medical school Heath went abroad, then he'd moved around, losing his soft Cheshire accent in the process, it seems. There were complaints filed, suggestions of inappropriate relationships with a couple of young patients. Overly friendly. But then he'd move on, to another short-term position. When he eventually settled back in Amberton, he had kept himself to himself. So no one at the surgery would have thought to check if one of the quiet young doctor's elderly patients was his mother—and that was only an irregularity, anyway.

But then Heath learned that Nicholls was looking into Sophie: I'd told him myself. And I bet *he* remembered *him*. It must have felt like the threat of discovery was getting too close.

"How is Mrs. Green doing?" Nicholls asked, breaking into my thoughts.

"Lily's OK, I think. It's hard to tell, but she seems much brighter. Clearer."

We don't really know what Heath intended with the drugs he gave her. He'd said that whenever she felt a bit lost or forgetful, she should take a pill. They kept her confused, certainly. But perhaps she'd been harder to manage than Heath thought. Asking too many questions about the little boy, or maybe my friendship worried him—what might she let slip? How easy it would have been for her to get mixed up, and take too much of her powerful medicine.

Because he'd been putting out feelers, they say, about work outside Cheshire, they think he was going to start again somewhere,
with Teddy. They searched his home, a neat little house on the
edges of Amberton, and found some of the stuff from the attic:
Teddy's clothes and toys, in bags in the loft.

It took a while to find out who Lily thought Teddy actually
was—I didn't want to upset her.

"Such a good boy," she'd said, a little wistfully. "A good boy,
underneath." She was talking about Heath. He'd told her that
Teddy's mother was a vulnerable patient, who just needed a little
extra help looking after him. But she couldn't tell anyone. "The
authorities, you know," she told me, her eyes owlish. "They might
take him away."

And it was the truth, in a way. Heath was hiding his secret in
plain sight. She'd long ago learned not to talk about her son, who
liked to keep his humble background quiet. Handy, too, when he
returned to Amberton, that no one would ask awkward questions.

Yet I wonder how much she knew about him, or had guessed
at over the years. I remember the way she pretended not to know
who Nancy was, the first time I asked. Of course, a housekeeper
would have learned not to gossip about the family she worked
for, and later to dodge curiosity about the painful past. And yet. I
know how far we'll go to protect the people we love.

In the end, I let it drop.

They had her new social worker break it to her that he was
gone, but I know she spared Lily exactly how. She seems to think
that Heath got mixed up in a fight. She gets confused, even now,
but she's out of hospital, where they put her under observation.
She's been moved into a new flat, where she's with people who
can look after her if she needs it, and we come and see her, Teddy
and I, and even Sophie's been once. I helped set it up: Heath's estate went to Lily, as it should have. He's had to go away, I tell her if
she asks, and once—and I hope she'd forgive me the lie—"Oh, he
sends his love." They found some of Sophie's stuff, too, a bit later.
He'd already taken it to the dump. If I'd done what he wanted, at
the end . . . I don't think he'd have kept her.

Suddenly I don't want to think about any of this anymore. I get up and put the kettle on again.

"So. Got any more safety talks planned at the Grammar, then? Maureen will be delighted."

Nicholls looks surprised, then laughs. "Maybe. You should probably be giving one too."

CHAPTER 50

Sophie, they say, is making a remarkable recovery, all things considered. I hadn't really understood how strong she is.

"Youth, maybe," says the counselor, Sally. "Teddy. And hope, that you'd find her." I'm seeing one again. I might as well, Sophie thinks it's good for me.

And Teddy? He's a little bundle of joy. We had to child-proof the house, of course. It is full of people now. Mark's here a surprising amount. Sophie likes it, so it's fine, and I feel bad for him. He's struggled with the knowledge that he stopped searching—that he gave up on her. But maybe, I thought the other day, it was neither of our faults. It came out of the blue, but something's loosening in me.

He's still nervous around her. And he keeps trying to say sorry to me, too. I was trying to be magnanimous, but it got to the point when I just wanted him to stop. "Mark, I forgive you, all right. Just please—stop following me about like a wounded puppy and make us all a cup of tea."

"Well," he said, the wind taken out of his sails, "there's no need to be so rude about it."

Incredibly, I heard a little laugh from the doorway. We looked round, both red-faced. I hadn't realized Sophie had come into the kitchen to catch us bickering. "You two don't change, do you?" But she didn't seem to mind. And the truth is, he doesn't need to say sorry to me. No one does.

Ben's been round again, too. Nicholls, I mean. He's good company, actually—funny, in a deadpan way. Maureen at the school was right; he has got something about him, when you think about it.

I don't know if it could be something more, one day. For now, a friend is enough. He knows what it's like to have something dark in your past that won't go away.

I've been so lucky. I almost can't believe it.

When I'm alone at night, my big house quiet again, everyone else asleep, and I'm in that drifting space between wakefulness and sleep, I still feel it: that cold familiar fear rising up to clutch at me again.

Because close your eyes and you know in your bones: Sophie never came home. The questions you nursed—the wheres, the whys, the what-ifs—were never answered. It's just you, alone, waiting. No change, no revelation, no daughter returned like something from a fairytale. Just more long years to endure . . .

And then I catch myself and realize that I am doing it again. Because if those dark years of absence came to an end, in a way they will never end for me. They showed me. They lifted the thin veil between the safe, normal world, the one most of us live in, and the world as I know it can be—a place of sharp edges and dangers, where bad people want to hurt my loved ones and me. So I hug my arms around myself, tight, and try not to think about that night in late summer, after the storm broke.

It's easier to do than you might think. They have stopped asking questions now, the official statements done. There were some uncomfortable articles in the papers about the first police investigation, how they were hoodwinked by the notes, the postcards, the rest of it; whispers of an inquiry by the police watchdog into the lessons to be learned.

But weren't we all deceived by Heath? That's the question I ask, as I tell everyone that we, as a family, want to move on, that we will address it all once we've some distance from the past. Maybe. And everyone accepts it. It's surprising what people will believe.

Most of them, anyway.

It was just something Ben said once, early on, when I still had to spend all that time at the station. I was sitting outside one of those little rooms, drinking sugary vending machine coffee. The duty lawyer who sat in with us had gone off to make a phone call, when he came by to say hello.

He asked how I was doing. "I'm fine," I said. It was true. "I can cope with all this." This, I didn't need to say, this was a walk in the park after the last two years.

"Of course you can." He stretched out his legs in front of him. "That was Heath's mistake, really, wasn't it. To underestimate you."

"What do you mean?" I turned to look at him.

"Just what I said," he said lightly. "To think that you would ever let her go. He didn't understand, did he? That there's nothing stronger than that tie. That there's nothing that a mother wouldn't do for her child. Her baby. Nothing at all." It was something in his eyes that told me. Not just sympathy, but—a question.

"You're right," I said. I couldn't look away. "There isn't."

The officer, Hopper, came back then, and told me it was time to go back in to continue with the interview, if I was ready. So we stopped there. I don't think we'll talk about it again.

We didn't plan it, Sophie and I. She wasn't in any state for that. They just assumed, from the start. My clothes were soaking, covered in blood. And I . . . let them. She was so young, so vulnerable, so traumatized. Of course it was me.

And I told them everything, just as it happened, until the very end.

"Then I saw the knife," I said, so many times in the days that followed, as we went over and over what had unfolded. "It felt like it wasn't really happening. There was no other choice, I couldn't stop him."

Because that's what he taught me. Hide the lie under a little bit of truth.

I'd known what I had to do from the moment I decided to go back inside, afterward, to pick up the knife, wiping the blade on my jeans. I'd wiped the handle, too, before wrapping my fingers back around it, making sure my prints were all over it.

I tell myself that I did the right thing. That I had no choice, that I couldn't fail my daughter. Not after what she did.

He was on me, his hands round my throat, when I got my hand free, scrabbling for something, anything. A rock, anything. But there was nothing, just bare floor. Nothing.

And then I saw her, over his shoulder; the knife held awkwardly in one hand, still tied to the other with tape. *She didn't leave. She didn't leave—she went to get it,* I realized with dawning horror. I'd thrown it away, as far as I could, with no thought of using it, just to get it off him. I couldn't believe it was happening, I felt almost like I was removed, just watching her from outside myself, and so afraid—*he'll notice, he'll hear her*—but he doesn't, he's lost it, completely, so she just comes up behind him, and quietly, delicately almost, she slides it in, between his ribs, before he knows it.

He groans. He's heavy; his fingers are still at my throat, but easing now, weakening. And suddenly I can roll him off; I can scrabble up from under him.

His blue eyes are glazed with shock, as he looks up at us both, standing there, our faces mirroring each other's horror. He slowly puts his hand on the wound, finally understanding what's happened: who did this to him. What he missed.

His blood is dark on the floor, already soaking into the earth.

Because she came back.

EPILOGUE

Today

In the car park, the woman struggles to find a space. It's one of those glorious autumn days, the crisp air smelling of leaves and smoke. Eventually she does, and pulls in gingerly. She's very young, not much more than a girl really, although—there's something about the set of her shoulders, the tilt of her head—you wouldn't call her a girl.

She's still not that confident a driver, not yet, but she told her mother she wanted to do this on her own. After all, it wasn't far. And she needs to do these things. She's got a lot to catch up on.

"Are you ready then?" She unbuckles the toddler in the back and heaves him out.

"Yes, Mumma." She takes his hand and they set off, her walking slowly, so he can keep up.

He's growing so fast now, the bloom in his cheeks so bright it's like he lights up from the inside. He's already forgetting that they ever lived anywhere else but Oakhurst, with Nana and the cat.

Now he's spotted what's in her other hand. "Nana flowers?"

"Not these flowers, Teddy."

His brows lower, his bottom lip sticking out. "Nana flowers," he insists. "Nana like flowers." The terrible twos, she thinks, here they come. She knows his birthday is around this time of year.

"That's right, Nana does like flowers. But these are special flowers, for someone you don't know. Someone who was called Nancy."

"Nan-cy," he says carefully. "We go see Nancy?"

"Kind of," she says. "Nancy's not here anymore. We're just going to leave them for her."

It is not by the place itself, she's glad to see, but in a pretty, shaded spot near the deer park entrance, at the foot of the first great oak tree off the path. Above the little pile of blooms and cellophane a lone balloon floats at half mast, its skin puckered.

"Balloon!" he says, now pulling her along.

It doesn't take them long. When they get there, she takes a moment before deciding to set the roses down at the back of the pile, wild hothouse blooms, peach and pink and yellow and white, out of season but beautiful, with their heady scent. There's no note: there's nothing she wants to write down.

The little boy stays close to his mother, uncertain now. Something in her solemnity has touched him. "Can I ha' balloon?"

"Not this one. This one has to stay here. But we can go and get you a new one. Right now," she says. She shivers.

"From supermarket?" he says hopefully.

She laughs. It's his favorite place: all the people, and sweeties, and the fifty-pence ride that bobs him up and down at a stately pace. "I think we could get you one from the supermarket. Are you ready?"

"Yes!"

"All right then. Let's go."

And they leave then to walk back to the car, the two little figures growing smaller and smaller, hand in hand, the sunset making the whole world glow before them. Neither of them look back.

ACKNOWLEDGMENTS

Thank you to John Scognamiglio and to everyone at Kensington who has supported my book.

Thank you to my UK editor Ben Willis, for all your energy, creativity, and hard work; to Francesca Pathak, for making things happen; and to the rest of the talented team at Orion. Thank you to my agent Clare Hulton, for your help and encouragement.

Thank you to those who were generous with your time in answering my questions about your working worlds, particularly Olivia Budge, Hannah Woodcock, Jennifer Twite, Lucy Oldfield, Robert Frankl and Rebecca Bradley. Any liberties taken with the usual professional procedures—or anything else—are mine alone.

Thank you to my family, friends and colleagues for all your support and enthusiasm. Special thanks to Helena Curran—I was and am so grateful for your insights. Thank you to Sarah Rowley, Zoe Rowley, Ian Rowley, Tom Colvin and Lis Mogul, for always cheering me on.

Finally, huge thanks to Liz Rowley, who helped me so much in the writing of this book. Unlike Kate, she knows this daughter is always at the end of the phone. In fact . . . Mum, sorry, I know it's late—but can we have a quick chat?

Connect with  **U**s

Visit us online at
KensingtonBooks.com
to read more from your favorite authors, see books
by series, view reading group guides, and more.

Join us on social media

for sneak peeks, chances to win books and prize packs,
and to share your thoughts with other readers.

facebook.com/kensingtonpublishing
twitter.com/kensingtonbooks

Tell us what you think!

To share your thoughts, submit a review,
or sign up for our eNewsletters, please visit:
KensingtonBooks.com/TellUs.